The Man from Shenandoah

Book 2: The Owen Family Saga

Also by Marsha Ward

That Tender Light
Gone for a Soldier
Spinster's Folly
Ride to Raton
Trail of Storms

Mended by Moonlight

The Zion Trail

The Man from Shenandoah

Book 2: The Owen Family Saga

Marsha Ward

WestWard Books

Payson, Arizona

WestWard Books
P O Box 53
Payson, Arizona 85547
www.westwardbooks.com

Publisher's Note: This is a work of fiction. Names, characters, places, and incidents are a product of the author's imagination. Locales and public names are sometimes used for atmospheric purposes. Any resemblance to actual people, living or dead, or to businesses, companies, events, institutions, or locales is completely coincidental.

Cover Design by SelfPubBookCovers.com/Shardel
Book Layout © 2017 BookDesignTemplates.com

Originally published in trade paperback by Writers Club Press, an imprint of iUniverse, Inc., and then by WestWard Books, with bonus material not found in the original edition. This third edition features new cover art and interior layout, as well as the revised placement in the Owen Family Saga book order.

The Man from Shenandoah/ Marsha Ward -- 3rd ed.
ISBN 978-0-9883810-2-5

Dedication
To my late husband, Rob, whose unfailing support and love
allowed me to explore my talents, and to rise toward
my eternal potential.

Acknowledgements
Among the dozens of people whose contributions made this
book possible, I must publicly thank three: Carol Crigger, Kerry
Blair, and Becky Rohner. Your inestimable suggestions, love,
and cheerleading helped me bring this project to fruition.

Contents

Introduction 1

Chapter 1 3

Chapter 2 19

Chapter 3 27

Chapter 4 39

Chapter 5 51

Chapter 6 59

Chapter 7 71

Chapter 8 81

Chapter 9 97

Chapter 10 109

Chapter 11 125

Chapter 12 137

Chapter 13 149

Chapter 14 161

Chapter 15 169

Chapter 16 185

Chapter 17 199

Chapter 18 213

Chapter 19 227

Chapter 20 243

Excerpt from *Spinster's Folly* 255

Introduction

Parole signed by Robert E. Lee on April 9, 1865:

"We, the undersigned prisoners of war belonging to the Army of Northern Virginia, having been this day surrendered by General Robert E. Lee, C.S. Army, commanding said army, to Lieutenant General U. S. Grant, commanding Armies of the Unites States, do hereby give our solemn parole of honor that we will not hereafter serve in the armies of the Confederate States, or in any military capacity whatever, against the United States of America, or render aid to the enemies of the latter, until properly exchanged, in such manner as shall be mutually approved by the respective authorities... The within named officers will not be disturbed by the United States authorities so long as they observe their parole and the laws in force where they may reside."

Signing this "parole of honor" marked the Beginning of the End of the American Civil War. But after General Lee surrendered to General Grant, a few military outfits, not hearing of the official end to hostilities, fought on past April 9. Other units, hoping against reality that the Cause was not lost, turned further south in join with forces in the Carolinas. One such group was the irregular cavalry outfit, Mosby's Rangers.

When the shabby boys of the unit finally disbanded and received their individual "paroles" as prisoners of war, they ceased to be soldiers, and were admonished not to wear uniforms of the Confederate States of America. An official determination was reached that when the embossed buttons were removed, the clothes they wore were no longer considered to be uniforms.

This story begins with one young veteran's introduction to that rule, and continues as he and his family find new direction for their lives after the end of the war.

Chapter 1

The gaunt-featured young man with the lanky build choked down the last of his moldy bread, then got to his feet and climbed atop the stone wall against which he'd been sitting. Carl Owen looked as far as he could see down the Valley Pike, about two hundred yards, but no one was in sight. Turning to look at the burned-out field the wall enclosed, he surveyed the gray-toned devastation made muddy by today's intermittent rain.

Rage rising in him, thundering in his ears as his heartbeat quickened in frustration and hate, he shook his fist at the sky.

"Phil Sheridan, may God spit in your eye for the ruin you brought to this valley. Rot in hell, Sheridan!"

"Get him!" he heard, just before he was tackled from behind, tumbling him off the wall and into the mud. Carl came up sputtering muck. As he wiped gluey sludge from his eyes, someone kicked him. He was hauled to his feet—arms brutally twisted behind his back—and dragged over the wall to where a huge, red-faced sergeant in a faded blue uniform stood waiting for him.

"Yankees," Carl groaned, berating himself for letting his guard down enough to miss their approach. Panic coursed through his belly. He tried to tear free, but two soldiers gripped his arms, and he finally quit struggling.

The sergeant stood with his legs spread apart, looking Carl up and down. "Johnny Reb, you're on the loose. We have a stout prisoner of war camp for you up in Washington City." He bent forward, laughing in Carl's face, who involuntarily wrinkled his nose and squinted shut his eyes at the overpowering odor of liquor fumes. The man frowned, drew a knife from a sheath on his belt, and tested it on his thumb.

"You look at me, Johnny Reb," he snarled. "Look at me when I speak to you!"

Carl opened his eyes and stared into the Yankee's mean eyes. "I have parole papers," he said, raising his muddy, stubbled chin in defiance.

"You're violating your parole, wearing the uniform of the Confederate Army," the Yankee said, and put his blade against Carl's throat, who sucked in a breath, then held it, careful not to move.

Just then, a burly soldier came up behind the sergeant. "Sarge, you told us we were going to find some Southern belles to entertain us," he complained. "Let's dump him in the woods."

"Keep your nose out of official business. I'll open him up a bit and teach him how to act around his betters."

From the north, a rider came pounding up the road, spurring his horse, then sawing on the reins to bring it to a halt. He alighted and ran to the sergeant.

"The major's coming down the road. You'd better not let him catch you cutting another Reb."

The sergeant cursed and turned back to Carl, grabbing the front of his coat.

"You got no right to wear a uniform, you dirty Rebel pup." He took a fresh grip on his knife and addressed the soldiers restraining Carl. "Hold him tight while I teach him a lesson."

Carl felt the tight prickle of fear racing up his spine as the soldiers freshened their hold on his arms. The sergeant looked around at the road, cursed again, turned to Carl, and cut the embossed buttons from his coat. He jerked the coat open, grinning evilly, and cut the buttons from his shirt, as well.

"Now you're not a soldier." The man cackled as he pocketed the buttons and sheathed his knife. "Let him loose," he ordered, motioning to the soldiers. As they dropped his arms, he looked Carl up and down once more, his expression changing to hatred.

The sergeant half turned away, then spun back, and with a massive fist knocked Carl flat. "Mount up," the sergeant barked, and strode toward his horse, weaving a bit.

Lying in the mud, propped on one elbow, Carl wiped blood from his jaw, tasting salt as he tongued his molars to see if they were still tight. He watched the patrol leave, hate burning his belly. He turned over onto his knees and got to his feet, wincing at the pain, then whistled for his horse. Looking around for his hat, he found it on the wall where it had landed when he was attacked. He brushed at the soft, shapeless felt, removing a splash of mud, then he jammed it onto his head.

Sherando came trotting out of the trees, gray coat glistening in the misty rain that had once again begun to fall. The horse jumped the fence to reach Carl and nickered softly. Carl checked to see that the Yankee rifle was secure in the scabbard. "Sure glad them Billy Blues was so drunk they didn't find you, boy," he whispered through raw lips.

He swung into the saddle and straightened his back, swiped at his face with both hands to remove as much mud as he could, then ran his fingers through the blond hair at the nape of his neck, tugging loose both tangles and mud. He hoped someone at home had a comb, for he had lost his personal gear in a wild, last-ditch ride for freedom with Colonel John Mosby. Carl's patrol had ridden into a Yankee camp to surrender after the war's end. Union officers gave the Confederate cavalrymen parole papers and turned them free instead of holding them as prisoners of war. Carl had stolen the rifle as he left camp, but hadn't had a chance to replace other gear.

Carl turned his horse onto the Valley Pike, laughing as joy surged through him. "Benjamin will have a comb. It'll be fine to see him again." Carl kneed Sherando to a trot, and launched into a tune he'd heard somewhere. "Oh Shenandoah, I'm coming to ya. I'm here, you rolling river."

Carl looked toward the shallow river flowing beside the road and grinned at the cleverness of his new words to an old song. "Hold up that head, horse. We'll show the folks that a passel of Yankees can't lick a Virginia boy. We're goin' home!"

"Ma!" Albert ran in yelling from the trees at the corner of the yard. "Somebody's riding in, mighty confident like," he panted.

Julia Owen looked up from the corn she was grinding and pushed back a loose lock of dark hair.

"Confident, you say? Does he look like a Yankee?"

Albert hung his head. "I mostly just saw him a-coming before I ran in, Ma. But he's riding real straight and sure of himself."

"Get your pa," she said, grabbing the Sharps rifle from the corner. "There won't be no Yankees set foot in this house."

Julia walked through the doorway with the Sharps in firing position and watched as a horseman neared the end of the lane from the pike. *Albert spoke the truth*, she thought. *That man rides bold.*

"Hold up right there," her voice rang out. "Put them hands where I can see 'em, and get down off that horse."

The mud-covered young man in the gray coat laughed. "You always did look fine with fire in your eye, Ma."

"Carl?" She took a step, lowering the rifle barrel toward the ground. "Carl! Is it really you? Lawsy, boy, we almost gave up on ever seeing you again." She swiped at her eyes with one hand. "Get off that horse and hug your ma." Her son dropped gingerly to the muddy ground and approached with long strides.

"Ma, I'm home." He grabbed her—rifle and all—and swung her into the air.

She caught sight of the wince that he tried to cover and the dried blood on his face, and immediately began to worry over his health.

Setting her on her feet, Carl brushed at the mud he had transferred to her dress. "I'm sorry about the mud, Ma. I had a little trouble with some fellers down the road a piece, and we wrasseled around a bit. Here, let me put that rifle aside. I reckon you don't want to put a ball into me."

"You ain't been hurt? What's that blood?" She followed him to the front of the house, where he leaned the rifle against the stone wall. "Here, let me look at you." Julia grabbed his arm, moistened the corner of her apron with her tongue, and dabbed at his face.

"Ma!" he protested. "It's just a little cut."

"And it needs tending to," she insisted, then hugged him again.

Roderick Owen came around the corner of the house, puzzled by the sounds in the front yard, but ready for Albert's Yankee invasion. He stopped short at the sight of a tall, very grubby man embracing his wife, and Albert bumped into his father from behind.

"Look here," Rod threatened, stepping forward.

Carl turned to meet him. "Have I changed so much, Pa?" He grinned under his smeared camouflage.

"Rod, it's Carl. He's home at last." Julia wiped the mud from her face with the apron.

Without a word, Rod enveloped his son in his arms. After a long embrace, he held him off to look at him, and shook his head. "By gum, you sure get your growth dashing around with Mosby. We thought you were dead, boy, not hearing from you, nor seeing you home yet."

"I took the long road home, Pa. The Colonel disbanded the Rangers about three weeks into April, but me and some thirty others wouldn't leave him, so he took us south to join up with

General Johnston in the Carolinas. The General gave up before we got there, so Mosby cut us loose and made us go in to get paroled." He paused a moment, scratching his nose. "They won't give him a parole, Pa. There's a price on his head!"

"I reckon there's mighty little justice around now, son. Your colonel won't get fair treatment since Booth shot the President. There's rumors Mosby had a hand in it."

"Somebody shot Jeff Davis?"

"The other president, Abe Lincoln."

"Is he dead?"

Rod set his jaw, turned his back on his son, and walked toward Carl's horse, his hand worrying the mud at the front of his shirt and pants. He picked up the horse's trailing reins and approached his son. "Yes, and it brings hard times upon us. There's no mercy in the boys running the country now."

"Mosby had no part in it. I rode with him day and night for over two years. He done no such a thing."

"I reckon."

"He didn't. That's all." Carl's stomach growled aloud, and he looked at his mother. "Is there anything to eat? It sure don't look like Phil Sheridan left much. We heard about his orders to burn out the Valley, Pa, but we laughed. Not one of us believed he could do it with you and Jeb Early's troops on home ground."

"They sent in two and three times our number, son. All we could do was pester them around the edges some."

"Well, I'm home now, and this ground will grow food—if we can get seed." Carl looked about the yard. Albert stood in the shadow at the corner of the house.

"Who's that young'un? I don't recollect leaving anybody that big at home when I left."

"It's me, Albert. I growed a mite."

"Can't be. You were just a little bitty sprout."

Albert came out of the shadow and stood where Carl could

see him. "I ain't a sprout now." His voice was a touch heated. "I'll be fourteen nigh on to Christmas time."

"You aged a right smart bit, Albert. Been doing most all the chores, I reckon."

"You left 'em to do."

Carl nodded. "I figured you three boys could handle the farm. When Peter died, I felt obliged to take his place in the fight."

"I reckon." Albert looked at the ground and kicked the mud.

"I didn't know James would go, too."

"They drafted him."

Julia moved forward and pulled on Carl's arm. "Come in and set, boy. Doubtless you're weary, riding all day. I'll finish the pone we're having for supper while you tell your pa what shape the Valley's in down south of here. He's been asking after news of the state of things since he got home."

"Now Julie, the boy's just got here. I can quiz him later while he eats." Rod turned to his youngest son. "Albert, take your brother's horse out back and put him in the pen behind the barn. See if you can find some grain. That animal's come far with your brother."

"Yes, Pa." Albert took the reins and led Sherando around the corner of the house.

After knocking the mud from his boots, Carl entered the house, shrugged out of his wet coat, and hung it on a peg inside the door. He pulled his shirt together the best he could and glanced around the room, savoring its warmth and cheerfulness. Then he took the stool his father indicated and moved it close to the fire before sitting.

"What happened to your buttons, boy?" Rod asked. "Were you obliged to sell them for food?" He also sat, and crossed one leg over the other.

"Naw. Some fat Yankee sergeant down the road a ways cut them off me. Said I was in uniform and didn't have the right."

"That's where you got the cuts and bruises and the mud, Carl?" his mother asked.

"I reckon, but they didn't hurt me none." He eased his rib cage from side to side to be sure.

Rod slapped his thigh in anger. "Yankees," he spit out.

Carl looked up, feeling a similar heat. "They ain't mannerly, that's for sure, but I came out lucky anyhow. Didn't lose nothing but my buttons. I hid my horse back in the willows along the creek, and they were too drunk to spot him, so they missed the rifle I snuck off the Yankee weapon pile after I got my parole."

"Drunk, you say? That sounds like the same Yankee bunch that's been back and forth through this part of the Valley, teasing and tormenting the folks."

"Could be them." Carl shrugged, then looked around the room once more. "Ma, where's Marie and the little girl? Ain't they supposed to help you?"

Julia smiled. "Your little sister is nigh on to twelve years old, boy. We kept having birthdays while you were away. You've had a couple yourself. Ain't you about nineteen now?"

"Closer to twenty, Ma. I ain't a young'un no more."

Julia looked at Carl's bearded face. "I see you been over the mountain, son." She paused to form a corn cake. "I sent the girls in to Mount Jackson to Rulon's place. Mary's not feeling well, and she's got Rulon to tend to, so they're helping out with young Roddy. You heard Rulon got hurt bad?"

Carl nodded.

"There's also more food in town," Rod explained. "Your ma has her wits scraped down to a nubbin to find us enough to eat since Sheridan paid his call."

"Clay went in with the girls," Julia added. "He's got a job at the livery, so there's just Pa and James and Albert to fix for."

"And Benjamin," Carl reminded her.

He watched his mother's body stiffen, and saw his father take a protecting step toward her. Silence hung in the room like a curtain made of combed cotton fibers, thick and heavy and oppressive. Then Rod spoke, his words muffled and measured.

"Benjamin fell at Waynesboro. I had no way to get word home. Your ma only found out when I got here."

The words bucked into Carl with the kick of a mule. He sagged on the stool and his head dropped against his hands. First, Peter had fallen at the Second Battle of Manassas, or Bull Run, as the Yankees called it. Then Rulon, the eldest, was sorely wounded in the siege of Petersburg last October. Now Benjamin was gone. Carl felt his ears ringing hollow, filling his skull with a soft buzzing.

He rose to his feet and faced his parents. "I'm powerful sorry," he said, holding himself still. "Benjamin was always such a lucky cuss, full of life, and all. It don't seem right he'd be gone."

Carl bowed his head, took a deep breath, and began again. "Ma, I know he was your favorite son, and I don't hold it against him. He was the favorite of everybody."

He took a step toward his mother, watching her white, crumpling face. With another step he had her in his arms, patting her head and shoulders. "There, Ma, you cry. It'll do you good."

Rod's arms went around the pair. "The boy talks sense, Julia. You ain't cried since you got the news. Let the tears wash out the grief you been carrying around." He continued gruffly, "I reckon I already done my sorrowing."

The men waited, suspended, as Julia's sobs tore the air. After a long time, she quieted, wiped the tears from her cheeks with her apron, and stepped out of the men's arms. Her face was changed, resigned. "I reckon that'll have to do for Benjamin, 'cause the living need their daily bread." She went back to the table, wiped her hands, and continued to fix supper.

Rod approached his chair and sagged into it, while Carl returned to his stool. Both men sat slumped for a time, saying nothing as the pain sat upon their shoulders. After a time, Rod threw back his head.

"Your ma's kept the family going whilst we were gone, son, and she's the one saw to it that we didn't starve when we returned. I got a leave to come home in December, on account of our mounts were starving for lack of forage, and I'll be switched if she hadn't outsmarted that cocky Phil Sheridan. She saved most of the corn by tying the sacks on the backs of the stock, and sending Clay and Albert to the hills with the animals. She saved the crop and the herd, both. I'm mighty proud of her."

"Ma, that was right canny thinking. I'd like to see Sheridan's face should he find out you outfoxed him."

Julia shook her head and continued with the meal.

"We ain't tooting our horn about the food we got, Carl," Rod said. "It's mighty little for our needs, and even so, we had to send the girls into town."

"How serious was Rulon hurt, Pa?"

"Well, he had a right smart mess of holes in him. The surgeon sent him home to die, but there ain't no quit in Rulon. That little wife of his nursed him along real well, too. He's mostly out of bed now, finally on the mend." Rod rose to his feet. "Say, come out and help me milk, son. That brindle cow the Yankees stole last fall wandered up to the fence today, bawling and kicking and carrying on to be let in the gate, but she's still half wild. There's a calf trailing her, so she must have milk."

Carl nodded. "Sure, Pa. I reckon a body don't forget how to do the chores."

As the men stepped out the back door, Carl glanced around

at what was left of the yard behind the house, and took in a rasping breath. The vegetable garden was a sea of mud, while out yonder, wreckage marked where the barn had been. All that remained were the burned beams and blackened supports that had fallen onto the floor. Two mounds of gray ashes, scattered by wind and rain, showed where the hay had been stacked. The animal pens were in ruins, poles broken and strewn about. Someone had piled brush in the gaps until new poles were cut.

Carl waved an arm at the view. "Was it like this when you got home, Pa?"

"Pretty near. The boys and I ain't had a lot of time to clean up much."

The brindle cow tied in the pen rolled her eyes and lowed in fright at the men's approach. Rod expelled his breath. "She always was skittish, Carl. I reckon she got away from Sheridan's soldiers and wintered back in the oak groves. She had her calf, then got lonely for home."

Carl stepped around behind the cow. "Mind that hoof." Rod spoke sharply as the brindle kicked out.

Carl dodged away and snorted. "She must be a Yankee lover. Welcome home to you too, cow." He patted her flank.

"Grab the pail and set to work, son. She wants milking."

Just then the hungry calf tied behind the remains of the barn began to bawl. Brindle pulled her head backward, and Rod reached for the rope to snub her on a shorter line. Lacking a stool, Carl squatted on his heels and began to milk.

The cow sidestepped, nearly catching Carl's foot. He avoided her hoof, and then she whipped her tail against his face. He turned away, saving his eyes from the coarse hair. Then she lifted her hoof and banged it hard against the pail, but Carl snatched it away in time to save the contents from spilling.

"Whoa, cow!" he yelled, as she swung her hindquarters against him. "You're right, Pa. She's gone wild." He scrambled out of the way, bringing the pail with him. "I call the job done. Let that calf come over here."

Rod grinned, went for the bawling creature, and untied the tether rope. "We're all out of practice of milking, son," he called. "I reckon I'd druther fight Yankees than get stepped on by a wild cow. I know James feels the same, after milking the white-face cow."

"Is he in one piece?" Carl asked, looking sidelong at his pa.

Rod turned the calf loose, and it ran to its mother. He grinned again as it began to suckle. Then his face went somber. "He got a flesh wound at Five Forks, outside Richmond, but it's healing clean. He can swing an ax, so I sent him up by the mountain to cut wood. Likely he'll be home tomorrow night with a load of fence poles."

"It'll be good to see him." Relief softened Carl's voice.

The two men headed for the house as the sun dropped toward the horizon. The rain earlier in the day had left the air cool and sweet, and a light breeze was blowing the final clouds away. Carl handed the milk pail to his father at the door.

"I'm all covered with mud, Pa. Best I wash up before I eat."

"You'll have to use the crick, son. The Yankees knocked the top of the well apart and dumped it into the shaft. I ain't got it cleaned out yet."

"Then I'll bring back some water."

Carl took two pails from the back stoop and slogged his way through the muck of the yard to the creek path. He felt like a small boy again, recalling the times he'd walked this path before the well was dug.

Carl came up to the creek, knelt, and dipped the pails into the deepest part of the water. After he set them high on the bank, he removed his shirt, tossed it aside, and plunged his arms into the water. Gasping with the impact of the cold, he splashed it onto his head and chest.

Once his face was clean, he wiped off his boots and rubbed most of the mud from his pants, then rinsed his shirt in the stream and wrung it out several times. He shook out the shirt and put it on, shivering when the cold, wet cloth made contact with his flesh.

Twilight took away most of the daylight as Carl paused to look into the water of the creek where it pooled below him. He saw a distorted reflection of the outline of his form in the dim light. Nineteen years had built his body well and tall, but the last four, with the privations of war, had hardened the muscles of his frame and made his features gaunt. His hair was too long, and the week's growth of sandy red beard itched. He'd have to hunt up scissors and a razor as well as a comb.

As night fell, Carl shrugged his shoulders to rearrange the damp shirt, picked up the pails, and headed back to the house, guided by the lamplight from the kitchen window. Breeze on the shirt chilled him, and he walked a little faster. At the steps he re-scraped his boots, then opened the door and went inside.

"We're just fixing to eat," Julia called. She turned and saw the water buckets. "Thank you, son. You saved me a trip."

Carl pulled up a chair to the table and joined Rod and Albert.

"It ain't much, Carl, but it'll keep you from blowing away." Julia waved her hand toward the food. "We're lucky to have greens. They popped up down by the crick, and I picked them late this afternoon. 'Course, there's corn pone, and we have milk, but there ain't no real coffee, just roasted chicory." She sighed as she sat at her place. "We'll have real food again once we get a crop up."

"That's something we need to do some talking about," Rod declared. "First, let's give thanks for Carl's safe return, and for this food we got."

At the end of the grace, Carl glanced across the table at his father. There'd been something in his voice that foretold serious business. Rod must have felt his stare, for he looked up, his beard wrinkling as he chewed.

Rod swallowed. "Tell me how it looks south of here, son. What did Sheridan leave for the folks in the south end of the Valley? You came from Staunton, I reckon?" Rod took a bite of greens.

"He burnt or pulled down homes, barns, crops, orchards, 'most everything, all the way to Staunton and beyond. It's a famine time. A crow flying by would have to bring his own rations." He paused to chew a piece of pone. "Ma, it's a wonder to me the Yankees left our house alone when they came back through."

"I had my good Sharps rifle, and I set right there in the doorway and wouldn't budge none. After a while they left me be and went out back to burn the barn."

"Marie could-a been killed," Albert said, frowning. "Them dirty Yankees didn't wait 'til she was out of the barn to set it afire." Albert's eyes looked dark and fierce. "I wish I'd a been down here shooting me some Yankees instead of up in the hills with Clay and all them cows!"

"Likely they'd have shot you, Albert," Carl said. "Praise God you was up there!"

Rod's mouth tightened. "What about livestock, son? What did you see?"

"I reckon we've got more cattle than any five stock men down the Valley, Pa. Maybe five pigs, thin stuff; not more'n ten hens anywhere. I reckon Grant didn't want no more supplies coming out of the Shenandoah. He meant for little Phil Sheridan to clean us out, and he did the job."

"Lucky I was warned some," Julia said, "or I wouldn't have had time to send the boys off up the hill."

Rod chewed his food slowly, his face looking thoughtful. "I reckon we're eating about as well as Rand Hilbrands. The

Yankees missed burning the store in Mount Jackson, so he still has food to put on his table."

"What happened over to Chester Bates' place, Pa?"

"He lost his barn, and the house is gutted out. They burned his fields bare. The Bates family is about wiped off the face of the earth, I'd say."

"Are they all dead?"

"They've got their lives and little else."

"That's sure a pity." Carl wiped his mouth with his hand. "They had the prettiest stone house I believe I've ever seen. Where are they living now?"

"Right on the place, in the old tool shed."

"Hush, that's a shame. There's no finer man than Chester Bates, 'cept for you and John Mosby, Pa."

"Andy Campbell says his pa's so mad about his place being wrecked, he wants to clear out and go someplace else," Albert reported.

Rod Owen cleared his throat. "That's just what I aim to do."

Chapter 2

Rod's words seemed to echo in the room, fading into silence. Stunned, no one moved or spoke for several seconds, then the air was split with the clamor of the family reacting to his declaration.

Julia raised her chin a bit as she stared down the length of the table. "This has been my home since we wed."

"Pa, I took an oath I'd come home and wait to be exchanged proper. I don't reckon the Yankees will let me leave." Carl shifted in his chair, sitting up straight.

Albert jumped to his feet. "But Pa, I was born right here in this house."

Rod waved away the arguments and held up his hand for silence. "I've decided to sell the farm and go to the Colorado Territory. You ma's brother Jonathan is out there somewhere, and we'll find him. There's gold and silver to be mined, but I been contemplating." Rod paused to lift his cup and try the chicory. He made a face, then drank some more before setting down the cup.

"There's no future for us here in the Valley. Since we're going to cross the country to make a new start, why not start a cattle ranch?" Rod looked around at his family. "We have good cattle here that we can sell as beef to the miners," he said. "There's a sight of folks out there that like to eat. I reckon raising cattle is as good a way to earn a living as digging in the ground for metal."

"I took an oath, Pa." Carl leaned forward. "I'm bound to stay here until my papers come."

"Carl, an Owen's oath is sacred word, but you saw the way of things out there. Since the Yankees paid their call, if we stay here our only choice is to starve. I reckon your oath is null and void."

Carl slouched against the back of his chair. "Who'll buy a burned-out farm? Nobody around here has any federal cash to give you."

"There was a feller here last week from New York State, looking for farmland. His brother was one of Sheridan's torch men, and told him all about the fine crops he set fire to. Well, the man offered a good price, and I took it."

"But Pa," Albert burst out, "he's a damned Yankee!"

"Watch your tongue, young'un. Yes, he's a Yankee, but he has good Yankee currency and coin to give me. Now that you're home, Carl, I aim to leave in two weeks."

"Two weeks!" Julia echoed. "We can't be ready by then."

"How long did it take you to send the boys off up the mountain with the corn?"

Julia stared at her plate.

"We'll be ready in two weeks, because Mr. Avery will take possession then. He'll be back from Washington next week with the money, then he's off to get his family to move them here." Rod slapped the table and stood up.

"You really sold the place?" Julia got to her feet. "You never thought to ask me?"

"We're bound for Colorado. That's all." His words were sharp, final.

Julia reached down for her plate and turned her back in silence.

Rod climbed into bed. Julia turned away from him.

"Still mad at me?" Disappointed, he reached out to touch her shoulder. She shrugged off his hand.

"I got a right."

"I figured you'd want to leave this place."

"I defended the house. I saved it, and I aimed to live in it." She turned over to glare at him.

"You need a change. This war has took your spirit, along with your boys, Julie. I figured you'd want to go."

"There ain't nothing wrong with my spirit, Rod Owen. I've plenty left to tell you what I think. It's a low-down, slimy, snake trick to take a gal's home away from her, without even a by-your-leave."

Rod pushed himself up with his elbows and stared at Julia. "You've changed a right smart whilst I was gone."

"I've had to fend for myself and the young'uns, Rod. I got so I was the boss around the place. I did my chores and yours, too. Now you come home and sell my place without considering my side of the matter. Yes, I've changed a right smart, and I'm mad at you." Julia turned away and hit the wall with her small, work-worn fist.

Rod sank back into the featherbed and let the air leave his lungs in one fast exhalation. When he spoke again, his voice was contemplative.

"I reckon we've both changed. Me, I got used to having my orders obeyed without a word of question coming back at me. It was do it right now or die. My guess is we've lost the habit of working together like we used to." He screwed up his face and rubbed his beard with both hands. "I just hope we ain't lost the habit of loving together," he added, barely audible.

"Um," she sighed, almost a sob, and after a long silence, she turned to look at Rod.

He put out his hand, touched her cheek, and said, "My Julie."

"I never got free of needing you to love me," she whispered. "We need to learn again how to get on with one another, is all."

"I give you my word I'll work hard to look after you like I used to."

"I don't need looking after like I did before the war took you away. I need you to work with me and think about my feelings and thoughts before you jump into something like this."

"I can't change what I did. The paper's signed."

"Oh, Rod, that means we have to leave Baby John lying over yonder in the burying ground." She clutched his forearm, then relaxed her grip to smooth the grizzled hair. "It about breaks my heart."

"Julie, I ain't an unfeeling man. I know it pains you to leave him, and Peter and Benjamin, too, but this is our chance to make a new start." Rod sat up, and the covers fell forward from his torso, exposing his long underwear. "We'll have the cash to buy an outfit to get to Colorado Territory. I'll try to shed my bossy ways, if you'll forgive me, and go with a willing heart."

Julia looked at Rod's back, gauging his excitement by the rapidity of his breathing. It finally returned to normal, and he sank back into the tick.

"Twenty-five years ago I made my vow to love you and to live with you wherever you went," she whispered. "Since you're bound to go, I'd best keep my promise."

Rod turned and looked at Julia. "I love you, woman," he sighed, gathering her into his arms.

Carl woke up in his bed. *I'm home*, he marveled, rolling over in the quilt. He was warm under the covers, barricaded against air chilly from the night's rain. Looking over at Albert, he saw the regular rise and fall of his brother's chest. *He's such a young'un*, Carl mused. *He's been doing all my chores for three years. It's time I took some of 'em back and let him sleep.*

He sat up and flicked the covers back from his bare legs. It had been a long time since he'd had a chance to get out of his pants at night. On the run with the Rangers, he had practically slept in his saddle. Carl got up and dressed quickly, yearning for a change of clothes.

He left Albert still asleep and went downstairs to stir up the fire. As he made it blaze to life, the chill around the fireplace faded, and he put a boiler of water on the hearth to heat for washing up later.

Carl crossed the room and got his coat before he went outdoors. From the doorway he looked at the morning sky. The clouds were thinning out, waiting for the sun to rise, and the rain had quit falling. Toward the east, the bulk of Massanutten Mountain rose up to prevent Carl from seeing the Blue Ridge Mountains, but he knew they were there, and he knew they were hazy and covered with fog on such a morning as this. He'd spent enough time dodging the Yankees, riding up into the sanctuary of the isolated gaps and hollows, that he knew the moods of the mountains.

The yard was under water from the night's rain, and Carl wondered how the animals would fare in the open in this weather. Then he recalled with a jolt that soon they would be used to it. There were no barns on the way to Colorado Territory.

Carl set about feeding the animals, and with courage born of morning freshness, he decided to tackle milking Brindle by himself.

"Cow, I been over the hill and down the river in the last few years. I ain't going to be licked by the likes of you."

Brindle promptly knocked him over, sprawling him into the mud and water. He scrambled up, soaked and sputtering, and went back to work, wiping his hands on his pants.

"I reckon I'll milk you, so you'd just as well surrender, you crazy cow." Carl set his jaw and grabbed a handful of teat. Brindle turned her head and rolled her eyes, unconvinced of Carl's prowess. He went on the attack, and the cow mooed with fright.

When he had a half-pail of milk, Carl figured he'd won the battle, and let the calf have its breakfast. He straightened his back, then probed the sore spot on his side where the cow had kicked him, but decided it was nothing to worry about.

Carl took the milk to the house and washed up with the water he'd left heating. Checking the wood box, he found it half empty and returned to the yard for an armful. From the looks of the stack of firewood on the left edge of the clearing, James had made more than one trip to the mountain for wood. Carl pulled some logs from the center of the pile where the wood was dry, and took them into the house.

Julia was up, tending the fire and baking bread for the day. She looked up at Carl, then down at his feet.

"Hush, Ma, I'm sorry. I forgot to wipe 'em. I ain't used to living in a house, but I'll try to keep the mud in the yard where it belongs."

Albert came into the room, yawning and stretching, and looked accusingly at Carl. "You left me a-sleeping. I got critters looking to be fed."

"You was up late, and looked like you were relishing your sleep. I took the liberty of doing your chores this morning. Set and eat."

"Thanks, Carl. Don't mind if I do." Albert sat and attacked his breakfast.

Rod came into the room, looking pleased with himself. He carried a list of purchases to make as soon as the Yankee money passed into his hands. He sat and greeted his family.

"Morning, Julia, boys. Fine day. Carl, you make ready to ride into town with me after breakfast. We'll fetch back your sisters to help your ma get the foodstuffs together." Rod paused to chew a mouthful of cornbread, then turned to his youngest son. "Albert, who did you say was willing to leave the Valley on account of his place was wrecked?"

"That would be Andy's pa, Angus Campbell."

"Pa," Carl broke in ahead of Rod's next speech. "How are we

going to get out to Colorado? Me and my outfit blew up so much track hereabouts, I reckon the railroad's useless."

"I been studying on that, son. We'll take wagons, like those who went to Oregon in the early days, and the Mormon folk in the forties. I reckon we'll keep off the northern trails. I can just see a Yankee farmer taking pot shots at us, calling us wild Rebs. Likely we can get through Kentucky and Missouri on the back roads and hit the Santa Fe Trail at the city of Kansas. We'll follow it along the Arkansas River into Colorado, then turn north and strike out for Denver City to find your uncle."

"We're getting a mighty late start."

"I know, and wagons are slow, but I figure we can haul more goods for less cost that way. I reckon we'll need four, five months on the trail, but the weather should hold pretty fair until then." Rod turned his head to his wife. "We'll take that old box of Jonathan's to him."

Carl's gaze shifted from his father's face to the leather-covered strongbox on the mantel. Uncle Jonathan brought it with him when he returned from his trip to the Territory in 'Fifty-nine. He told his sister it was hers if they ever got word of his death. Then he went back west to his gold fields. The box had never been opened, and sat, padlocked and dusty, where he'd placed it.

"How long since you heard from Uncle Jonathan, Ma?" asked Carl.

"It's been a couple of years, but mail has been real chancy with the war on."

"It'll be good to see him again." Carl rose from the table. "I'll saddle the horses, Pa."

"I'm nearly through here." Rod paused to wipe his mouth. "Albert, you'd best get to shelling the corn. Your ma will need to make it all up into cornmeal before we leave."

"Yes, Pa."

Chapter 3

Carl rode with his father down the Valley toward Mount Jackson, feeling a wrenching in his gut at the desolation and ruin in the homesteads they passed. These folks had worked for years, generations even, and now everything was gone, wiped out by the advance of Sheridan's army. Some of these farmers might listen to Pa's plan to go west.

As they rode through the gray mist and green trees, they approached Mount Jackson, which sat near the Shenandoah River. The damage here was not so heavy. Old stone houses still lined the streets of the residential section, where the town folks were scratching out a post-war living. An occasional empty lot in the business district gave testimony of a wooden building gone up in smoke.

Rod pulled up his horse at an intersection and turned to Carl. "We'll go to Rulon's house first, let the girls know to pack up their bundles. Then I'll go talk to Randolph Hilbrands. He could make a pile of money with a store in Colorado, and he's always been partial to money." Rod chuckled. "Let's see how long it takes me to convince him."

Rulon lived on a quiet back street in a brick house owned by his father-in-law, the same Randolph Hilbrands. Rulon and Mary had lived there since he was sent home to die.

As Rod and Carl rode up to the door of the house, someone pulled aside the curtains of a window on the ground floor and peeked out. The men dismounted and tied their horses to the fence, then the door of the house was flung open, and out boiled two young females.

"Papa!" Julianna, fair colored and exuberant, with the energy of eleven years, threw herself into Rod's arms.

"It's Pa," squealed Marie. "And Carl's here, too!" Despite the decorum she had gained in sixteen years, she wrapped her arms around Carl, nearly knocking him off balance.

"Whoa, hold up there, Sis." He put out his hand to steady the two of them against the fence. "You've growed up," he said, astonished.

"Sure have." Marie giggled, tossing her dark head. "And you're a man, looks like." She backed away for a long appraisal.

Carl went hot with embarrassment. His sister was looking at him with woman's eyes.

"I'm just real skinny," he protested. "It makes me look taller."

"Wait 'til the girls get a look at you," laughed Marie. "You'll have to drive 'em off with a hay fork. It's been a long time since we've had any suitors around."

"Suitors! You and your friends ain't never had no suitors. You was just babies when us men went off to fight." Carl took a deep breath, on home ground now that he was bantering with Marie.

"That's all you know," she replied.

Julianna dragged Pa toward the house, so Carl grabbed Marie's hand and followed.

Mary Owen stood in the doorway, offering her hand to her father-in-law, who gave her a bear hug instead. She looked pale, and a crease appeared on her forehead as she endured the hug.

"Roddy," she called to a small, dark-haired child playing by the hearth. "You come over here. Your granddaddy just came. Give him a welcome."

The boy looked up, then jumped to his feet.

"Poppy!" he cried, and ran over to grasp Rod by the knees. Rod bent down and boosted him up onto his shoulders. The boy whooped, and held on to Rod's ears.

Julianna plumped a pillow in the best chair in the house, saying, "Papa, come an' set down."

Rod put the youngster on the floor, and Roddy scampered off to play with his blocks.

"Pa, it's right nice to see you again," Marie said, hugging her father. "Carl, come over here and set a while," she urged her brother, placing a chair for him.

The men sat, and Julianna tiptoed behind Carl, then ambushed him with a big hug, startling him into standing again.

"Jule! You'd best not surprise a man thataway. I might've hurt you."

"Carl's home, Carl's home," she sang, dancing her way around the room, heedless of his discomfort.

Rulon, hearing all the uproar, came down the stairs, leaning against the wall for support. Upon seeing his father and brother, he lowered the pistol he carried and entered the room. Mary glanced up and gave a little cry of alarm, but he waved aside her concern.

"I'm fine, Mary," Rulon grinned, sweeping his hair out of his eyes. He tucked the pistol into the waistband of his trousers and held out his hand to his father. "Just the sight of my kin makes me feel strong."

Rod arose and took Rulon's outstretched hand, then passed him on to Carl, who carefully embraced him.

"You look a mite thin, Rule, but likely you'll never get as skinny as me." The younger brother measured himself against the older, found himself to be taller, and grinned with delight. "Seems you've shrunk a mite, too."

"Taller don't make better, Carl. I still outweigh you in a wrestling match. Wait 'til I get my strength, and we'll have a go at it." Rulon stepped back to look at Carl's spare frame. "'Pears to me you're healthy. Did you catch any Yankee lead?"

Carl grinned. "Colonel Mosby kept us riding fast enough to beat the bullets. That's not saying we didn't lose a few men here and there." His expression changed. "We lost more than a few. I reckon we paid a powerful price."

"Amen, brother."

"Leastwise, you made it home, Rule. Pa just told me about Ben yesterday. That's a mighty blow, I tell you."

Rulon nodded, clapped Carl on the shoulder, and took a chair. "Pa, what brings you into town in the middle of the morning?"

"I've come to fetch your sisters home to help your ma. We've got a right smart job of work to do in the next fortnight. Well, so do you, come to think of it."

"What's that you mean, Pa?"

"I've sold the farm, and we're going to the Colorado Territory to hunt up Uncle Jonathan. I aim to thumb my nose at these Yankees, light a shuck out of here, and make a new life growing cows for all them miners to buy."

"Do miners need lots of milk and butter, Papa?" asked Julianna. She looked around, confused by the hoots of laughter that greeted her question. "Well, do they?"

"I don't mean milk cows, daughter. We're going to raise beef critters."

"Are you asking us to go with you, Pa?" Rulon asked.

"I'd like it, Rulon. It'd be best to keep the family together. You need good clean air to help you mend proper, and Mary here could use a change, her feeling so poorly just now."

Mary sank to her knees beside Rulon's chair, looking anxiously up at him. "I don't feel like I can leave Pa and Ma and go traipsing over the countryside dodging Yankees, Rulon. Please say 'no'," she implored him.

"Don't you go to fretting, Mistress Mary," Rod chuckled. "I aim to fix things with your pa right now. Marie, you girls gather up your things into a bundle and get ready to leave with us."

Rod turned to Rulon. "I'll leave Clay to help you get things together. He's a handy young'un, for his age."

Marie wagged her finger at her father. "Pa, don't let Clay hear you talking like that. He's done more than his share of the work since Carl took off to ride with Mosby. Then when James got drafted, well, he was the man on the place, and he's mighty proud of the job he done."

Rod laughed and tipped his hat onto his head. "Coming, Carl?"

"Ready, Pa." Carl rose to his feet and accompanied his father through the door.

"We'll go over and catch Rand in his store. He won't know what hit him." Rod laughed as he mounted his horse.

When he entered the Hilbrands Mercantile a few minutes later, Carl sniffed the spicy odors of the candy counter, just as he had in years past. This was a friendly place, as well known to him as his home or his saddle.

Rod walked in as though he owned the mortgage, moving with an easy, strolling gait. "Rand," he greeted Mr. Hilbrands, hand outstretched.

"Well, Rod Owen, you old nag-rider, you found you another son." Randolph Hilbrands took Pa's hand and shook it. "Seems like a new one comes home every day."

"Just got in yesterday. Colonel Mosby kept his boys in after school let out."

"You, with five sons left to you, you can joke. Me, with five daughters, and only one married, well, I'm past laughing." Mr. Hilbrands stroked his thin black moustache.

"Now Rand, it hardly seems likely that your girls are all of a marrying age. Why, wasn't Amanda just having a child about the time I left for the fighting?"

"That would be Eliza. But Ida, now. She fancies herself quite a lady, and her not yet seventeen. Always going around worrying about when she will marry. I'm afraid Mandy's filled that girl's head with a mess of nonsense." Mr. Hilbrands shook his head and eased his tall, fleshy frame back onto his stool.

"She's just the age of my Marie. I reckon she's the same way."

"Not like my girl Ida. You never heard the like of the plans she makes to catch her a beau. It'd curl your hair, Rod."

Carl felt the heat of embarrassment creeping into his face, and turned away from Mr. Hilbrands' somber description of his daughter's antics. Looking around at the displays to find one out of earshot, he bumped into the saucy Miss Hilbrands herself, who had just entered from the street.

"I declare, you are the clumsiest—" As Ida got a good look at the object of her verbal attack, she backed up a step and started over. "I *am* so sorry," she drawled. "Silly me, can't help but trip on this old floor. Now let me think. You must be Carl Owen, Rulon's brother. I declare, you *have* grown up so nicely."

Carl stared at her, hoping his mouth wasn't open. Ida Hilbrands had grown up very nicely herself. Above a pair of merry blue eyes was the blondest, silkiest mop of curls he had ever seen. Her nose was tiny, with a hint of mischief to its tilt. Her mouth looked as though it laughed a great deal of the time, and was just now curled upward as she smiled gaily at her prize.

Ida threw back her head and gave a little sigh, and Carl became aware of other curved portions of her body.

"Carl Owen, I declare, has the cat got your tongue? You haven't said one little word since you bumped into me!" Ida smiled encouragingly, tapping her foot.

"I— I'm truly sorry, Miss Ida. I'm not used to being home yet, and in the company of such a pretty little thing as yourself. You have surely changed since last I saw you." Carl vaguely recalled a female child with long braids and knee-length skirts.

"Have you been home long?" Ida inquired sweetly.

"I arrived last evening. Got my parole last week near Charlottesville."

"All this talk of paroles! Makes our men folks out to be a passel of criminals."

"We was prisoners of war. The paroles mean we're on our honor to come home and wait for an exchange. I got my parole, like I said, then snuck me a Yankee rifle. Almost got caught, but I slipped away."

"Well, I never heard of such a thing," Ida exclaimed. "Why on earth would you want a dirty Yankee rifle?"

"Because it's an almighty good one, a repeater. I needed me a good firearm."

"I don't know anything about rifles and such," Ida murmured, looking at Carl with dreamy eyes.

"I have to see if Pa needs any help," Carl gulped, anxious to be away from the gaze of those eyes. "It was wondrous fine to see you again, Miss Ida."

"You'll have to come around and see us from time to time, now that this nasty war is over," she countered.

"I'd be pleased to," Carl nodded. He looked down and stared at his boots.

Ida tossed her head, greeted her father, and went into the back room of the store, sending one last smoldering look towards Carl.

He dropped a sigh of relief, then walked over to where his father and Ida's were deep in discussion.

"I've got my store," Mr. Hilbrands said. "I can make a living. You go ahead on. I'll not set the Yankees to your trail."

"I hope you'll give it a bit more thought, Rand. You've got goods here for a store in the Territory. Look around you and see the conditions hereabouts. Folks are starving, and all you can do is hand out credit and pray they'll get a good crop to repay you." Pa paused to scratch his nose. "Those miners in Colorado Territory have good hard money, gold dust and nuggets, mostly, and dug fresh out of the ground by their own hand. The things they lack are the goods you have right here. It don't seem right when you could make a bunch of money, were you in Colorado. It's not fair, somehow."

Carl wondered how long the silence would last. He glanced at Mr. Hilbrands, and nearly laughed out loud at the hungry look that came across the older man's face.

"Gold dust and nuggets, you say?" Mr. Hilbrands passed his hand over his face. "I'll go with you Rod, but with all this inventory and my house goods, too, I'll be needing an extra driver, and I'm willing to pay a good wage. Will you give me Carl, here?"

Pa turned and looked at Carl, his eyes twinkling. "Will you drive Mr. Hilbrands' wagon, son?"

"I reckon. You've got help a-plenty with the other boys."

"It's done then, Rand." Pa shook hands with his friend. "Have your wagons ready to go in a fortnight. We'll meet at my farm, and get an early start."

"Good. I want to get out there before some other merchant garners all the business." Mr. Hilbrands chuckled, and rubbed his hands along his apron front.

Pa waved good-bye and left the store, followed by Carl, who waited until they were outside, then said, "It didn't take so long to change his mind."

"I reckon I saved the best for last, son. I knew Rand Hilbrands could never stand the thought of good hard gold a-slipping through his fingers." Pa mounted his horse.

"It surely was comical to watch his face change." Carl swung into his saddle. "Who else do you aim to see here in town, Pa?"

"I'm going over to speak with the blacksmith. I hear he's been itching to go west since his wife died last winter. If he goes with us, Tom can take his little ones along, not leave them with the Campbells."

"Isn't Tom O'Connor some kind of kin to the Campbells?"

"Closer than most. Mistress Molly is Tom's sister. Now if Angus will agree to go with us, the whole passel of them can stick together and make a new start in the Territory."

"Why don't I go give the girls a hand, Pa? You don't need me to talk to Mr. O'Connor."

"Have them ready to go when I get back. Look, there's Angus Campbell himself, crossing the street up yonder. I may be gone for a while, son. I'll see you back at the house." Pa nudged his horse into a trot, and little puffs of dust arose as he went up the street.

Carl turned off toward Rulon's house. The sun had come out bright and strong, and it felt good and warm on his back. He grinned. "Hush, we're going west."

As he reached the corner, Carl saw a group of mounted men dashing up the cross street in front of him. Panic rose in his throat as he recognized the Yankee patrol that had jumped him, and he wheeled his horse to find a place of concealment. Then he realized where he was, turned Sherando again, and tried to calm his pounding heart. The soldiers were probably racing through the streets of Mount Jackson to make a ruckus, and he felt foolish to be caught in their trap.

"Easy, boy," he told his horse. "It ain't likely they'll take after me in town."

The Yankees drew up at the far end of the street, then turned and started back to town. As they thundered toward him, Carl noticed a young girl opposite him, evidently trying to decide whether to cross. She hesitated a moment, then bolted out into the street. In the middle, she looked around at the approaching soldiers, tripped, and fell into the road.

Without thinking, Carl spurred his horse into the street, leaned out from his saddle, and plucked the arising girl from the muck. Sherando carried them across the road while the Yankees whooped and whistled as their horses rushed by, venting their disappointment. Carl got down the street, turned a corner, then pulled up and set the girl on her feet and slid off his horse.

"Hush my mouth! That was the foolest thing I ever seen a body do!" Carl made no attempt to stop the hot words from tumbling out of his mouth. He glared at the girl, standing in the street with her chin up and her eyes flashing, auburn hair disheveled, the front of her clothes mud-caked and dripping. "You surely could have been killed, and that's a fact! You keep clear away from that gang of Yankees, you hear? Darn fool girl, anyhow." He got on his horse and left her standing there, pridefully biting back tears of relief. Then he rode away, shaking mud and slime off his arm, and muttering to himself.

Carl dismounted at Rulon's fence and tied his horse, then rapped on the door. Marie answered and looked him over a moment before letting him enter.

"Did you fall off your horse, brother?" she asked, arching an eyebrow.

Carl glared at her. "Don't start in a-teasing me, Marie," he warned, stalking into the room. "Where can I clean up?"

"The well is in the back. I'll bring you soap and a towel if you'll tell me how you got so dirty."

"Keep them. I ain't going to give you the satisfaction." Carl left through the kitchen.

Marie heard the squeak of the windlass as she headed toward the stairs. "Stubborn," she proclaimed. Before she had gone up two steps, someone rapped on the front door again. Marie sighed, came back down, and opened the door.

"Ellen Bates! Whatever happened to you?"

"Please let me come in. I'm afraid those nasty Yankees will bother me again." Ellen's voice quivered dangerously, and Marie stepped back to admit her. Then she closed and bolted the door.

Ellen Bates was covered in the front with a slimy layer of mud. She stood by the door, shaking and dripping on the floor. Marie grabbed her arm and led her to the fire.

"Set here by the hearth while I get some water to clean you up." Marie went toward the kitchen, then halted. "Ellen, my brother Carl just went into the back yard with his arm all covered with mud, and in such a rage. Does he have anything to do with the state you're in?"

Ellen moaned and covered her face with her hands. "Is that who he was? I'll never be able to face him." She got up and moved toward the door. "I have to leave."

"Oh now, you ain't going anywhere." Marie barred her way. "I won't let you go out there looking like you fell down in the road. Oh lawsy! That's what happened, ain't it."

"I was crossing the street in front of those stupid Yankee soldiers running their horses down the way, and I tripped and fell. Your brother kicked that big horse of his and fetched me out of there. Then he set me on my feet and cussed me up and down. He really flapped his tongue some at me," she mumbled. "You've got to hide me before he comes in."

"You're not afraid of Carl, are you?"

"Not afraid. Just shamed. It was highly foolish of me to try to beat those Yankees across the street, and to get plucked out of the mud like a rag doll." She shuddered. "I'll never be able to hold up my head around him my whole life long."

"That's likely, but you can't keep from seeing him. He's here to take me on home. Ma needs me right now. We're going—" Marie looked sideways at Ellen. "I mean, we're going to be busy with . . . the planting."

"Marie, you're telling a fib. What's happening?"

"I'm sorry, Ellen. I can't say." She sighed. "But I will tell you, real soon, I promise. We'll clean you up, and I'll find some clothes so you can go home."

Marie left Ellen by the fire and went into the yard. She found Carl washing his shirt in a bucket of water. As she approached the well, Carl flicked drops of water at her and grinned.

"I'm sorry I was so fierce with you," he said. "Seems like ever since I got home, I've been muddy more than clean, and it's wearing on my nerves. Once, a cow knocked me into the mud, and now I'm filthy on account of a dumb girl."

"Well, that 'dumb girl' was coming to visit me, and she's out in the parlor dying of fright that you'll cuss at her again. Carl, how could you?"

"What? She's here?"

"She's my best friend."

"You surely do pick dumb friends."

"I ain't looking to fight with you, Carl. You had no business yelling at her, though."

"She nearly got us killed by a bunch of Yankees I had trouble with once before." He held up his dripping shirt. "Look at that. I was on my way home and they cut off all my buttons. Claimed I was violating my parole. I do not favor them casting their eyes on me again, seeing as how they're running the show hereabouts."

"Ellen knows she done a fool thing, but she's sorry. You'd best come in and make amends for yelling at her."

"Not me, Sis. Let her die of fright. I ain't apologizing for giving her something she earned." Carl put on his wet shirt and tied it closed with some bits of string.

"I see. Well, she needs to clean up, so if you don't aim to meet her, you'd best remain out here."

Carl mumbled something.

"What did you say?"

"You don't want to hear it."

Chapter 4

Two hours later, Rod Owen whistled as he tossed little Roddy into the air.

"Please, Mr. Owen," Mary cried out. "The baby is so delicate."

"Mistress Mary, you worry too much. This young'un is strong as an ox. And he'll need strength where we're going."

"You're still trying to get us to go with you? Rulon, tell him we can't go," she pleaded.

Rod continued. "Would you druther stay here and bid good-bye to your folks? Your pa agreed to go with me. Not only him, but Tom O'Connor, Angus Campbell, and Ed Morgan are going. I figure we need only one other family, and I'll talk to them on the way home."

Mary found a chair and sank down into it. Rulon crossed the room to squat by her side, and lifted her chin with his blunt fingers. "It won't be as bad as you figure, Sugar. I'm getting stronger every day, and you'll have your ma and sisters along. Look here, it'll mean a good start for us, and we've never had one, with this war. Mary, we're four years wed, and all we have to show for it is Roddy and some pots and pans." He got up and turned to his father. "Pa, we're going with you."

"Rulon, I'm pleased. You won't regret it none. Well now, are those girls ready to go home? I expect I'll need a wagon to haul their things."

Mary got up, sighing heavily, and went to get the girls, and as she passed her husband she gave him a long, despairing look.

"Afternoon, Mary," a young male voice called from the kitchen.

"That's Clay home for lunch," Rulon said. "He likely don't

know you're in town, Pa. Clay," he called. "Come here a minute. Someone's here to see you."

A slim youth entered the room with his hat still on his head, brushing specks of straw off his colorless homespun shirt and faded brown trousers. "Pa!" he exclaimed, hastily taking the hat off his blond head. "When did you get into town?"

"I been here all morning, son. I bring happy news. We're pulling up stakes and heading for Colorado Territory."

"We're what? Where Uncle Jonathan lives? What do you want to do that for, Pa?"

"I've sold the farm, Clayton. We need a fresh start, and I'm sick of the sight of Yankee soldiers."

"You sold the farm? Our home, Pa?"

"I've decided, son."

Clay stood silent for a while, then said, "All right, Pa."

"By the way, your sisters are going home with me, but you stay here and help Rulon get ready to travel."

"What about my job, Pa?"

"Give in your notice this afternoon. Your brother needs you full-time, him not being so spry yet."

"Oh lawsy," Marie interrupted, coming down the stairs. "This house has been full of people all day." She came into the room with her bundle, trailed by Julianna, Mary, and Ellen, whose dignity had been restored by a wash-up and a change of clothes.

"How're you going to get us home, Papa?" Julianna did not like to walk if she could ride.

"I'll hire a team and buggy with Clay to drive us," Rod teased.

"Papa," Julianna wailed. "That takes money, and the Yankees have all of it."

"You'll ride behind me, and your sister will double with Carl." Rod looked around the room. "Where is Carl?"

"He's in the yard being a blue-nosed, stubborn fool," Marie told him.

"He's angry on account of me, Mr. Owen," said Ellen.

Rod finally noticed the extra face. "You're Chester's girl. Is your pa home?"

"Yes, sir, he was when I left this morning."

"Well, we're heading out to your place, so you can come along with us. You can ride with Marie, and Carl can walk."

"Oh, please, Mr. Owen. I'll be happy to walk. You don't need to bother Carl none."

"He's already almighty bothered." Marie giggled into Ellen's ear.

"We'll work something out," Rod declared.

As Ellen walked down the pike with Marie, she daydreamed herself onto the back of Carl's horse. She imagined she felt the hard muscles of his torso under her encircling arms, bit her lip, and gave a shudder of delight. Then she realized her arms were wrapped around her own front. "Pleased, God," she prayed under her breath, "let him forgive me for being a fool." She squeezed her eyes shut in her fervor.

"Miss Ellen, are you ailing?"

Ellen jumped, and opened her eyes as Rod Owen came alongside her, leading his horse with Julianna aboard.

"You were making such a face, I wondered if you was feeling poorly."

"Oh, no," she hastened to assure him. "I was doing a mite of thinking."

"Would you favor riding for a spell? You can hop up there with Julianna and the baggage."

"I'm fine, Mr. Owen. I like to walk."

"You don't always do it so good," a scoffing voice broke into the conversation.

Ellen whirled around, her face flushing with anger. "That's not fair, Carl Owen. Tripping was an accident. You wasn't invited to busybody your way into my bad luck. Better for me had the Yankees run me over." She turned and ran off a ways before walking once more.

"You do have spunk, I'll say that," Carl called after her.

Rod scowled at his son. "That's no way to treat the little lady. You apologize to her."

"Pa!" Carl protested. "It's a misunderstanding betwixt her and me. Them Yankees were hooraying her in town, and I got some riled at her for getting in their way."

"No son of mine ever spoke to a girl in like manner, Carl, and you ain't going to behave in a new fashion because your temper's short. You get along and make sure she's smiling when she gets home."

Carl shrugged his shoulders and set out after Ellen, frowning as he trotted his horse up the road. Ellen had gotten about ten yards ahead of his sister even though Marie called for her to wait and ran after her.

Carl slowed his horse to a walk alongside Marie, who was breathing hard and holding her side. "Save your breath, Sis. Go back and walk with Pa."

Marie looked up and giggled. "You're going to apologize, ain't you. Afraid I'll listen?"

"You'll try. Go along back to Pa. This is all his idea."

"I told you to say you was sorry, but you wouldn't listen to me."

"Go along, or I'll help you," he threatened.

"I'll go. I obey Pa better than you." Marie wrinkled her nose and stuck out her tongue, then stopped walking to wait for her father and sister.

Carl heeled Sherando into a faster gait to catch Ellen. As he came up beside her, he slowed the horse again and looked down at her angry, set face. "Say, you ain't still sore at me, are you?"

Ellen kept walking.

"I was mean as a mad dog to you back there in town. I'm sorry."

Still she walked, facing front, giving no notice to his words.

"I was worried about you. Looked like you were going to get yourself killed."

She stopped, hesitated, then looked up at him, shading her eyes. "You were worried? Why?"

Carl reined in the horse. "That was no way to treat any girl, especially a Southern girl. Them Yanks figured to hurt you. That scared me."

"You were scared?" She began to walk again, and Carl followed, walking his horse.

"Yes. You was, too."

"I saw them horses coming faster than I had figured, and that's what made me trip. I about died of fright."

"You about died of trampling!"

"I'm sorry you got so muddy, and worried, but I'm most sorry I didn't get a chance to thank you. You saved my life, I reckon."

Carl was silent for a moment, wondering why the conversation was so easy. *One thing*, he told himself, *this girl don't talk funny like that Hilbrands gal, playing a man like a fish on a hook*. After a while he asked, "Is your pa planning to rebuild the farm?"

"What choice does he have? We got to put the crops in, and I guess the barn goes up after that. But I reckon we don't need much of a barn, since the Yankees came through and took almost all the stock!"

"You've got you a temper, girl. Almost as bad as mine." He laughed.

"That's what my ma keeps telling me. She says, 'Girl, you're never going to catch—'" Ellen's face turned red again.

"What's that she says?"

"Never mind. Not important." Ellen walked faster.

Carl nudged Sherando to a faster gait and caught up to her.

"If you're in such a hurry, you can ride behind me for a ways. Likely Marie's bag is soft enough to sit on." He put down his hand to help her up.

Ellen stood still in the road for a moment, then she accepted Carl's offer, took his hand, and he boosted her up on the baggage behind him. "Hang on tight," he advised. She slowly put her arms around his waist, and he felt the warmth of her body against his back. Then she rested her cheek against him, and he noticed that the thud of her heart matched the beat of his.

"Chester, you been wiped out. Come with me to Colorado. You can grow acre after acre of wheat there." Rod Owen sat in the Bates' front yard on a tree stump, looking from Chester to his wife, Muriel.

Chester Bates was a mild, weather-beaten man, thick of chest and shoulder, but with no spare fat on his bones. His reddish hair was thinning a little on top, and his square jaw made a proper floor for his square face. Rod had seen the light fade from his dark blue eyes when he returned from the war to find his wife and daughter living in the former tool shed, compliments of the Yankees who burned his home. Now the light was back.

Chester glanced from his dark, matronly wife to his friend. "You're a God-send, Roderick Owen. I'll go with you," he replied. "I'll leave this place and go with you, and the Yankees be damned!"

"Chester, the young ladies," Muriel scolded, smiling.

Ellen pounced on Marie. "This is your secret," she burst out. "And now we're going with you. Lawsy me, if we didn't go, I'd just die!"

~*~*~

"James is back," Julia greeted Rod. "He brought in all that wood. What are we going to do with it? It's no use to us on the road."

"We'll sell it. Likely there's some lazy man around who'll take it off our hands. Did Albert get the corn shelled for you?"

"That boy's been working his fingers to the bone—not to mention his tongue—with all his questions. I reckon he's anxious to go west." Julia hugged the girls. "How's Mary? Were you a help to her? Is Rulon on the mend?"

"He's up and about, Ma," said Marie. "Soon he won't even limp no more."

"Mama, Clay's going to quit his job. Papa told him to," Julianna reported. "Mary always looks sick, and she didn't want to go when Papa told her about his plan."

"I wonder what's making that girl feel so poorly?" Julia glanced over at his husband, catching his eye. "Just how well is Rulon?"

"Well enough, and surely home enough, I reckon," he replied, winking over Julianna's head. "And high time, too."

"Hush now, Rod," Julia cautioned.

Carl took the horses to the pen and stripped off the saddles. Hearing a faint scraping sound behind him, he crouched in the brush. A short ways off he saw a young man seated on the bank of the creek, stropping a razor. At his side he had a basin of water and a pistol. After a while he laid the strop down and began to remove the curly black beard from his lanky face.

"James!" Carl called out. He rushed from the bushes and ran to the creek. The younger man threw down the razor and grabbed the pistol, then dropped it and gave a rebel yell.

Meeting on the bank like two young bulls, the brothers crashed together in a welter of arms and heads, wrestling each other to the ground.

Laughing, Carl declared, "You're just the feller I want to see. And you got you a razor, besides." He rubbed his red stubble while James punched him fondly in the side. "You be through shaving when I'm finished with the horses, you hear?"

"Carl, you coon-faced old lard bucket, we thought you got took prisoner or something. Pa was ready to go to Washington City to see what become of you."

"You're joshing me!"

"No sir, not me. He and Ma were sure worried some. I never seen them so worked up about a body. I reckon Ben going and getting himself killed there at the end of the fighting took some of the sand out of both of them."

"You old liar, you. Pa never had more sand than now. He's ripping us out of this valley, lock, stock, and barrel, and taking us to Colorado. Says we're going to raise beef cattle for the miners."

"He's what?"

"We're going to find Uncle Jonathan and set up a cow ranch, or something like that. Pa's spoken to a bunch of men, and they're going with us."

"You mean we're leaving Ma and the young'uns here?"

"No!" Carl tapped James on the head. "You got mush for brains? We're all going west. Ma and the girls, and everyone. Rulon, too."

"Which men did he talk to?"

"Rand Hilbrands, Ed Morgan, um, Angus Campbell, and Chester Bates."

"Not Joseph Bingham?"

Carl frowned at his brother. "Mr. Bingham lost his legs at Petersburg, James."

"I know that."

"Even though he's Pa's good friend, he's not fit for a trek over the countryside. I'm sure that's why Pa didn't ask him."

"Then I'll speak to Pa. I can tend to a wagon and chores for the Binghams. I have to change Pa's mind."

"You're fussing about something, James. What's nettling you?"

"Miss Jessica. I can't leave here without her."

Carl nodded. "You've been sparking her, I take it?"

"She's let me walk out with her. I think she'll marry me if I ask her."

"You've got yourself a lot of talking to do, brother. Good luck on changing Pa's mind."

"I'll take the offer of luck. Hey, you better finish with them horses, or you'll need the luck back with Pa after you. You know he sets great store by dumb animals."

"That must be why he was so worried about me," Carl quipped, rising to his feet. "Mind, as soon as you're done shaving, it's my turn."

Carl returned to the horses, fed and watered them, and brushed their coats down with an old rag. Then he went back to the creek bank and picked up the basin and razor.

"James, what I need is a bath and a change of clothes."

"Can't wait for Saturday, huh?"

"That foolish brindle cow keeps pushing me in the mud."

"Brindle always was a mite spooked. Well, I got a spare pair of trousers that might do. We're near the same length, looks like. Maybe Ma has an old shirt tucked away that Ben or Peter left behind."

"It's going to be hard to ask that of her."

"Yeah. But you need the clothes."

"Well, I'm bound for that old swimming hole downstream. Thanks for the loan of the razor."

As Carl turned away, James stopped him, holding something out. "Brother, don't forget the soap."

James had to wait two days before both courage and opportunity to speak to his father coincided. As they worked together reinforcing a wagon, James said, "Pa, did you forget to ask Mr. Bingham to bring his family with us?"

"You mean Joseph Bingham, son?"

"Yes. He's your friend."

"He is my friend. He's a kind and gentle man."

"Then he and his family should come with us."

Rod put down his hammer and looked across the wagon bed at James. "He's a cripple. He can't go."

"He's getting better all the time, Pa. I can drive his wagon, do his chores."

"What would he do in Colorado, son? He has a home and a business here, and his wife can manage the bakery. He's not up to building again in a different place." Rod picked up his tool and began to pound a nail into a sideboard.

"Then give me your leave to ask Miss Jessica to go with us."

"What? Leave her family? Why?"

"I'll be her family. I want to ask her to marry me."

"That wouldn't be fair to her, asking her to go across the country where she'd never see her kin again. No."

"She'd do it, Pa. I've been sparking her on Sunday nights."

"I won't break up a family. Since Joe can't go, no one else of his kin goes."

"Pa—"

"No, James. They don't have time to get ready."

~*~*~

Rod turned over in bed in the middle of the night and whispered in his wife's ear. "Julie."

She sat up with a rustle of the tick beneath her, eyes blank and staring in the moonlight that poured into the room from the un-curtained window. Rod pulled her down beside him.

She released a rush of air. "You startled me, Rod. What do you need, this time of night?"

"Julia, I've been thinking."

"In the night? Thinking?" She squirmed into the hollow of his elbow. "You're almost too old for anything else, I reckon." She chuckled, then yawned largely.

Rod squeezed her, then released her shoulders, slipped his arm free, and sat up. "We got to have a wedding before we leave."

"What?" Julia sat up again, wide awake.

"Yes. I've been thinking on the matter of our journey. For one thing, it'll take several months, and for another, it'll take us into land that isn't settled."

"What does that have to do with a wedding, Rod?"

"We've got us a couple of young men who need good wives. We're also taking several young ladies along with us, and they need men to take care of them."

"Roderick Owen! You're not thinking—"

"When Carl met young Ida Hilbrands, I reckon some sparks flew around her pa's store. He's going to drive a wagon for Randolph, and he might as well marry into the family, same as Rulon did. Since James has a hankering to marry, Chester's girl strikes me as a strong, likely match."

Julia sat mute.

"It's a good plan, Julie. You know it is. We won't have a lot of carrying on if the boys are safely wed, and it'll make tight bonds between our families."

"You're meddling where it isn't wanted, Rod," Julia finally managed to say. "You know James is heart-broke that the Binghams aren't coming with us."

"Nonsense, Julie. I'm sorry I can't accommodate his yearning. He'll get over the Bingham girl."

"I fear you're going to live to regret such thoughts. This will stir up more trouble than a bear putting its paw into a bee tree."

Rod laughed softly. "I'm not wrong, dear wife. The more I think on it, the better it sounds. I know Rand is anxious to marry Ida off, and I'll give Chester that wagon I picked up the other day in exchange for his word on his daughter's hand."

"Oh, I never heard the like. That's just— I don't know what to say about such conniving, Roderick Owen."

"Come on, Julie. You want them boys settled into their lives now that the war's over, and those are good girls. Well, that Ida is a mite flighty, but Carl can handle her fine. James is a tad distracted right now, but he and Ellen will get on very well, I wager. I'll talk to their fathers later this week." He idly rubbed the sunburned flesh below his Adam's apple.

Julia sucked in her breath. She held it a long time, then let it go in a rush of sound, bowing her head. "I'm near speechless at your meddling, Rod, but I know you're bound to try to work your will. I hope it don't return to bite you like a water moccasin."

Chapter 5

The next days sped by. Rod was here and there, at one farm or another, directing the preparations for departure. At last night fell, with only one day left to complete the work before they left the Shenandoah Valley forever.

Rod sighed deeply and settled into the tick that lay on the floor of the bedroom. "It's all set, Julie. Tomorrow, late in the afternoon, we will gather at Hilbrands' store to check the final details and see that everyone has their instructions. I've arranged for Reverend Halsey to come and speak the marriage words for Carl and James. I can trust Halsey not to say anything. The young people will have their wedding nights together before we all leave the next morning."

Julia slowly brushed the surface of the quilt with her hand three times, then said softly, "Wouldn't it be a good idea to tell the boys?"

"I don't want to spook them, especially James. You know he is still half ready to stay here."

"Rod, you're going to have to pay the piper someday."

He laughed and nuzzled her neck. "A man needs a wife, Julie. With good luck, they'll have love, too. No, I'm sure of it. Love will come along for both those boys."

Julia sighed. "I pray that will happen. I can hardly stand to look at James's long face. I hope he don't end up hating you, Rod."

He chuckled. "I'm right in this. He'll come to see it."

~*~*~

Rod paced the floor of the Hilbrands' store, then turned to glare toward the two couples standing uneasily at the counter in the back of the room. All the members of the company were present except for Clay, who Rod had dispatched to find out what had happened to the Reverend Halsey. They stood around in family groupings, talking quietly.

"Damnation! Where is the man?" Rod fumed, ignoring the furrowed brow that Julia turned toward him. "He's late. I paid him good money, and he's not here."

"What time did you say?"

"He's two hours late, Julie. If he doesn't come soon, the whole plan will be ruined."

Chester Bates approached Rod. "Not ruined, surely. Just put off for a while. We can find someone farther down the road to marry the young people."

Rod pressed his lips together, his beard bristling. He grunted.

Chester went on, his voice pitched lower. "Mayhap it's a good thing they don't wed yet. We'll need to build houses and get crops in the ground. If those boys are working hard to build homes for their brides, they may not take it into their heads to go somewhere else to settle."

Rod growled a surly reply, then looked up as Clay came through the door. "Speak up, boy. Where's the minister?"

"He went off into the hills to give comfort to Mother Whitwell. She's dying."

"Humph!" Rod snorted. "When will he be back?"

"Mrs. Halsey didn't know for sure, but thought he wouldn't be back until after the burying."

Rod groaned, then gathered his wits and addressed the gathered company. "We'll put the weddings off until later." He shrugged his shoulders. "I suppose it's best that the young ladies don't have to travel with buns in the oven."

Several shocked faces turned his way.

"Well, git on home." He made a shooing motion with his hands. "We meet mighty early tomorrow."

After he set fires in the house and walked to the waiting wagons, Rod did not look back. He mounted to his place on the seat, turned to look at his wife, and gathered the lines into his hands.

"Avery can't live in your home now, Julie."

"Oh, Rod! Did you have to burn it?"

He let out his breath. "Hard work is what's needed, Julie. We can't undo the war, nor bring back our dead sons, and the land belongs to Avery now, but we can begin a new life where we won't have cruel memories."

He started the team, and the wagons of his neighbors turned into a line behind him. Albert and Andy Campbell, driving the livestock, took up the rear, and the animals provided the only island of noise amid the silent pioneer party.

They were anxious to get on the road, and to avoid the pursuit that might come when Malcolm Avery discovered that all he had bought with his Yankee money was land.

Julia sat on the seat of the wagon, hearing the stern command of her husband not to look back, but her body turned with a will of its own, to look at her home for one last time. She watched in fascination as the flames caught on the roof of the house. The fire rose in fingers of red and orange, falsifying the dawn and lighting up the bulk of Massanutten Mountain. Then her trance was broken by Rod's hand on her arm.

"Julie, don't!" he pleaded, and she turned around on the seat.

"Rod, it's my home," she said, feeling tears run down her cheeks. She drew herself up, setting her back rigidly against the glow of the fire.

Rod pulled on the lines, bringing the team to a halt. He set his jaw and put his arm around his wife. "It'll be ashes and rubble soon, just like the rest of the buildings, and we must be on our way." He looked down at her head, made his voice rough, and continued. "Let's go on, Julie. We'll get through this pain."

"I know," she whispered.

Julianna huddled with her sister in the back of the wagon, numb from the long journey down the Valley Pike. She could not recall a more dismal experience than sitting in the wagon hour upon hour, cramped and jostled by the churn and the provision box. Their father had cautioned them to stay in the wagon, for he wanted to travel as fast as possible this first day.

She eased her muscles the best she could, and wondered how soon they would stop for the night. Passing scenery no longer amused her, and she wanted to stretch her legs.

"Jule, do you remember Uncle Jonathan?" Marie asked.

Julianna turned to look at her older sister. "I remember his beard. It always scratched me when he picked me up." She yawned. "But that was such a long time ago."

"I remember when he put his box on the mantel. I didn't want him to go back to Colorado." Marie sighed. "It's been so long since his last letter came. I reckon that's because of the difficulty lately."

"Marie, do you reckon he could be—dead?"

"No. Not Uncle Jonathan. Ma says the mail's been cut off with all the fighting. She says we'll catch up with him sooner or later."

Julianna yawned again, and wished Pa would make a rest stop.

~*~*~

The light of the afternoon sun slanted sideways through the trees when Rod sighted the meadow. A small stream ran through it, and oak limbs were blown down in the surrounding woods. They didn't need anything else for a campground.

The wagon came even with the edge of the forest and Rod pulled his team off the road. He drove on a ways, back into the meadow where the forest put out a feeler into the grassland. Hauling on the lines, Rod stopped the wagon close to the stream. The others followed, stopping their wagons alongside his. Rod jumped down from the seat and helped Julia climb down from the seat as the men from the other wagons gathered.

"We'll make our first camp here, with two small fires, and two guards out toward the road."

"You're not still in the Army, Rod," interrupted Rand Hilbrands.

"Caution pays, Rand. We don't know who might follow us, or when they'd come."

"Not for a couple of days. You must be joking," Rand scoffed.

"I burned my house," Rod reminded him. "Most of us are paroled soldiers. There may be someone who'll object to our leaving."

"There's still soldiers going north," Chester said. "Some I've seen are hungry and mean. You can't trust them not to take what little we've salvaged. I'll take the first watch, Rod."

Rod laid his hand on Chester's shoulder and gripped it. "Thank you. Rulon will join you. Somebody will bring your supper, so don't get spooky and shoot them."

Carl got down from the last wagon and helped Ida Hilbrands to the ground. "Now you, Missy," he said, and swung down Eliza, her youngest sister. The girls gave their thanks, and walked off in the direction of their family wagon.

Even though their wedding had been postponed, Ida had insisted that she should ride on the seat of the freight wagon with Carl so they could "get to know each other better." Her mother agreed, as long as she took small Eliza along for "company."

Carl stretched, then shook out his tired arms. He hadn't driven a team in nearly three years, and today's trip had been extra-long. He took his Spencer rifle from under the wagon seat, sought out his father, and volunteered to get firewood. Being still unused to the company of women since his war service, he was a little shy of Ida, with her head tossing and giggles, and was anxious to be off by himself in the woods for a while.

He jumped across the creek and strode into the trees. Carefully, he circled back toward the road and scouted the area, checking for signs of other travelers or pursuit. When he was satisfied that the group was alone, he returned to the vicinity of the camp and began to gather deadfalls and dried limbs for fuel. He arranged his load to leave his right hand free to carry the Spencer, and turned back to the camp. As he came out of the woods, he noticed Ida standing on the bank of the stream, waiting for him.

"Yoo-hoo," she called. "I've come to help you gather wood."

Carl approached the bank and grinned. "Seems you're on the wrong bank. I've got plenty, thanks."

"Oh-h-h," Ida pouted. "I couldn't get across this river."

Carl laughed. "Well, I can't let you go back empty-handed." He shifted his load to get a chunk of wood into his other hand, then awkwardly tossed the piece across the creek. It hit the bank and bounced into the water, and Ida scrambled after it, lost her footing on the slick bank, and landed in the water with a little cry.

Carl dropped his load and waded into the creek to retrieve her, struggling to stifle his laughter. Gathering her up in his arms, he became conscious of how the wet bodice of her dress accented her shapely form. His body reacted, and uncomfortable, he looked away from Ida and hurried to get her out of the stream.

"Are you hurt?" he asked, placing her on the bank. He stepped back and linked his hands together in front of his body.

She sighed. "Only my pride."

"You'd best get back to camp and dry off. You could take the ague, wet like that." Carl turned and splashed back through the creek for the wood, grateful the water was cold.

After supper, Rod approached Carl and squatted on the ground beside him.

"You and James take the second watch. Get some sleep, and Rulon will wake you. I gave him first watch so he could sleep the rest of the night through."

"He seems much improved, Pa."

"There's no quit in Rulon, not even for a Yankee mortar shell. I can't figure why his wife's feeling so poorly, though."

"Woman's complaint?"

"Woman's ways, likely. Changeable creatures, they are. Take your ma. She was colder than wet socks when I told her I sold the farm, but she calmed down, and took right to the victual making and all. Except this morning, she was broke up some about leaving. She didn't like to see the house burning."

"You told her not to look, Pa."

"Well, she did."

"There ain't no accounting for women, Pa. I can't figure out Ida Hilbrands."

Rod chuckled. "I've seen the way she acts. She ain't had a man to work her womanly wiles on since she grew up and learned them, son." He placed his hand on Carl's shoulder. "You be cautious. Don't let her work you into a dither. If you fool with her before you have the marrying words said, Rand will take a shotgun to you. Mind my words."

"I will remember. Goodnight, Pa."

Carl crossed over to the Owen wagon and got his bedroll out of the back. He picked his way through the sleeping camp to the spot where James was already stretched out in his bedding. Carl unrolled his own blankets on the ground. He sat and pulled off his boots, then lay back and drew the covers around him.

"Night, James."

"Wake me when Rulon comes," James mumbled.

As he drifted off to sleep, Carl recalled the feel of Ida in his arms, the sight of her clinging dress. He groaned as his body betrayed his good sense, and half-woke James, who stirred in his sleep.

Carl sat up and shook his head to clear out the thought of Ida.

"Remember what your daddy said," he told himself, turned over, and eventually went to sleep.

Chapter 6

The city of Kansas lay ahead, hot in the sun, as Carl drove the freight wagon through the ford at Blue River. Three months of exposure to wind, dust, and sun had weathered his face and forearms to a dark brown. Three months of driving the mule team made it a matter of routine to urge the animals up the riverbank and into the meadow.

Those same three months of Ida Hilbrands' company had broken through some of Carl's reserve, and when he had pulled the team to a halt and applied the brake, he stood up, threw off his hat, bent over, and grabbed Ida off the seat. She squealed and grabbed for the wagon, but Carl held her fast and squeezed her.

"Look at that, girl. We made it all the way to the beginning of the Santa Fe Trail, this here town. Purty soon we'll be on the last leg of the trip."

"Well, I declare, Carl Owen," she protested. "You put me down! I don't hanker to fall off this big old wagon."

"Hush, I ain't going to drop you." Carl let go of Ida's waist with his right arm to prove his strength, holding her with his left.

"Put me down! I'll have Papa speak to you." Ida struggled and kicked against Carl. "You ain't to be trusted!"

"Ida, you make me laugh. Your pa has trusted me for three months now with no complaints, and you been left in my entire care and keeping the whole time."

"You put me down, or I'll go ride with my mama and the other girls. I would be hurt real bad was you to drop me."

Carl frowned and eased her down to the seat. "Go along if you care to. I'll not stop you." He hoped she would ignore his retort and say something bright and witty, but she flounced down on the seat beside her little sister and folded her arms across her chest.

He swung down from the tall wagon, then put up his arms to help Ida get down. She was gone, climbing down the other side, taking Eliza with her. He fisted his hand and punched the wagon rim, then shook his hand and sucked his sore knuckles.

"This is a fine mess," he muttered, scuffing his boot through the dust. He sighed, and wondered what he'd done wrong.

Ida was fun to be with, most of the time. She excited his imagination, calling his attention to fantasy details in passing clouds, and had been an amusing and entertaining companion through the long, wet days of flight through Kentucky. Ida had kept him awake while he drowsed his way up the old King's Trace in eastern Missouri, feverish and weak. She had made him feel like a man, and many times he had had to dig his heels in and think "whoa" before he grabbed her and stole a kiss. But times like these confused him, with Ida willful and quarrelsome. He wondered what kind of a trick she was playing on his this time. Finally, he shrugged his shoulders and turned away from the wagon to find his pa.

As he walked along, a female voice called his name, and he stopped to find the speaker. Glancing around, he saw Ellen Bates peering from the back of her father's wagon. She was on her knees, searching for something, and her sunbonnet hung down her back, letting her auburn hair spill over her shoulders. Carl thought how pretty and peaceful she looked, and wished that Ida were as gentle.

Grinning, Carl approached the wagon. "Hello, Miss Ellen. Seems like forever since we last spoke."

"There ain't been much need." She looked down at her hands. Then she raised her head, looking him straight in the eye. "You been busy, driving that big wagon, and looking after the Hilbrands girls."

"It's been a lot of work, getting the knack of it, but I manage pretty well with the mules now. The girls ain't been too much trouble."

"Do we make camp here?"

"I was on my way to find out." Carl noticed for the first time the little flecks of brown in Ellen's green eyes. "I'll come back and tell you, if you like."

"Oh, don't go to any bother. Likely Pa will come back and tell us."

"You sure now?" There were also little flecks of brown across the bridge of Ellen's nose. *Sun freckles, like as not*, he thought, liking them.

Ellen nodded and disappeared into the wagon.

Hush, she's a fetching looking girl, he mused, never suspecting the hot tears that she wept onto her blanket at night, raging against Ida's good fortune.

Carl found his father and asked, "Is this our campground?"

"Howdy, son. No, I want to get closer to town before we settle in, but you can unhitch your mules and water them. By the way, I'm riding in to town later on to get some supplies. I'd be pleased if you boys would ride along with me."

"Sure, Pa. How much longer you figure before we hit Colorado?"

"If we don't have no major breakdowns, I reckon we got a month or forty-five days' travel ahead of us. Git going, son, and tend to your animals."

"Yes, Pa." Carl returned to the wagon and unhitched the mules, then drove them down to the river. Albert was there with the loose livestock, and Clay came down the bank with the spare horses.

Carl's horse, Sherando, caught his master's scent and tossed his head, whinnying in greeting. Carl waded over to his horse and patted the big gray gelding on the neck.

"Sherando, have you been keeping out of trouble? Hush, I miss riding you, you old war horse!"

Sherando nickered softly, pushing his muzzle into Carl's chest. Carl took a step backward and kept his balance.

"Oh no you don't, boy. I'll take a bath when I've got the time."

Albert came and patted the gray's flank. "He's a mighty fine horse, Carl. Why'd you name him 'Sherando?' It ain't a name I ever heard."

"It's the name of an old Indian chief, Albert. There's a legend that the Shenandoah Valley was named after him."

"An Indian, huh? In the Shenandoah?"

Carl ruffled the boy's hair. "It's so, Albert. There used to be Indians all over the woods and valleys, about a hundred years ago."

Bidding his brother and his horse good-bye, Carl returned to the mules and drove them out of the water. He took them to the wagon and re-hitched them. Somewhere from his belly came the pinching cramps of hunger, and he climbed up to the wagon seat to retrieve a packet of cornbread from underneath.

By gum, I never figured to eat cornbread again once I left the army, he thought, then shame swept over him as he remembered that he would be starving now if it hadn't been for his mother's quick thinking and courage. He finished the bread in silence.

"Tarl, lift me up," a small person with a lisp demanded.

Shoot, she sounds just like Ida, he thought, helping Eliza into the wagon.

"Where's your sister?"

"She's helping Mama. I'm 'posed to tell you that India is coming with us now."

Carl groaned. Ida was making good her threat. "Girls!" he exclaimed, and dropped to the ground, leaving the child on the seat.

He found Ida next to her father's wagon, doing nothing more needful than rearranging her hair. Silently, he caught her by the wrist and pulled her along with him, out into the meadow, away from the wagons. She didn't resist him physically, but protested a little with squeaks and squeals as they went along.

Carl stopped suddenly and spun around to face her, gripping her by the shoulders. "It's time we stopped the game-playing, Ida. You started it, but I'm ending it my way." He bent down and kissed her full on the lips. "That's how I feel about you. My pa arranged our betrothal to suit himself, but I like you a lot, and I reckon I want you for a wife. We can wed once we're settled in Colorado, but I'm telling you now, you stop picking fights with me!"

Ida stood rooted to the ground, looking up into Carl's eyes, and he watched the changing expressions on her face. He waited as she thought over what he had said, still holding her shoulders.

"I'm sorry I riled you," she blurted out. "I'll be a good wife to you." Ida gave a little gasp and clapped her hand over her mouth. "Carl, why don't we get married in the town? I know Papa will be much happier, and Mama will be glad to see me married safe."

"My pa wants me to ride with him into town in a little while. I'll see what I can arrange."

"Oh, Carl. It'll be so much fun!" She turned and ran back towards the wagon, and Carl slowly followed, his head reeling and his heart thumping in his chest.

"It surely does feel fine to ride this horse again," Carl said to James as they followed their father and younger brothers into town. "I don't know as I would favor becoming a freighter for good. I would miss riding."

On his other side, Rulon rolled his shoulders, stretching them in a circle. "I'm surely glad I've got well enough to ride. Mary gets a bee in her bonnet from time to time, and it's a relief to get out of the wagon for a while."

"The old married man," James laughed. "Tell me, what makes her so touchy?"

"Why, she's making us up another young'un." Rulon's grin almost split his face in two.

"You don't say! Rulon, who would've figured you mended so quick?" James rode his horse up by Rulon and punched him lightly on the shoulder.

Rulon slugged him back. "Keep your nose wiped, little brother. Your time will come soon enough."

James made a growling sound deep in his throat. "I'm none too happy with Pa's meddling. If it weren't for Ma, I would have stayed behind. I'll never see Miss Jessica again."

Rulon reached out and patted James' shoulder. "I'm sorry your plans got thrown away, brother. It's hard to take leave of such good friends. Our family has to stay together to survive, though. Pa's right about that."

James only grunted and made a dour face.

Rod Owen pulled his horse to a halt by the tie rail in front of A. G. Boone's store. He dismounted and waited for his sons to join him before he spoke.

"Rulon, you take James and Albert and hunt up the law in town. We missed the trading caravans to Santa Fe by a long time, so find out what measures we need to take for safety. Carl and Clay, you come with me. I'll hunt up Mr. Boone. Your Uncle Jonathan told me to trade with him if ever I got this far west."

Rod wrapped his reins around the rail and swung under

it, stepping onto the board sidewalk. Carl and Clay followed him, while the other three went off down the street.

Before entering the store, Carl turned and surveyed the bustling street. Even though the traders were gone, the traffic seemed constant. He glimpsed some soldiers up the street, loading a wagon with supplies, and recalled that his father had mentioned Fort Leavenworth up north a ways.

Wagons passed the store, narrowly missing each other in the intersection, their drivers yelling obscenities at one another, filling the air with strident shouts. Then the street was empty for a moment, and Carl's attention was drawn across the street by a group of three men lounging outside a saloon.

From the loudness of their talk, Carl guessed they had already visited the bar at some length. Two of the men were of average height and weight, wore nondescript trousers and shirt, and had full beards and shaggy hair. The third man was swarthy, tall, and of a powerful build. He wore tight black pants of a cut Carl had never seen before. His shirt was white, topped by a black vest that was embroidered with a light-catching thread. On his head he wore a hat with a wide brim and flat crown. The hat, too, was embroidered, with colored threads in fancy designs. The man's face was clean-shaven, except for a full-flowing moustache.

Carl gazed at the man for several seconds, until the dark, fancily dressed man removed the thin black cigar from his mouth, chuckled, and said something amusing to his companions. They laughed, and looked over at Carl, who noticed the whiteness of the big man's teeth beneath his moustache. *I reckon he's a Mexican*, he thought, and turned and entered the store.

He glanced around the crowded establishment. Three areas of commerce—dry goods, hardware, and groceries—shared the room, crowding the shelves and aisles. Pa was headed for the hardware counter, where a solidly built redhead in his fifties minded the store. Clay looked like he was enjoying himself browsing through the dry goods section, and Carl joined him.

Rod stopped at the counter. "I'm looking for A. G. Boone. You be him?"

"I am not. Mr. Boone is out to lunch. I am his clerk, Samuel P. Flaherty, at your service."

"Well, it ain't anything you can't handle, I reckon." Rod looked around the empty store. "You don't have much business today."

"It's the lunch hour. If you want to see business, sir, stick around until the end of the month when the traders return. Then you'll see business!" Mr. Flaherty bobbed his head in anticipation.

"I don't plan to stay that long. I'm here for provisions. That's my list. Can you fill it?" Rod put a bit of paper on the counter.

The man took up the list and peered at it. "Surely. If we don't have it, you don't need it." He looked up at Rod. "You going far?"

"We have kin west of here," Rod answered warily.

"Well, I wouldn't presume to ask, except if you're going to the Colorado Territory, you'd better check your supply of guns, powder, and lead."

"Is that a fact?"

"Yes, sir. The Indians are on the warpath out there. Seems some militia colonel named Chivington wiped out a bunch of Cheyenne and Arapahoe at Sand Creek last winter, and three or four tribes took exception to the action. They're raiding all the way from the Platte to the Arkansas, and on east into Kansas." Mr. Flaherty stopped to pull some cans from the shelf. "Indians favor sneaking up on a body when they attack. It's almost like they're invisible until they're on top of you." The clerk scratched his chin.

"Dangerous fellows," said Rod.

"Yes sir. I see you're not wearing handguns. Handguns are right handy to have when an Indian is five feet away and swinging a hatchet at your head. I expect you're a rifle man, yourself. Well, a rifle'd just get in the way with an enemy so close and set on revenge. Some of them don't care if they lives or dies, just so their kinfolks is avenged."

"You don't say."

"But I do say. If I was you, I would outfit my entire party with handguns, belts, and holsters. That's if I was you and going out to the Colorado Territory." Mr. Flaherty folded his arms and leaned forward on the counter.

Rod looked at the clerk, waiting there for a sale. He said nothing, but tucked his chin into his chest for a moment, then moved over to the dry goods section of the store.

Carl had spent his time admiring the clothes on display on the counter. There was a pair of blue jean trousers, waist overalls, that would suit him fine. He wished he had a couple of coins to rub together, or better yet, to spend on new trousers.

His father looked around for Clay, who had moved over to examine the candy counter. He saw Carl looking at the trousers, and approached him.

"They would look mighty nice, son, and you surely do need them, but I can't spare the cash right now. If what the clerk says is right, looks like we'll be needing handguns worse than a change of clothes." Rod looked chagrined. "I was hoping to get a little keepsake for your ma, but I reckon our safety comes before trinkets."

"Trouble on the trail, Pa? Outlaw?"

"Indians. Somebody broke a treaty, and the whole east part of Colorado Territory is running with blood. We might have to fight our way in." Rod grinned and winked. "Don't mention it to Rand Hilbrands. He's not much for fighting."

"Now, Pa," Carl responded. "Mr. Hilbrands ain't so bad. I don't reckon he's a cowardly sort. He just spent the whole war behind a store counter, and didn't get the chance to harden up like we did."

"That's so. And he saw a right smart lot of Yankees going up and down the Valley, but he sometimes wears my patience mighty thin."

"Pa, speaking of the Hilbrands, don't you think we could rustle up a preacher in this town so Ida 'n me can get married?"

Rod looked sharply at Carl. "Are you sparking on that wagon seat, boy?"

"I'm driving. Ida does the sparking." Carl grinned. "It's time I got wed, Pa."

"I'll see what I can do. It's surely a shame that preacher never came around back home. He put a bad crimp in my plan." Rod gripped Carl's shoulder and turned away toward the counter where Flaherty was loading his order into a couple of emptied grain sacks. "What are you asking for a handgun set?" he asked the clerk. "I might be persuaded that I'm interested if the price is right."

"Well now, we've got a mighty nice piece of goods for twenty-five dollars, complete with belt and holster. It's an Army model 1860 by Colt, .44 caliber with six shots. It's your standard percussion cap revolver, ain't been used much. Twenty-five dollars, ammunition extra." He brought out a big revolver for Rod to examine.

"If it saw action in the war, it's been used more than a mite." Rod looked it over, checking the cylinder and the heft of the nearly three pound gun in his hand. "You got any more like this?"

"Some. The Army dumped them on the market a while back, and they've been selling good."

"Let me have my pick of six pistols, you throw in the belts, holsters, and a thousand rounds of shot, with caps and powder enough to shoot them, and I'll give you a hundred dollars, Federal cash."

"Done!" said Mr. Flaherty.

"Hallelujah, Pa! You got me a gun!" Albert's voice cracked in his excitement. "You really got me a gun, a humdinger. Thanks, Pa." The boy lifted the pistol in two hands, sighted down the barrel, then put it back into his holster.

"Albert, we're likely to run into some trouble up the road. I expect you to learn to use that pistol, but it's for protection. I won't stand for gun play. Don't forget that!"

"No, Pa, I surely won't. Boy, wait until I show this to Andy. His eyes will pop out of his head."

Rulon hitched his gun belt to a more comfortable position. "It feels strange, Pa. I'm more at home with a rifle."

"Rulon, it's mighty handy to have a weapon strapped on with enemies coming right at you. Mr. Flaherty spoke of Indian raids in the Territory. If we aim to find your Uncle Jonathan, we'll need guns at hand, I reckon." Rod hitched up his own belt.

James swung into his saddle, and retrieved his pistol as it slipped loose. "Pa, how do I keep the revolver from falling out of the holster when I'm mounting, or jogging loose as I ride?"

"Look at this thong, here. Loop it over the hammer, and the gun will stay in there real snug. If you expect trouble, just slip off the loop, and you're ready."

James fixed the rawhide thong as Rod had directed, then kneed his horse into the street. He cantered down a block, dodging wagons, then waited for a clear moment and returned at a gallop.

He pulled up before his father and brother, checked his pistol, and declared, "That works right fine."

Rod caught Carl's arm and spoke confidentially. "I found a preacher, son. He's willing to speak your wedding words this evening."

"That's good, Pa."

"See if you can talk James into marrying Miss Ellen, too."

Carl nodded and got on his horse. "Pa, I reckon I'll ride ahead and give Ida the news. She'll be happy to hear it."

"I'll go with you," Rulon volunteered. Rod and the others mounted their horses, and rode out of Kansas town in a cloud of dust.

As they completed the first mile of their ride back to camp, they heard gunfire and rode forward cautiously. Before them in the road, the big Mexican with the fine clothes trotted his horse in a circle, shooting his gun and laughing, while his two cronies followed him, enclosing three young women, who huddled together in fright.

Carl and Rulon, ahead of the other men, looked at each other, anger darkening their features.

"That's Marie, and Ellen Bates," Rulon shouted.

"And Ida Hilbrands," finished Carl.

Chapter 7

Carl spurred his horse into the midst of the rowdies, knocking the guns from the hands of two of them before Rulon arrived. As he whirled Sherando to face the man in the black vest, Carl saw the gun pointed at his chest.

"Do not be foolish, señor," Black-Vest warned him. "I shoot very fast, and I do not miss." He drew back his lips in what passed for a smile, and his teeth, white beneath his moustache, seemed large as headstones.

The other Owen men arrived, and noting the gun covering Carl, sat their horses in stolid silence, hands held carefully in sight. The two bearded men dismounted and retrieved their pistols, laughing as they brought them to bear on the Owen party. One man stepped backward and tried to caress Marie's cheek with his free hand. Marie shrank back and cried out.

Ellen's eyes went dark and glittering, and she snapped at the big Mexican, "What kind of cowards are you, picking on girls and honest men?"

Black-Vest's smile vanished. "Coward! You will see that Berto Acosta is not a coward. I withdraw my gun." He holstered the weapon and lifted his hands. "Now you see I am no coward. *Joven*! You with the quick temper. Let us see if your hand is as quick as your anger." He motioned to Carl to try to outdraw him.

Carl shrugged his shoulders. "I can't beat you. I just got the gun today."

"Ah," said Acosta. "But when a man puts on a gun he must be prepared to use it. What do we do now?" His hand dropped toward his gun.

"You're still a coward, or you'd let us go," Ellen hissed.

"That little one has fire," Acosta said, then leaned over to stroke Ida's blonde curls, "but I choose this white little goddess."

"No you don't!" shouted Carl, looking at Ida's chalky face. "I can't meet you with guns, but I sure can beat you with my bare hands!"

"A champion," laughed Acosta, baring his teeth. "*Mis amigos*," he addressed his friends, "we will have here a fine contest, and all will know I am no coward. If he wins, they will all go free." He threw back his head and laughed a long time. "But I will win, and then we shall enjoy the spoils!"

Carl flung himself off Sherando and stripped away his gun belt and shirt. Acosta seemed confident, dismounting with a lazy grace that spoke of long, hard muscle and great control. The big man gave his holster and belt to one of his companions, but he made no move to take off his vest or shirt.

As he looked at the Mexican, Carl imagined him holding Ida in his arms, and a cold rage welled up into his throat, nearly choking him. He stepped up to the older man and threw the first punch with his right fist. Acosta ducked and laughed, and hit Carl a short, sharp jab to the stomach. Carl backed up, sick from the powerful blow.

Acosta followed and slugged him again. When Carl doubled over, Acosta chopped down from above, aiming for the back of Carl's neck. The youth twisted out of the way, and Acosta's joined fists glanced off his shoulder. Carl stumbled sideways, knowing his opponent was following him, then he thudded up against Sherando. He gasped for breath, then moved out to meet Acosta's attack.

This time the blows caught him on the face, and he tried to escape by ducking as Acosta had done. The Mexican swung into air, and Carl, surprised by the success of his maneuver, followed up by butting Acosta with his head. Caught off guard, the rowdy went down, Carl on top of him.

They rolled together, dust filling their lungs and coating their bodies and clothes. Carl broke away first and got to his feet, coughing and shaking his head.

His rage was now a steady, burning drive to defeat the older man. He tasted blood as he licked his upper lip and realized that the Mexican was still unbloodied. "I'll change that now," he muttered, setting himself for the next attack.

Acosta got to his feet, threw back his head in anger, and cried out, "You have soiled my clothing, *señor*. This I do not forgive."

He's prideful, Carl thought. *It makes him angry to be mussed.* Carl raised his arms to turn aside Acosta's renewed attack, then hit his foe in the face as hard as his work-toughened muscles would allow. He heard the crunch of the nose breaking, felt the moistness of blood on his knuckles, but he hit again, with his left, opening a gash over Acosta's right cheekbone.

Stunned with the blow, unused to having his own blood flow, Acosta panicked, jabbing ineffectually at Carl's body. He paused once to wipe the blood from his ruined nose, and the sight of it on his hand seemed to cause him more alarm.

He swore at Carl, words that lost no venom for being in a foreign tongue. "You have ruined my face," he finished.

Carl gathered his strength and punched Acosta on the side of the head. The Mexican went down and stayed down, and Rod and young Albert pulled their pistols, covering the three rowdies, while Carl climbed on Sherando and his brothers boosted the girls up behind them on their horses. They all left at once, as the two men tried to revive their unconscious amigo.

When the Owens arrived in camp, Carl slid off Sherando and ran to gather Ida into his arms as Rulon lowered her to the ground from his saddle. Carl held her close to his dusty chest and stroked her hair, feeling the shivers that seized her body.

"There now, Ida," he soothed, calming her with little pats and strokes. "I took care of him. He won't never bother you again."

"Oh Carl, I thought he was killing you." She sneezed from the dust, then peered at his bruised and bloody face, and patted the puffiness under his left eye. "Oh, Carl!" Ida covered her mouth with her hand. "He spoiled your handsome face."

"I left him more a mess than he left me," he said, flexing his swelling hands.

Marie and Ellen slipped to the ground and tried to get to their wagons, but Rod Owen barred the way, and he was soon joined by Chester Bates. Then Julia and Muriel ran up, with the rest of the party close behind.

"Marie," demanded Rod. "Why were you on the road back there?"

The girl took one look at her father's contorted face and began to blubber hysterically. Ellen put an arm around her and tried to smile.

"Ida said she needed to get some things from the store, and we agreed to go with her. We was almost there when those men rode up and began to torment us, shooting off their guns and making rude comments." Ellen looked up and saw Ida in Carl's arms. "If Carl and the rest of you hadn't come just then—" She turned her face and broke into sobs.

"Ellen," Marie cried out, and wrapped her arms around her friend. "You been so brave, and you talked back to that awful man. Don't cry."

Ellen shook her head and wept on, throwing her arms around Marie's neck.

"There, now," Muriel soothed her daughter. "We'll take you over to the wagon, you can lie down a spell, and you'll feel better tomorrow."

"No," she sobbed. "Leave me be." Then she whispered through her tears into Marie's ear, "Take care of your brother's face. It wants cold cloths, and Ida sure ain't going to think of that."

Marie drew back and gave her a sharp glance, then looked over at Carl and Ida. "I'll take her, Mrs. Bates," she volunteered. "We'll both be fine with a little rest." Marie took Ellen's hand and led her away from the buzzing group.

When the girls arrived at the Bates' wagon, Marie turned to Ellen. "You're not crying because you're scared. You're crying over my brother!" She scrutinized Ellen's face, not allowing her to cover her eyes with her hand. "You like my brother. I do declare!"

Ellen wiped her tears. "He saved my life. Twice, now. And I can't go over there and fix him up. You'll have to tend to that."

"You're right. Ida won't think of it, and Carl sure won't bother. Why, he ain't even got the sense to put his shirt back on. And I reckon his hands could use some tending, too. Ellen, you bathe your face, and I'll tend to Carl's."

Rod spoke to the men gathered around the blowing horses. "We'll likely need extra guards tonight. I don't know if them rowdies have other friends, nor if they'd be foolish enough to attack an armed camp, but we'd best be prepared for them. Clay, Albert!"

"Yes, Pa," responded the two boys.

"You bunch the stock and put them on pickets, those you can. We'll give you more guards. Folks, let's form a square with the wagons. Angus, you and Ed put yours on the east side, Tom and Chester, take the south. Rand, you pull into the west, and Rulon and me'll make the north side."

"Rod, I reckon I need some supplies," Tom O'Connor said.

"This is a good time for everyone to take stock. Look over your goods, and if you need victuals, or extra shot, go into town together to buy." The men dispersed, except for Rand Hilbrands, who approached Rod.

"Where's Carl? My driver?"

Rod gestured toward the family wagon. "Getting his wounds tended. Say, Rand, the young ones wanted to get wed today, but I don't think it's a good idea now. Will you let Carl know?"

Rand grimaced. "I will." He walked up to Carl, who was seated on a barrel of cornmeal undergoing Marie's ministrations. "Carl, my boy, you done a fine, brave thing. I'm mighty grateful to you for rescuing my girl Ida from those thugs." Rand reached into his trousers pocket. "Here, take this coin with my thanks." He pressed it into Carl's puffy hand and continued. "Your pa said to say today's not a good time to wed."

"No, I—" Carl began, but Marie muffled her brother's voice with the cold cloth she held tightly to his mouth as Rand walked toward his wagon.

Marie removed the cloth when Rand was safely out of hearing range. "You were going to get married today?"

"Yep. That Acosta fellow surely messed up my plans."

Marie bit her lip, and ached for Ellen. When she had finished with Carl's face, she said, "Your hands are a mess, your lip is split, and you'll likely have a black eye for a spell, but you'll soon make Ida's heart go 'pitty-pat' again."

Carl squinted at his sister and gave a quick shrug of his shoulders, then got up from the barrel. "Thank you for tending my face. You didn't have to do that."

"I know it. Put your shirt on. You surely look foolish parading around half-naked." She put her fist on a hip. "Then go thank Ellen Bates. She's the only one of us who thought of caring for your ugly mug."

Carl felt his swollen lip with bruised fingers. "That was right sisterly of her."

Marie stared at her brother, unable to think of a proper response.

"What do I do with all this money, Sis? I've got my eye on a change of clothes, and I want to get something pretty for Ma, but I expect I'll have a bit left over."

"It's your money, and I reckon you took a beating to earn it, but I wouldn't fuss if you was to bring me a bite of something sweet."

"The store has a candy counter. I'll do it. I reckon that'll pay you back for washing up my face."

"Mind you, it was Ellen's idea. If you bring me some candy, you have to bring her some likewise."

"I wonder why she didn't fix me up herself?" he asked, putting on his shirt.

Six cautious men went back into town to buy provisions, and Carl was among them. He picked out his clothes quickly, and then lingered over a selection of gifts for his ma, finally choosing a bright yellow Spanish shawl with colored embroidery and fringes around the edge. He spent a whole quarter dollar at the candy counter, and came away with plenty of sweets for the young people at the camp.

On the return trip, Chester Bates matched the gait of his horse to Carl's. The furrows between the older man's nose and mouth deepened and widened as he smiled at Carl and motioned for him to slow his mount.

When they had their horses walking, Chester put his hand out and gripped Carl's shoulder. "I'm beholden to you for defending the girls today. My Ellen has a strong mind and will, but she's no match for a bully of that kind. I thank you."

"Your daughter spoke out well for the girls. She is a brave one, Mr. Bates. If she had been armed, likely there'd have been no need for my help."

"You're a modest lad, and well-spoken yourself. Your pa can be proud of such a son."

Carl squirmed under this praise, knowing he had not earned it for defending Ellen or his sister. He said nothing, and Chester nodded to him and rode off up the trail.

When he reached camp, Carl went directly to his family's wagon and changed into his new clothes. As he dropped from the wagon box, his mother straightened up from the fire and looked him over.

"Don't you look fine! I count myself lucky that my sons are as fair of deed as they are of figure."

"Oh, Ma!" he protested, then advanced to the fire and placed a bundle into her busy hands.

"What's this, Carl?"

"Something I thought you'd like, Ma."

"For me?"

"You're the only ma I got."

She moved to the barrel beside the wagon and sat, smoothing the paper wrapping. "For me?" she asked again.

"Go ahead, open it, Ma."

She worried over the knots, until Carl stepped forward with his knife and cut the string. Then she wrapped it into a ball over her fingers and tucked it into a pocket of her apron.

"Come on, Ma," Carl urged.

She spread apart the paper, and the yellow silk burst into the light. Julia caught her breath. "Oh, Carl, it's lovely!" She laughed and held the shawl to her face, pressing the softness of the fabric against her cheek. "Where'd you get the coin for this, boy?"

"Mr. Hilbrands gave me a little 'thank you' present. He was grateful Ida wasn't harmed."

"And well she might have been." Julia sighed. "I don't know what got into those girls, even to think of going into a strange town without a man to escort them. I'm glad you boys happened along in time."

Basking in his mother's grateful reception of his present, Carl went in search of the girls.

"Here you go, Sis," he said, and gave Marie a twist of paper. "Thank you." He turned to Ellen and presented her with a similar paper twist. "I reckon thanks goes to you, too. Marie says so."

Ellen looked at Marie. "What's this for?"

"Tell her, Carl."

"Marie says you sent her over to fix up my wounds. I'm obliged."

Ellen turned to her friend. "Marie!" she protested, fidgeting with the paper in her hands. Then she held the candy out to Carl. "I didn't do nothing. I can't take it."

"Nonsense. It's for keeping your head, like."

She looked down. "Thank you."

"Enjoy your sweets."

Carl turned away, and Marie whispered to Ellen, "Look there, he's bringing you presents. And Ida ain't married him yet. He's still fair game."

"Marie, he treats me like he treats you. I'm an extra sister, to his mind."

Marie took hold of Ellen's upper arms and shook her. "Don't give up, Ellen. Sometimes he's a bother, but Carl is a good catch. You keep in his sight. Don't let him forget you're around." She let go of Ellen's arms. "Mind you, Ida's fun, and I reckon Carl thinks so, too, but I don't think she'll make him a good wife out in the Colorado Territory. She ain't the pioneering kind."

Ellen held the twist of candy over her heart. "But there's James to consider."

Marie sighed. "There's nothing wrong with James," she said. "He's nice enough: he's kind, and he's brave—he's got a bayonet wound to prove that."

"I don't want James," Ellen said, shaking her head, her face gone somber. "He's got that grin, and a quick wit, and I feel so ashamed that I can't find a morsel of affection for him." She hid her eyes behind her hands for a moment, then added, "I was so glad when Reverend Halsey didn't come. I know James was, too. But now he comes to our fire and sits with me, and tries to pretend he's happy a-courting me. He'll even kiss my hand from time to time before he goes back to your fire, but there's no...no loss in my bosom when he leaves."

Marie's eyes were wet with tears. "Oh, Ellen," she sniffed. "Why is life so hard?"

"They will regret they ever came to *Ciudad* Kansas," the Mexican swore, breathing with difficulty through his smashed nose. "The young one, he will watch Berto Acosta have his way with the girl." He drained the beer from the mug he held in his fist, then turned and shouted, "I will follow them, and the *muchacha* will be mine!"

"You need rest, Berto," Willy murmured, taking hold of his arm.

"Shore, that nose won't heal proper if you sit here drinking all night," Rankin agreed, grabbing the second arm. "Let's get some sleep. We'll pick up their trail easy in a couple of days. Them tenderfeet are always easy to track."

Chapter 8

For several days after leaving the city of Kansas, the travelers had the road to themselves. Although stage stops and farms stretched all along their path, the other men agreed with Rod that camping and cooking their own food was both cheaper and safer than stopping to eat ready-made meals. However, Rod did inquire for news of Indian movements along the trail ahead.

A week later, the party came upon a fork in the trail, and Rod pointed out to Julia the branch angling off toward the northeast.

"That there's the road to Oregon. There used to be a sign here, telling folks which way was what. It was mostly a joke."

"But we don't go that way?"

"Nah. We take the left fork, keep going west until we hit the Arkansas River."

"Looks easy to follow, Rod."

"Should be. This trail is over forty years old. I reckon we could hold to the road in a snowstorm. The tracks are worn deep and wide."

"How come there is more than one trail going to the same place, like over there?" Julia gestured toward another track 50 yards away.

"I've been told folks would strike off on a path to one side, or where the grass was thicker for the stock. All the trails go to the same place—Santa Fe."

"I like the trees along here. They remind me of home." She pointed to a stand of oaks interrupting the waves of blue-stemmed grass.

"Enjoy them now, woman. There's a long stretch ahead of us without trees at all, and it goes for hundreds of miles. Jonathan said folks call it the 'Great American Desert'. That's where all them buffalo are supposed to cover the land from one horizon to the other."

"Rod, ain't there no trees in the Colorado Territory?"

"We'll have trees, Julie. I promise you we'll have trees if I have to plant 'em myself."

"That'll take years, Rod. I'd hanker for shade."

"You'll have it. I didn't bring you out here to pioneer forever. We'll have all we had back in the Shenandoah, and more. I figure to make a heap of money. I aim to have my share of this country, especially since the Yankees took as much of mine as they did. If I've got to start over, I mean to end big."

"Rod." Julia changed the subject. "I've been watching that dust cloud out there on the horizon, and it's growing mighty fast. Somebody's in a powerful hurry."

Rod studied the dust for a moment, noting how it boiled up out of the distant roadway. "No telling what trouble that could be. We'd best get off the road and circle the wagons."

Rod directed his team off the road, and the others followed him, wondering what was causing the delay. At Rod's explanation, they drew the eight wagons into a tight circle, unhitched the teams, and led them into the center along with the extra livestock. Then they found their rifles and waited as the dust cloud drifted nearer.

A few minutes later, a loud thundering sound accompanied the dust. Soon, the nervous watchers made out a dark, bulky shape, like a covered freight wagon, bearing down on them at high speed.

As it drew closer, Rulon called out to his father. "Pa. I reckon that's the mail stage." He walked nearer, and continued in a lower voice. "I reckon I forgot to tell you it was expected about now."

Rod expelled a lungful of air, and looked at his eldest son.

"No harm done, I guess. Next time I send you to a stage stop for information, it would pleasure me if you would tell me all you dig up, boy."

"I'm sorry I forgot to give you that word, Pa. I reckon I ain't a boy no longer, though. Not with a wife and young'uns."

"You'll always be my boy, Rule. That's the way of fathers." Rod suddenly focused on his son's face. "Wait a minute. You said 'young'uns'?"

"You been preoccupied, Pa. Mary and me, well, Mary, anyway, is a-brooding chick number two. We reckon it'll hatch just before spring."

"That's why she didn't want to come west. A gal gets mighty particular about her nest during these times. Is she taking this traveling well, son?"

"Well enough. Look at that stage, Pa."

Six horses pulled the coach abreast of the wagons. The stage, blue- and red-painted sides gleaming through the dirt, sped by with only a wave of the hand from the guard, and then the stage, passengers, guard, and driver all blended into the dirty ball of dust following them.

Edward Morgan laughed. "That's a good joke on us, Rod. We're sitting here all ready for Indians."

"Practice makes perfect, they say," Rod said, his mouth set in wry lines. "Let's hitch up and get on the road again."

Several hours later, Ida turned to Carl on the wagon seat. "What if that had been Indians?" she asked.

"What?"

"Back there. The stage. What would we do if they did come down on us?"

"Ida, a lot of us came through the war because we were pretty good with our rifles. That, and lucky. We've been practicing with our new revolvers, too. I reckon we'll fight them off, girl. A bunch of Indians can't be much different than a bunch of blue-belly Yankees."

Ida sighed. "I expect I'd die of fright. I still shudder when I think what might have happened to little ol' me." She gave an illustration of her best shudder.

Carl clamped his mouth shut against angry words. Her games grated on his nerves, what with the edgy feeling he'd had as soon as he woke that morning.

Ida continued to prattle on about her fright, and when he could bear no more, Carl turned his head to stare at her, trying to get his anger under control before he spoke.

Ida arched her eyebrows and remarked, "You're a cranky ol' fuss-budget today, Carl Owen. What ails you?"

Carl turned back to the lines, thinking, *I got a bad feeling*, and when James rode up alongside the wagon, Carl hailed him.

"Hey, James. Come take the mules for a spell."

James looked surprised, but traded places with Carl and greeted Ida, who sat frowning next to Eliza. "Hello, Miss Ida. Bet you could use the sight of a handsome face for once."

"Hello, James," she said in a monotone.

"Well, you'll get over that snit," he replied. "You always do."

"Humph," she replied, and bounced nearer her sister.

Carl rode off on James's horse, breathing deeply, feeling his anger drop away as he put distance between himself and the wagons. He headed east, checking the back trail, easing off toward the north. Searching the prairie, not knowing what he expected to find, he gained composure in the act of working.

After a few miles of riding through tall grass, Carl turned south again, and stopped to let his horse breathe. A rider approached from the direction of the wagon train, and he sat the horse and waited. Once he made out Rulon's blunt face, he walked the animal forward to meet his older brother.

"Find anything, Carl?" Rulon drawled.

"Nothing. And what's more, I don't know what I expect to find, but I been nervy as a bird waiting for the cat to pounce. I sure would admire to know why."

"I felt the same. Say, did you ride all the way back to that knoll over yonder?"

"Not yet."

"Let's go check it."

After riding for a time in silence, they reached the hill and cautiously circled wide behind it, approaching from the rear side. Rulon pulled up his horse, and pointed toward the east.

"See where that grass has been pushed aside? Somebody rode through that blue stem, probably early today."

The brothers dismounted and let the reins drag, ground-tying their horses. Rulon took the east approach, and Carl the west, and they advanced slowly, eyes sweeping the earth at the foot of the knoll.

"Look here," Rulon sang out, excitement registering in his voice.

Carl arrived to see Rulon down on his knees, picking up the stub of a thin black cigar. The grass was trampled in a large area, and included sign that several men and horses had met. Deep heel tracks marked where someone had squatted down. He had drawn in the dirt, then smoothed away the drawing.

"Did they watch the trail?" Carl asked, looking up at the knoll for signs of ascent.

"I reckon. I'll go up and see what's to be found there."

As Rulon climbed the hill, Carl walked over the area again, searching for more sign of what had taken place. He found a spot where a man had stretched out on his back, and the grass was still bent over, showing the outline of his body.

Rulon gave a shout as he skidded down the last few feet of the hill. "Somebody bellied-down there for quite a spell," he puffed, then caught his breath and went on. "Watching for us, maybe. The way I read it, they came before daylight and waited until we passed by, then up and returned the way they came." He gestured around. "How many do you figure in the party, Carl?"

"I count two over here, then two more came up. How many climbed up yonder?"

"Just the one, and he smokes these thin cigars. I found three more stubs up there. Something puzzles me, though. I thought maybe these folks might be those toughs from back yonder in Kansas town, but the feller up the hill didn't mind getting a little dirt on his britches. Your Mexican friend was powerful upset when you dusted up his clothes, so was it really him and his cronies?"

"I mussed up his fancy duds, but he's not likely to wear them on the trail. I got a crawling up my back tells me we got Berto Acosta and his pals tracking us."

Rulon took one last look around the base of the knoll. "Well, we'd best get back. I'll report to Pa. I've a feeling he won't like what I have to tell him." He laughed and shook his head.

"There ain't nothing funny about this, Rule."

"Only funny thing is that you have to sit up there day after day alongside the girl who brought this whole mess upon us."

"What're you saying?" Carl demanded.

"Mary's fool sister couldn't wait for an escort to get into town, so she drug the other two girls along with her, and almost got the three of them despoiled. I'd say that makes her to blame for this mess."

"I'd just as soon take a poke at you here and now, Rulon. Ida didn't mean anything, heading into town. If anybody's to blame, it's them three rowdies, especially Berto Acosta. Ida's blameless, and I won't allow you nor anybody else to pin the fault on her."

"You got yourself a case of hot blood there, little brother. Mind it don't get you into trouble."

"Don't push me, Rule." Carl climbed on his horse and started back toward the wagons, biting his tongue in regret at his hard words. He didn't know why he felt compelled to defend Ida, because he knew she was partly to blame for the trouble.

Carl relieved James at the lines of the freight wagon, and spent the rest of the morning in grim silence. When the wagons stopped for the nooning, Carl helped Ida down from the wagon seat and looked at her gravely. "I ain't been good company this morning, and I'm sorry for it."

Ida smiled. "I'll pay it no mind, Carl."

"I've got to go talk with my brother. You stay put. No wandering away from the wagons, you hear? It's important, girl." He looked sternly into her blue eyes, and wagged his finger under her nose for emphasis.

"You're mighty serious, Carl," she giggled.

"I'm mighty serious," he agreed, nodding as he escorted her and her sister to the Hilbrands' family wagon.

"Sorry I left you out there, Rulon," Carl apologized stiffly once he located his brother. "I reckon my fool temper is stronger than my sense. Did you talk to Pa?"

"Yep."

"Well, what did he say about our watchers?"

"He thinks we're most likely right about who they are and who they're laying for."

"Well? What's he going to do?"

"He didn't say, Carl. You know Pa. He'll contemplate on the situation for a spell before deciding what action to take. We'll have to wait."

"That's so."

~*~*~

Before the travelers hitched up for the afternoon march, Rod sent word around that he wanted to talk to the men. When they had gathered, he told them what Carl and Rulon had discovered behind the hill. Rod rubbed his beard and squinted around the horizon.

"There's no need to alarm the women folks. I reckon if we keep a sharp watch behind us, we can go along about like we have."

"Are you crazy, man?" Rand Hilbrands sputtered, his face red and mottled. "I say we should stay here and circle the wagons, wait for them ruffians to appear, and meet them from a position of strength."

"We could sit here for a week, waiting for trouble to find us, our food and water running out, when we should be miles down the road toward the Territory. That's not good tactics, Rand."

"You think because you were an officer and I stayed home, I don't know anything. Well, this I know: I'll not run from a fight. You go along with your two wagons, if you're too scared to stick and defend yourself and your women folks."

"Don't be a fool, Randolph. If they want to make trouble, together we have twice their number. You'll sit here and divide us up with your fool talk, and make it easy for them to wipe you out."

"I ain't going, Rod Owen. I aim to stay right here and fight it out, and yes, with your boy at my side. I paid for his work, and I'll keep his rifle here." He turned to the other men. "Tom O'Connor, you never ran from a fight, either. Stay with me."

The brawny blacksmith nodded. "I never ran, for a fact. I'm bound to back a man who'll stand and fight."

"Will the lot of you sit around and burrow into the trail then, waiting for those men to spook you like a bunch of rabbits?" Scorn thickened Rod's voice. "Devil take the ruffians. Who'll go on with me to Colorado?"

"I'll go, Rod," answered Chester Bates. "I see no sense in waiting for trouble to find me."

"The farther we go, the nearer we are to home," observed Ed Morgan. "I'm with you, Rod. You have my son Tom's rifle, too."

Angus Campbell glanced around at the angry faces. "I'd favor going on, Rod, but I can't leave Tom and his little ones. I reckon I have to stay with my kinfolks."

"You're a good man, Angus. I'm sorry to lose you. Godspeed to you, then. We'll go on." Rod turned his back on those who elected to stay, and took Carl by the shoulder.

"You ma will take this parting hard, Carl, but you've a duty to stay and see that fool and his freight wagon get on the way again. He's putting us in double danger, splitting our firepower, but I won't sit and wait. The season is late enough now."

Carl nodded dumbly, his throat choked tight with shock. He shook hands with his father, then, as Rod walked away, Carl called out.

"Pa! How'll I find you in Colorado?"

"Follow the trail, son. Once you catch sight of the mountains, you look sharp for my sign."

Carl got his gear and his saddle out of the family wagon, dumped it in a pile, and tied Sherando to the back of the freight vehicle. The day burned hot, with no beauty to temper his misery, and Carl felt dull-witted while the Owen group got under way. He stood gazing at his family as the four wagons turned miniature in the distance, finally being swallowed up in a cloud of dust. Then he turned and sat down against a wagon wheel, his rifle across his knees.

Rand Hilbrands swaggered a little with his new position of command. The other men hitched up their teams and drove them into a square. He walked around and around the puny shelter of the four wagons, assigning men to stand watch.

"You there, Carl. Get some rest. You'll have the first watch after nightfall."

Carl got his bedroll from the pile where he'd dumped his gear. He unrolled it and lay down beneath the wagon, but sleep would not come in the afternoon heat. Turning over on the blanket, he opened his eyes to see the hem of Ida's skirt.

The girl bent over to look at him. "I'll rub your shoulders, Carl, help you relax a bit," she offered.

"It wouldn't be seemly," Carl said, "you scooting under here with me."

"Fiddlesticks!" she declared, and crawled under the wagon beside him. "You're my man, and you need to get your mind and body laid to rest before you can sleep. I reckon it's my duty to help us all, you going on watch later, and all."

Carl looked up at her, keeping silent.

"I'm sorry your pa took off in such a hurry, Carl. If that nasty brute is following us, we could use a few more guns to chase him away. I think my pa is so brave to set here ready to stand him off. I am so thrilled."

Carl sighed wearily and declined to answer.

Ida leaned over him and began to rub his shoulders. He sensed the nearness of her body to his, smelled a faint odor of lilacs, then willed his muscles to go slack under her hands. Soon, her kneading manipulations eased the pain of tension. "That feels mighty good," he grunted, not caring any longer about the possessive way she was touching him. If Ida didn't care that her pa saw what she was doing, he wouldn't care either. Then, he succumbed to the heat and his fatigue and shock, and slept.

When he awoke, the sun was gone and supper was ready, cooked over a large campfire. Uneasy at the amount of light cast upon the prairie, Carl looked around for his father to protest. Then, remembering the split that the group had undergone, he shrugged his shoulders and yawned.

Ida smiled at him across the camp as he crawled from under the wagon, and a shiver of warning went up Carl's spine. *By gum, that girl has something on her mind, and I ain't got no taste to find out what it is just now*, he thought. He arranged his blankets into a neat bed, then stood, got his plate, and approached the fire.

Amanda Hilbrands served him a scoop of beans, some biscuits, and a mug of chicory coffee, eyeing him from under her pale brows. "You slept well enough after Ida tended to you, I see," she said. "My daughter has healing hands. Her daddy sent her to rub those tired muscles of yours. He says she's got a real talent."

Carl stared woodenly at Mrs. Hilbrands, thinking he had not heard right, then walked over to a barrel and sat. He ate silently, gulping down the hot brew in his cup. When his food was gone, Carl drained his mug and threw the grounds into the fire. He dropped his plate and mug into the washtub, wiped his knife on his trousers, and got his rifle from the wagon wheel. Then he walked out a ways from the hubbub of the camp and took his turn on watch.

Gradually, the noises of the camp subsided as the women washed and put away the dishes and the travelers retired to their beds. Glad when the fire died, Carl walked around the outside of the wagons, listening to the night sounds, alert for any unfamiliar noise. He took up a position for a time, then circled the wagons again, never keeping to a set pattern that a watcher could count on.

He listened as the night insects chirped early in the evening, then they, too, went to sleep and he was left in the solitude.

Dwarfed by the immensity of the night sky, Carl wondered where his family was that night. He drove his fist into his hand in frustration at the lowly rank he held in this company that kept him from talking sense into Rand Hilbrands. In Rand's eyes, he was barely more than a kid, a hired driver, not yet a son-in-law, and not worth listening to. Besides, he was Rod's son, and right now, that was a count against him. How long would they be here, perched on the side of the road, waiting, and sitting, and eating up the food and drinking the water barrels dry?

When his hours of watch were up, he awakened Tom O'Connor, then prevented him from throwing an armful of fuel onto the fire.

"Let's don't show them were we are, Mr. O'Connor."

"Right, lad. I guess I'm still used to a roaring fire in the hearth of the smithy. It comforts a man, somehow." Tom went off to take up his position, while Carl returned to the freight wagon to crawl into his blankets.

The next day, Carl spent several hours in Sherando's saddle, scouting the back trail. He wished Rulon was with him, with his tracking experience, but even without him, he was sure he had not missed anything when he returned and reported to Rand.

"There's nobody out there, Mr. Hilbrands. Not a sign of folks watching us, not a cigar stub, not a blade of grass bent down for miles around."

"You're sure you missed nothing, boy?" asked Angus Campbell. "If they're not out there, we might as well go on, don't you think, Rand?"

"No! We'll wait and fight them from a position of strength!" he trumpeted. "They're out there, all right. They're just waiting for a weak moment, a wavering on our part, to close in and destroy us. We'll wait, I say, and outwit them."

Carl turned away and went to rub down Sherando. *The man is hell-bent on staying until we all take root*, he thought. *There's no turning his mind to the righteous path.* Grumbling to himself, Carl worked with his horse, cooling it down from the exercise of the morning. Tom O'Connor walked over, and rubbed the horse's nose.

"Nothing to be seen, lad?"

"Maybe they went back to the last stage stop to drink some courage," Carl mumbled. "Acosta saw we were well armed when he spied on us, Mr. O'Connor. He'll have to make a plan other than 'catch up and shoot'."

Tom clapped Carl on the shoulder with his massive hand. "That's thinking, boy. We're ready for anything, here. But things have changed. There's less of us now."

"And he doesn't know it yet. I don't reckon there's any chance of fooling him when he shows up. Eight wagons, take-away four leaves us with the odds about even, and he'll know it sure as daylight spills over the edge of that prairie when the sun rises."

Tom's black brows drew together. "I'm beginning to think twice about this plan of Rand's. We should have stuck together."

Carl spun around to face the blacksmith. "It's too late to change your mind now," he said, gritting his teeth against striking out at the man. "You should've said that when Pa gave you the chance. We're double-dyed fools to sit here and waste time."

"Wait a minute, boy. Are you calling me a fool? Better think twice, yourself."

Carl stood himself up straight. "We're all fools, one day or another. And I ain't a boy, Mr. O'Connor. I ain't been a boy since I joined Mosby." He jabbed his finger into Tom's chest.

Tom grabbed Carl's fist, sucked in a breath, held it, and let it out slowly. "I reckon you're riled some, Carl. I can't see as I blame you, getting cut off from your kin." He loosened his grip on Carl's fist and dropped it. "If my babies was split up from me, why, I'd—"

"I'm sorry I let go of my manners, sir," Carl interrupted. "I guess one day or another I'm still a boy."

"Well, it takes a man to own it, I reckon," the blacksmith drawled. "Here, let me take that saddle."

Carl staked Sherando on a fresh patch of grass, then, with his arms full of tack, followed Tom back to the wagons. He dumped the headpiece, bit, and other gear in a heap beside the freight wagon, and accepted the saddle from Tom, who took his hat off, put it back on, then left.

Douglas Campbell wandered up as Carl inspected a loose cinch buckle on his saddle. "Ma says you're invited to eat dinner with us, come noon."

"Thanks, Doug. I don't mind if I do," Carl replied, recalling that Molly Campbell made the best biscuits he'd ever eaten. "Does your ma have any flour?"

"Sorry, no. But she's going to open a tin of peaches, I believe. She got it out of the supply bin."

Carl grinned. "I'll be there."

The day was long in passing, and the enforced idleness weighed heavily on the members of Rand Hilbrands' rear guard. A quarrel developed between the most tolerant of men, Angus Campbell, and his brother-in-law, Tom O'Connor, over where their stock should be picketed. Rand tried to smooth over their feelings, but he lacked Rod Owen's mediating skills, and bad feelings persisted into the next day.

Again Carl scouted the surrounding area as soon as light broke over the eastern grasslands. He found nothing, even though he went farther afield. When he returned, he gave his report to each of the three men at the camp, for they were not willing to endure each other's company in order to hear his news at one time. Disgusted, Carl sought his bedroll before noon, and tried to sleep amid the noise of fighting children and quick-tongued wives.

He woke when someone called his name in an urgent whisper, and he sat up hurriedly, bumping his head on the bottom of the wagon box. He swore, wincing at the pain, and rubbed his head.

"Carl Owen, I declare," exclaimed Ida. "You oughtn't to say such words in the presence of a lady."

Carl groaned and shook his head. "Beggin' your pardon, Miss Ida. Somebody woke me up real sudden like, and now I've got a headache would make a lap dog turn vicious. Whew!" he shook his head again. "What do you want?"

She slid under the wagon and sat beside him. "Only some company. It's so boring sitting out here, getting hot and sunburned, and swatting flies and 'skeeters and other horrid little bugs." She grimaced. "Mama made me scrape some meat this morning. It had maggots on it, and she made me touch it." She shuddered. "I don't think she will find me under here with you."

Carl moved around in his bedroll until the sitting was comfortable and he could face Ida. "Seems like not long ago this setup pleased you mighty fine, your daddy being in charge, and all."

"Well, it's dreadful boring now, just like I told you. I'm sorry I ever let him talk us into staying."

"I didn't think we had much choice."

"Fiddle-dee-dee! I could have talked Papa into going on, if I'd have wanted to. I just didn't want to, at the time."

"Know your own mind, is it?" Carl's voice grated in his own ears as he looked Ida up and down.

She flushed. "You're making fun of me, Carl Owen. It's not fair for you to tease me."

But a woman can tease a man all she wants, and nobody says a word, Carl thought. "I was trying to get some sleep, girl," he said, hunching his shoulders and preparing to lie down again.

"Let me stay here beside you so Mama won't make me help her again. I fair liked to faint, working this morning." At Carl's scowl, Ida put on a smile and put a pleading note into her voice.

"Please, Carl. I won't say another word, just sit real quiet and watch you sleep."

"Ida, you got the dangedest notions. It ain't fitting for a girl to stay around when a man sleeps, not unless the two of them is wed."

"I don't care. We were supposed to be wed by now. Twice, even. Let's pretend we are. Then I can cuddle up beside you and get some—"

"Ida Hilbrands! You get along with you. Scoot outta here! I won't play them kinds of games with you, not here, and not likely anywhere else on this trip. You git!"

Ida went, reluctantly, but finally. Carl let out a shuddering breath, wiping his sopping forehead on his sleeve, and ran his moist hands down the front of his shirt.

He swore mildly, and thought, I'm set to marry one forward gal. We're sitting here under God's great sky, not getting one foot nearer to Colorado Territory. I'll never get that cabin raised before winter sets in. He shook his head and sighed. And I won't take her to wife, or anything like unto it, until I have a place for us to call our own.

Chapter 9

The next day dragged on like the three before it: hot, humid, and full of quarrels. Carl again went out to scout, but this time, Angus insisted on going along with him.

They didn't say anything much to each other; there wasn't a lot to say about riding large circles through the dusty grass, squinting into the sun looking for trampled grass or hoof prints, and feeling the sweat dripping down their chests, backs, and arms. They stopped from time to time to share a gourd of water or to rest their animals, but they still didn't talk.

Carl and Angus rode all the way back to the knoll where the brothers had discovered the signs of pursuit several days before. The younger man got down from his horse and walked around, looking at the bare patch of ground where men had met and plotted.

He squatted on his heels for a time, backtracking his and Rulon's movements to determine if there was something here that they had missed. He climbed the hill, stood on the top of the rise, took off his hat and wiped the sweatband, replaced it on his head, and looked out toward the north. A half-mile away, a band of chewed-up earth stood out from the blue stem, catching his eye. *Rulon and I came up from behind the hill*, he thought, *but we didn't make them tracks out yonder*. He stared toward the track in the grass, then turned and ran down the knoll to where Angus waited with the horses.

"We've got trouble." He bowed his head, his chest heaving, then looked up. "No, Pa's got trouble. Those fellows didn't go back to town."

"What?"

He gestured to the north, then around the area. "There's a big track out there Rulon and I didn't see before the grass died. They stopped here and had a discussion, and if I'm reading sign rightly, left toward the east, then circled around out that-a-way, rode hard, and set up an ambush for us along the road a piece." He swore and scrambled into his saddle. "My family and a lot of other good folks moved right into it, and I don't think they're going to come out alive, because we're sitting here on our thumbs waiting for the moon to rise blue!" He clucked to Sherando, and started for the wagons.

"Now, calm down, son. Maybe they did go back after they saw how strong we was," Angus called.

"No chance," Carl threw back over his shoulder. "I saw the hate in that man's eyes when he flung them strange words at me, and he ain't one to quit on us."

Angus got his horse started as well, and caught up to Carl. "Maybe he thought better of it after a time," he shouted.

"You weren't there, Angus. He's after my blood, and the blood of my kin, and the girls, too. He won't give up on the girls," Carl yelled, his words bouncing out of his mouth.

When Carl and Angus rode into the camp, Tom and Rand were standing nose to nose, shaking fingers in each other's faces. Carl slid off his horse and ran up to the overheated men.

"Stop it! Stop it right now," he commanded. "Rand, if you want to prove how much courage you've got, then you'll have to go down the road a piece."

Randolph turned on Carl. "You're crazy, boy. We'll fight off them ruffians right here."

"Well, they ain't coming here. They holed up ahead, laying for my ma and pa, and my brothers and sister, and your daughter and little grandchild, and all them good people."

Tom turned to him. "Speak plain, boy."

Carl threw out his hands. "Berto Acosta and his bunch circled around and got ahead. My folks could be dead right now."

"Well, what're we sitting here for?" Rand sputtered. "We'd better get on the road." He turned on his heel and strode toward his wagon, then wheeled and returned. "How do you know, boy?"

"The sign all adds up now. Besides," he continued in a low voice, "I got a feeling in my bones."

Rand shuddered and moved away, bawling out orders for breaking camp.

They got underway, pushing the animals hard to eke out extra miles of travel. Carl looked around at the waving grass, and wished the wind would push them along with as much speed. He glanced at Ida. She sat scowling, holding on to the seat of the jolting wagon as he coaxed the mules to pull a little harder, move a little faster. Eliza played with her doll, looking like she was content to be moving again.

When the road made a curve around a stand of trees, he looked back the way they had come and caught sight of a mass of dark clouds on the horizon. *Rain*, he thought. *Good and bad, both. Cool us off, but it'll muddy up the road.*

Later, Carl saw the clouds again, but instead of growing upward to pile high into the heavens, these clouds grew sideways, spreading out to cover a good part of the eastern skyline.

Carl stared a moment longer at the cloud, then a mounting dread filled the pit of his stomach as he realized the blackness bearing down on them was not cloud, but smoke. He stopped the mules, threw himself off the wagon to the sounds of Ida's protests, and ran up the line to Rand's wagon.

"Rand, hold up a minute. Look at that," he shouted, pointing to the smoke enveloping the east. "That's a prairie fire, or I'm not my father's son."

"Prairie fire!" Rand exploded, then went white in the face. "What'll we do, boy?"

"We've got to make for the next stream and drive the wagons down into the water. Hurry, man, we ain't got much time to outrun it." He left Rand's wagon and ran back down the line, shouting, "Angus, Tom!" The men started to halt their teams and climb down from their wagons.

"No, keep moving," Carl yelled, waving his arm. "Fire! Get down to the next creek. Move on."

He ran back toward the freight wagon, calling out to Andy Campbell. "Throw them stock animals ahead of us. If they stampede, maybe the teams will follow."

Carl climbed to the seat and cracked his whip. The mules were reluctant to start pulling, and Carl assaulted the air again with the whip until he had provoked the animals into a shambling sort of hurry. He wished the girls weren't on the seat with him. Maybe then he'd feel like telling the team what he thought of their efforts.

Looking back at the smoke, Carl gauged the fire's advance. He could see flame now, growing dark orange as the fire paused to engulf a grove of trees. The smoke became black, towering upward into the blue heaven.

Hush, he thought, we ain't going to outrun this fire.

He turned to urge the beasts onward at a faster pace and caught sight of Ida's white, set face. She stared straight ahead, fingers tightly gripping the edges of the seat.

"We'll make it," he grunted, forcing himself to sound confident. "I ain't come this far west to burn up in no fire!"

Ida gave no sign of having heard him, but continued to stare ahead. Carl took his gaze from her face and whipped the mules a little faster. The trotting animals smelled the smoke on the wind from the east and lurched into the hames, frightened by the volume of the odor.

He turned to check the fire's progress again, and a groan escaped his tightly compressed lips, startling Ida out of her trance. She turned and hurled herself against Carl, grabbing him around the neck and cutting off his control of the team.

"Carl, Carl!" she screamed. "Don't let me get burned. I don't want no scars!"

He struggled with the panicked girl, trying to loosen her hold on his neck, trying to catch his breath. His right arm came free of her grasp and brushed against his holstered gun. Slipping off the rawhide loop, he drew the Colt and held it overhead, then fired one shot.

Ida jumped at the report of the gun, shrank back from Carl, and huddled on the lurching wagon seat.

At the sound of the gun, the mules took on a new spirit of cooperation and stretched out in a lope, faster than before. Carl replaced his pistol, and seeing that Ida was safe, tried to sooth her with quiet talk.

"Ida, settle down. You're going to be just fine," he said softly, his words jolted and cut up from the movement of the wagon. Smoke billowed on all sides of them now as the wind blew fiercely from the rear. Carl's belly twisted as he realized that time was short, too short, before the fire overtook them.

Like a sentinel of salvation, a lone oak tree stood out against the western sky just ahead. Carl's heart swelled with hope, and he stood up and popped his whip.

Andy Campbell already had the stock running in the direction of the tree, and the wagons followed, with Carl's bringing up the rear. He whooped for joy when he saw Rand's team drop from view into a valley. Then Angus and Tom and their wagons and teams also disappeared, and Carl cracked his whip once more to drive his team over the lip of the declivity.

In a second, it seemed, Carl took in the entire scene. Flowing water gleamed in the bottom of the cut, reflecting the billowing tops of three wagons parked on the stream's bank. A fourth wagon stood jacked up in the water with goods scattered on both banks, and both rear wheels lay on the ground alongside a shattered axle. The wagons of the second party still careered down the slope.

Recognition flamed in him. Carl heard a voice yell, "Pa!" and from the rawness of his throat, knew it was his own voice. Relief washed over him as his father's bearded face appeared next to the freight wagon.

"Prairie fire, Pa!" Carl picked up Ida and handed her down to his father, then dangled Eliza to him also. Julia hurried over and took the frightened girls to the stream.

Rod quickly glanced at Carl's smoke-blackened face, then turned to shout, "Ed, Chester, boys, get those wagons into the crick. Grab your shovels and buckets. Fire's comin'."

Mary Owen cried out, "Fire! My bed! My food!" and Marie and Julia ran to help her gather up as many of the goods on the near bank as they could handle, and piled them at the edge of the creek.

Tom and Parley Morgan and the Campbell boys helped Chester Bates push the parked wagons into the water as Ed Morgan showed the latecomers where to drive into the stream.

Elizabeth Morgan and Muriel Bates set the girls to wetting quilts and blankets in the water, and Molly Campbell passed them to the men to carry to the top of the slope where they would use them to beat out the rapidly approaching fire.

"Julianna," called out her mother. "You take the babies and little ones to the other side of the creek out of harm's way. Keep them happy, daughter, so they won't take a fright."

The girl ran to scoop up Delia Campbell and her two brothers, their cousin Joshua O'Connor, and her own nephew Roddy, and herded them into the stream. "Let's play a game," she said, trying to keep her voice calm. "Come over here, children. I know a story."

Rida O'Connor followed her, calling out, "I can tend the young'uns, too."

Rulon hurried over to consult with his father. "Pa, let's set a back fire and burn off the grass up there on the rim. It might help us turn the fire away."

Rod nodded. "Take James and Clay. The women'll keep the grass and the wagons wet down here. Carl, show them how to wet down the wagons." Rod grabbed a shovel and ran up the slope, shouting for more assistance.

Once he had driven the freight wagon into the water, Carl started to climb down, but his tensed muscles gave out, and he collapsed into the stream. Wiping the water out of his eyes, he arose, dripping, and grabbed the bucket tied to the side of the wagon. He dipped it into the river and pitched the water over the canvas covering of the freight.

Rand Hilbrands saw what Carl was doing, and cried out, "Stop! You can't wet my cargo."

Carl looked wearily up at him from the stream.

"I can let it burn, if you'd druther."

Rand waved his hand in concession, and his shoulders slumped from exhaustion. Amanda pressed a bucket into his grasp.

"Forget about the store goods," she shrilled. "Look out for our own things."

The wind carried thick, black smoke and sparks down into the valley, as Rulon's fire caught hold ten yards past the rim. He and his brothers nursed the flames in the direction of the rim, scuffing the earth behind the burned section with their shovels to make their firebreak. Ed Morgan sent his sons with filled buckets to help control the burn. "Wet the sides of the bank up there at the top," he called. "Keep the slope soaking wet."

Ida shivered in the stream, wrapped in a drenched blanket. Her sister Eliza, busy splashing water from a bucket onto the family wagon, looked over at her and sniffed.

"Ida ain't working, Mama."

"Pay her no mind, 'Liza," her mother called. "She's no use to us now. Keep the wagon wet!"

"Here it comes," James yelled, tumbling over the rim as he retreated from the extreme heat, with Clay and Rulon hard on his heels. The Owen brothers, faces streaked with sweat and grime, came down to the water, wiping the gritty smoke out of their eyes.

"All that smoke puts me in mind of a battleground," grunted Rulon as he sluiced water up the hill. He paused to rub the back of his neck. "It sure brings back bad memories." Then he bent to the water again.

Nobody but Ida had time to sit and listen to the crackle of the burning vegetation and the roar of the flames. Nobody but Ida noticed the change in volume of sound of the fire as it veered away to the south. Nobody spoke to Ida, so Ida told no one.

Then Carl saw that the smoke had thinned out, and he straightened his back to look up at the rim. The towering clouds of smoke were gone, and he dropped his bucket and scrambled up the bank of the creek to the top of the slope.

"Pa," he shouted. "The fire's gone off to the south. Looks like Rulon's back fire did the trick!"

His older brother climbed the hill to join him, and Carl glanced back to watch him come. Rulon had discarded his sooty shirt, and for the first time, Carl saw the angry purple scars of his brother's war wounds.

"It's a wonder you made it home, Rule," Carl said gravely. "What did you run into that made so many holes?"

Rulon stopped on the edge of the valley. "You ever hear of a mortar shell? Them things explode into a right smart number of pieces when they hit. Shrapnel, they call 'em." He fingered the largest scar. "I was too close to one that last day, and caught a bunch of shrapnel."

"Whatever they are, they didn't do you no good. Mary's lucky she ever saw you again."

"Most of 'em are still in there. The surgeon figured I'd die, so he didn't bother to dig the iron out," Rulon added, and rubbed the scar.

Carl turned and surveyed the blackened east, wiping his hands on his shirtfront. "Makes me ache inside to see all that grass gone. What a ruin!" He hung his forearm over his shorter brother's shoulder. "Did you come across any surprises out this way?"

Rulon's head snapped around to look at Carl. "You mean like that Acosta scum attacking us in this valley? Yeah. We had some surprises." He spat into the ashes at his feet. "We buried Ed Morgan's little girl, and put her brother Harry into the wagon with a bullet through his thigh. Real nice surprise for a ten-year-old."

Carl dropped his arm from Rulon's shoulder, clenched his fists, closed his eyes, and swore. He stabbed his shovel into the earth several times. "Anybody else hurt?"

"Couple of near hits, but the Morgans got the worst of it because they was out wood-gathering when the men rode down on us." He paused for a moment, wiping the sweat from his dripping forehead with the back of his hand.

"How'd it happen?"

"Ed sent Tom out with the kids. The gang rode in from over that rise." Rulon gestured with his hand. "We heard the shots and came a-running with our rifles. We dropped about half of them outlaws before they pulled out for good. Rode on south."

"Gone to Texas?"

"Likely. Good riddance. We'd been here a day when they attacked, on account of my axle."

"How'd that happen?"

"Went off the bank wrong, hit a boulder in the creek. I had a feeling about that axle being flawed when I got the wagon, but I didn't have much choice."

"Where did you get it?"

Rulon smiled crookedly. "I stole it off the Yankee who bought the livery for taxes. Clay helped, but he wasn't real happy about it."

"I guess nobody's happy lately. I'm sorry about the Morgans' loss."

They stood for a moment, looking and thinking, then Carl spoke up slowly, still looking off into the distance.

"Is Mary Hilbrands a good wife to you? Does she make you . . . feel like . . . a man?"

Startled, Rulon raised his eyes to look at Carl's face. After a time, he said, "That's a mighty strange question, brother, but since you make bold to ask, I'll answer best I can."

He paused, evidently searching for words. "Mary was barely scratching at fifteen years old when we wed. I was such a—" He closed his eyes briefly, then shook his head before continuing. "I reckon I was in a hurry to marry her, leaving soon to join the cavalry as I was. We didn't have time to learn much about each other as married folk before I rode away." He clicked his tongue. "Then I didn't see her again for four long years, not 'til I woke up in a strange bed with a mess of holes in me, with Mary's dear face—" He stopped and looked at Carl. "You sure you want to know all this?"

"Yep."

Rulon sighed and squinted and made a little scoffing sound, but continued. "Mary's a good wife, a dutiful wife. After I got home, all shot up and obliged to lie in bed day and night, she kept the house and cooked the meals and tended Roddy, as well as bringing me through the pain and the nightmares and back to living." He paused again, his face working. "She tended to my needs, all of 'em, Carl, and yes, I know I'm a man."

He cuffed Carl on the jaw with a gentle fist. "Now you know more'n you should about Mary'n' me. Mind you, keep it silent."

Carl nodded and swallowed hard. "Do you reckon you love her?"

"I have no doubt on that score, no doubt at all. Despite all our troubles, I'm confident she feels the same."

"Like Pa and Ma?"

Rulon nodded. "Like Pa and Ma."

Carl turned to look down the grade. Ida seemed so tiny and forlorn, standing on the side of the stream, and his throat pinched to see her clutch the damp blanket around her shoulders. "No more questions," he said, and started down the slope.

Carl gently took the damp blanket from Ida's stiff fingers. "You'll take a chill, wrapped in that thing," he said.

She hung her head, turning away from his gaze. "Don't look at me," she cried. "I'm all dirty and wet."

"Well, I'm liable to break a looking glass myself. Let's go set in that patch of sun up the crick a ways. We both need to get dry." Carl took her arm and firmly led her away from the wagons.

He sat her down in the full sun, on a rock that jutted out over the bank of the stream, then collapsed into the grass at her feet, spreading full-length on the soft green sod.

"We've had us a time lately, girl. Near calamitous for us all," he said, staring at the sky. "Especially for the Morgans. Did you hear what happened? They lost their little girl to them unholy ruffians from back down the trail." Carl gazed into the sky, blue and white with wispy clouds drifting overhead. "Now, I don't blame your pa for having his own opinion, but that ain't any comfort to Mrs. Morgan, I reckon. Your pa came near ruining our whole enterprise with his notions. We all got to stick together and listen to the leader, and that's my pa. We can't take any more bickering, if we're to get to the Territory before winter sets in."

Carl looked up and saw great tears flooding silently from Ida's blue eyes. He sat upright, got to his knees in front of her, and took her into his arms.

"Hush now, darlin'. I didn't mean to go on so about your pa. You had a mighty hard time out there today, and here I'm just rambling on with a mess of foolish words."

Ida broke into sobs.

"Ah, don't cry on me, sweetie-pie," Carl pleaded with her, alarmed at her tears. "I ain't had much practice with crying women." In his discomfort, Carl began to smooth her hair and wipe the tears from her eyes. He felt clumsy and bumbling, and tried to kiss her forehead in apology.

Ida shut her eyes and tipped back her head, a little shudder moving her body. With her motion, Carl's lips accidentally met hers, and he kissed her gently. She responded with fiery hunger, and a shock went through the Carl's system as he realized that she had led him into a trap.

He rose to his feet and pulled her to hers, alarm battling with the stirring in his blood. "We have to go back," he insisted firmly. "I should have looked after the team by now."

Ida picked up a rock and flung it into the water, then stiffly followed him to camp.

Chapter 10

"Rule, let James do that lifting," Rod instructed. "You don't want to tear nothing loose." The two brothers splashed through the water to change places at the rear of the wagon. "Get set with that wheel, son. On the count of three."

James and Carl gathered their limbs beneath them, and at the count, they lifted the wagon atop their backs and Rulon added the wheel to the new axle. Rod placed the pin in the hub and secured it, and the younger men eased the wagon down.

"Glad that's done, Pa," James wheezed. "It must be supper time."

Rod laughed. "Likely. You boys put the tools away and load the wagon, and I'll go see if your ma is ready to feed a bunch of hungry wolves. We'll be on our way first thing tomorrow morning."

"Thanks, Pa," Rulon rubbed raw knuckles. "Next time I cross the country, I'll make sure I have a prime wagon."

"Or bring a spare axle," Carl added.

Soon the men had the tools and the waterlogged wagon out of the creek, then set about gathering Mary's wide-strewn belongings and restoring them to the vehicle. Afterward, they scattered to prepare for supper.

"Mary," Rulon called to his wife from the far side of the stream. "Look here. Our things are back together."

Mary picked her way over a path of rocks that Albert had put in the stream for the use of the ladies and the children. "Oh," she sighed. "That's better. And Ma and Pa are back with us. I reckon I can rest peaceful this night."

Rulon drew her to his side and walked her behind the wagon when they could speak in private. "Are you feeling poorly?" he asked, his voice low.

"No. I've been so worried about my folks and about our wagon. Now at least those cares are swept away." She took his arm. "Rulon?"

"Yes?"

"Are we close to where we're going?"

He sat her down on a barrel that had been left beside the wagon, got his shirt from the wagon seat, and slowly put it on. "I'm sorry, Mary. We have a fair piece yet to travel."

Mary placed her hands on the middle of her bulging abdomen and smoothed her apron over the roundness. "I can't keep doing this, going, and stopping, and traveling on, every day of my life, Rulon. We've got to find a place to stop and stay."

He caught one of her hands and lifted it to his lips. "I know it's hard on you, but it can't be helped. This place ain't Colorado yet. We must keep going." He put her hand on his chest, over his heart, and held it there.

"Does it have to be Colorado?" She took back her hand.

"It does if we're going to settle around our kin, Mary." He leaned over and stroked her cheek. "Isn't that worth a little discomfort?"

She inhaled. "Yes, but will I have a home before I bear this child?"

Rulon's forehead furrowed and he stooped over her. "Are you feeling pains?"

"No, no. That won't happen for a while, but will we be there before the time comes?"

He patted her shoulder. "Pa thinks another four weeks should see us into the Territory. You can hold out that long, can't you, Sugar?"

"I don't know. I yearn for a bed to lie in, a place to rest this heavy body." She caught Rulon's hand under hers. A flicker of a smile touched her lips. "It appears you want the same." The smile retreated. "Will this journey ever end?"

He cringed at the pain in her voice. "Oh, my Mary," he said. He pulled her gently to her feet and enfolded her in his arms, slowly stroked her hair. "You'll feel better after you eat. That'll put spunk into you."

Mary closed her eyes and snuggled her head under his chin. "I want a home of our own," she whispered.

Several days after the fire, Rod directed the weary travelers to set up camp beside Diamond Springs, where water flowed from a hollow rock.

When the evening meal was done and they lay in their blankets beneath the wagon, Julia asked Rod, "When are you going to make your peace with Rand Hilbrands?"

"He owes me the first word of apology," he mumbled.

"The way I see it, both of you were wrong. He divided us, but you didn't see the attack coming."

"But I did, Julia. If I'd had the man-power, the sentries, we wouldn't have been surprised."

"So you keep thinking that, and put off healing this wound in our people?"

"Julie. It's not that way."

"You're a fine, strong man, Rod, and you served well in the war, but you can't court martial your friends because they make mistakes." She sought his hand with hers, and squeezed it. "Rand is a good man. Make peace with him."

"You're a wonder, woman. What do you know of court martial?"

"Being a woman doesn't make me stupid, Rod."

"I didn't say that."

"Well, I'm not ignorant, either, but that's beside the point. I want your promise."

"Julie!"

"Rod, I mean it."

"I reckon you're in the right," he muttered a minute or two later, giving in. "We ought to live in harmony... for the next month, at least." He snorted. "To keep the peace, I'll do it."

"Thank you." She squeezed his hand again.

He turned over and looked at her in the quavering light of the dying fire. "I missed you." He carried her hand to his lips.

"What?"

"All that time I was gone. I missed my woman, my helpmeet, my wife."

She stirred in the blankets, moving against him. "Times were hard," she replied.

"Not anymore." His arm slipped around her waist. "Do you love me?"

"Forever and always, Rod Owen."

"That's a long time."

"Even when you're a stubborn, mule-headed man," she whispered, then laughed softly, deep in her throat. "Who would've known this quilt would cover us twenty-five years."

He kissed her, then growled, "Shut up, woman."

Julia laughed again.

At Turkey Creek they ran out of firewood.

"Jonathan Helm warned me this day would come," Rod chuckled when the women brought the lack to his attention. "From here on we gather these here things." He turned over a dry, flattened circle of matter with his boot-tip. "It's called a buffalo chip, and it'll burn quick and hot. But you'll need plenty, for they ain't much more than grass."

Amanda Hilbrands protested. "Why, that's just— It's not fitting for fuel," she finished. Robert Campbell and Joshua O'Connor laughed, and Amanda turned to glare at them. "And you'll be the first to gather them," she declared.

The "gather" was made, gingerly, that first day, but continued without further thought as time went on. Then after days of travel, the party reached the Great Bend of the Arkansas River. Ed Morgan lost the frown he'd carried since the skirmish at the creek, whooped, and threw his hat into the air at the sight of the river after so much dry land.

"Look at them trees." Little Catherine Campbell gave a great sigh. "No buffalo chips tonight."

Cottonwood trees grew in profusion on the little islands in the middle of the river, so Rod sent several of the men and older boys wading over to the nearest island to chop enough wood for a two-night stay.

"All this wood and water does my heart good," he told them all before the supper began. "We'll have singing and dancing tonight."

They set up camp on a sandy yellow ridge several hundred yards from the river. Swarms of small bugs filled the air and bit whatever exposed flesh they landed on, and snakes rustled in the grass around the camp, but the abundance of water made these nuisances bearable.

Albert Owen and Andy Campbell beat the brush with long sticks and shot all the snakes they could find. They took their trophies home. Their mothers, gritting their teeth, took the reptiles, skinned them, cut them up, and threw them into the supper-pots.

After the dishes had been washed and put away, out came the instruments. Edward Morgan's fiddle lacked the low G-string, but he played a merry tune, his fingers flying up and down the remaining three strings.

James produced a small metal object. "This here's a jaws-harp my buddy taught me to play. I was obliged to take it from his pocket before the fall of Richmond." He stopped for a moment. "He had no further use for it." He ducked his head and wiped his nose.

Andy Campbell polished up an old harmonica and introduced the travelers to some of the songs he used to entertain the stock as he drove it along.

"Let's dance with everybody tonight," Rod exhorted. "Have a good time, and don't let any girl sit too long."

The music was lively, and Carl was right in the middle of the crowd, trying to get to Ida, but enjoying a dance with his sister Marie. He claimed Ida for the next dance, but at one point, Tom Morgan, Edward's eldest son, swept by and caught Ida in the exchange of partners, and Carl found himself dancing with Ellen Bates.

Carl grinned at the redheaded girl, relaxed, and forgot Ida for a while. Recalling the last time they had spoken, he bent and whispered in Ellen's ear. "How was that bit of candy I brought you?

She smiled up at him. "It was wondrous sweet." Then she fell silent once more as Carl led her into the next step.

The music died, and Ellen smiled again. "I saved some candy to share with you. It's over in the wagon."

"Lead the way," he said, laughing. Carl went to the big campfire, took a long stick that was blazing at one end, and used it to light their path to the Bates' wagon as the dancing resumed behind them.

Ida saw him go, stamped her foot, and glared after his departing back, but he didn't catch any of the reproach sent his way.

Ellen went around to the dark side of the wagon and stepped up onto the wagon tongue. "I need a little boost," she said.

Carl lifted her up, and she climbed over the seat, then disappeared into the darkness under the wagon cover. He heard her moving around, and soon she poked her head out of the opening and smiled.

"I have it." She held up the small twist of paper, then slipped it into her skirt pocket. Climbing once more over the seat, she stepped to the edge of the wagon box.

Before he could reach out to help her down, Ellen tripped, and dropping the torch into the sand, Carl caught her, going down on his back to break her fall. For a brief moment he held her to him, feeling the quick, hard beating of her heart against his chest.

"Oh! Please . . . I," she stammered, blushing in the wavering torchlight. She struggled out of his arms, whispering, "I'm sorry, I had no thought to— Oh lawsy!" Then she would have fled into the sand hills, but Carl grabbed her hand as he got to his feet.

"Wait." He stopped her flight. "It was an accident. No harm done." Taking her by the shoulders, he sensed the fluttering of her heart as she shivered with embarrassment. "Don't go." He reached out to pull a leaf from her hair. Brushing the red gold strands with his fingertips caused a hot sensation to rush through his blood.

"What about the candy?" He felt the sand, the bank, the earth shift under his feet, and wondered if her lips were as soft as they looked. Longing to touch them, he fought for control as she recovered the sweets from the depths of her pocket. With a shaking hand she held out a piece of the candy, and he took it and bit off a small chunk.

Chewing slowly, he watched the shadows flicker over her grave face. The torch sputtered out in the sand, and she shivered in the darkness.

"It seems you're always saving my life." Her voice sounded thin and shaky, as though someone were squeezing her throat and shaking her by the shoulders at the same time. She shivered again. "Thank you."

The music started up and Ellen turned to listen. "We best go back to the fire."

"Stay a minute. We've missed a dance or two already." He took her hand.

"No!" She pulled loose, and turning, left him.

"Ellen," he whispered, but she was gone, and her leaving brought a sharp ache to his soul. He followed, stomach churning in turmoil, and as he stepped into the firelight, he glanced around. Ellen was nowhere to be seen. At the far side of the party, Ida laughed merrily at James and Tom Morgan. The latter young man took her hand and led her off to dance.

Carl walked over to Marie and startled her by whirling her off balance into his arms. She stumbled a little as he moved her into the dance, but he helped her to recover, and gripped her hands tightly in his, fighting both anger and guilt that rose in him.

"Carl!" Marie tried to free her hands. "What ails you? You're hurting my hands."

Surprised, he loosened his grip. "Sorry," he mumbled.

Later, as Carl sat on a stool someone had placed in the shadows by a wagon, resting his feet from the unaccustomed labor of the dance, he sensed someone beside him, and he turned his head, whispering, "Ellen?"

"Not hardly," replied James, speaking low. The younger man massaged his left shoulder with his right hand.

"Are you weary?" Carl got up from the stool and motioned for James to sit.

"I don't need that. I want to talk to you, brother." James paused and flexed his left arm.

"Shoulder bothering you?"

"Not nearly as much as it might later," James said, and Carl shivered a bit at the menace in his voice.

"You said you wanted to talk. Do it."

"I saw Miss Ellen a piece back, and she didn't look very happy. Fact is, she looked like a mule run over her, she was that white and fearful looking." James stopped talking and moved closer to Carl. "That was just after you took her out back of the wagons, brother."

Carl turned to face James. "Meaning?"

"What did you do to put that face on her?" He held his crumpled fist in front of Carl's face.

Carl flushed, remembering. "It ain't your business, James."

"I'm here to remind you it is. You have you a girl you're going to marry—Miss Ida Hilbrands. Miss Ellen is betrothed to me. Stay clear of her." James jabbed Carl's chest lightly with his fist every few words. His face blazed red in the glow from the campfire.

"What do you want with Ellen? You don't love her." Carl sneered.

James hit him in the belly, hard enough to double him over. "That's 'Miss Ellen' to you," his low voice continued, harshly, as Carl remained curled over, guilt constraining him from throwing a punch of his own. "Pa set up the match against my will, but you don't have my leave to break it. Keep your distance."

James turned and stalked away, and Carl took a huge breath. "He means it," he said to himself, and gritted his teeth.

The party lasted until very late. Carl could not sleep, and he lay staring into the dying coals of the fire. Ida had not danced with him for the remainder of the night, though she smiled and claimed it was not her fault, but that "the boys" wouldn't let her go for even a minute. Carl made a show of bowing to the superior numbers of "the boys," and did not press her. Once he turned his head suddenly and caught her staring petulantly at him, but usually she kept a smile on her face.

Ellen had appeared toward the end of the party, but she didn't speak to Carl. One time he walked toward her to ask her to dance, but she turned her back and he pretended to be on another errand.

Now Carl rolled onto his back and saw by the left-hand position of the Big Dipper that it was past midnight. The air was warm and still he could not sleep, though he turned in his blankets and shut his eyes.

Half an hour later, Carl tossed the blankets aside and reached for his boots. He shook them upside down in case anything had crawled inside, then pulled them on. Grabbing his gun belt, he stood and strapped the weapon around his hips as he walked toward the edge of camp.

Edward Morgan was on guard, and turned as Carl came up to him. "I thought young Tom was going to take the next watch." Ed yawned and rubbed his neck, then squinted at the stars. "You're an hour early, Carl."

"It isn't my watch, Mr. Morgan. I can't sleep. I reckon I'll go down to the riverbank for a spell. Maybe take a swim."

"It's a nice night for swimming, being so warm." Ed sounded sleepy. "Keep a watch for them snakes."

"I brought my shooter," Carl replied, walking down the sandy slope in the darkness.

The closer he got to the river, the louder he could hear the rush of the water over the sandy bottom. The continuous sound felt easy to his ears, and he sat on the bank watching the stars' reflection in the endlessly rolling water.

Carl gazed at the ripples before him, and thought of Ida and her laughing eyes, how they sparkled when she was happy, and the curve of her lips when they entertained a smile. Then he recalled her shocked state while he fought the fire, her lack of help, and fear of getting scarred. Remembering her panic brought back the feeling of protectiveness.

I don't wonder she didn't want no scars, he mused. A pretty-looking young thing like her don't care to be disfigured.

He thought of her lips, and how soft they had been back on the meadow outside Kansas town. Carl stretched out on the sandy bank, arms behind his neck, and closed his eyes and recalled how it had been, holding her in his arms, feeling her heart pounding against his chest. He felt again the sting of fire leaping through his veins as he touched her flame-like hair. He remembered her trembling perplexity, her flight back to the safety of the dance, and he opened his eyes, confused at the vision.

Suddenly he sat up, realizing he dreamed of Ellen in his arms. He groaned, then said aloud, "No! I'm bound to marry Ida!"

He got to his feet. Blood pounded through his temples as he stared into the sky. "Pa arranged it, but we both agreed," he shouted into the void. "I've said my piece to her, and she agreed to be my wife. I won't go back on my word." He shook both his fists at the stars. "I can't betray my brother," he added, his voice dying away to a whisper.

Carl's arms fell to his sides, and for a long time he stood there—the pulse of his pounding heart moving his torso slightly—listening to the water surging past him. He half expected Ed Morgan to come investigate his outcry, then realized his words had been covered by the sound of the waters.

At last, disquiet seeping out of his veins and his resolve firmed by the regular rhythm of the river, he turned and went back to camp.

~*~*~

Carl avoided Ida during the next two days that the travelers spent alongside the big river. He spent his time caring for the team and riding Sherando out into the Great American Desert, a place of wind-whipped plain and short buffalo grass. There was no more tall, waving, blue-stemmed grass, no brilliant wild flowers, no escaping the eternally blowing wind. At the end of the second day, Carl returned from his hours of solitary riding ready to accept responsibility for his actions, willing to make the best of his future with Ida.

He went to Ida that evening, quietly insisting that she walk with him along the river. She followed him reluctantly, and he sensed her resentment toward him.

Carl walked along with his hands in his pockets, thinking over his words. Finally he stopped walking and turned to face the silent girl.

"I reckon you're unhappy with me, and I figure you've got a right. I left the dance the other night with another girl, and I owe you a mite of explaining. Ellen Bates went to get something for me from her wagon, and I tagged along."

He stopped, leaving the telling at the bare bones, deciding to spare her the shame and the pain of his struggle, his turmoil over divided loyalty.

She stood with arms akimbo, head thrown back to fully see his face. "Well, I reckon I am a mite peeved with you, Carl. I know we're not wed yet, but folks know it will happen sometime. I expect you to burn your bridges."

Her words hit a guilty spot in his soul, boring into it, and a cloud passed over his lean brown face. "We've both got some making up to do, Ida. You were having an almighty fine time with the boys, seemed like."

"It just looked like it to you," she said, tossing her head, making her curls bounce. "My heart was a-sorrowing something pitiful."

"Well, my heart is turned to you, Ida. I have a powerful liking for you, and I still want you for my wife, if you're willing." He held his breath.

Ida looked at her feet for a moment. She looked up. "My heart's feeling some better. I reckon I'm still betrothed to you." She beamed her most brilliant smile upon Carl.

He sighed, then took her arm to escort her back to the wagons.

The next morning, Rod Owen got his party moving again. The wagons toiled along the sandy valley of the Arkansas, day after day. From time to time Rod sent two or three men to hunt for fresh meat. Often they were gone for several days, returning with heavily laden pack horses.

One day toward the middle of September, James came tearing back from the hunt, riding a lathered horse, with Albert and Clay hard on his heels.

"Pa," James yelled. "Hold up them wagons. There's a herd of buffalo headed this way." He stopped his horse and jumped off, then caught the alarm in his mother's eyes. "Great snakes of the sandy hills, I didn't mean to scare you. They ain't stampeding or nothing like that. They're just moving along, grazing, but there's a powerful lot of them, and it makes an awesome sight."

"Well, Julianna," Rod said over his shoulder to his youngest. "Here's your chance to see a buffalo up close." He took off his hat and scratched his head. "I reckon we'll make camp here, for I been told a buffalo herd can hold up a train for days."

Julianna shook her head. "Papa, I don't want to see no buffaler. Clay says they're 'most as big as monsters, and have long hairy claws coming out of their feet. He says they got a humpback, and make a screeching sound that'll raise the hair off my head as good as any red Indian might. I don't want to see 'em."

"Clay is teasing you, daughter. I heard some of them stories he told you that night, and he's put a mighty lot of nonsense into your pretty little head. Buffalo isn't nothing to go having a fit over. Calm down and enjoy the sight."

The great, hairy, humpbacked creatures came from the north, and browsed slowly along, crossing the trail and the river as though nothing was in their way. For the next two days the women camped, washing clothes and baking. The men stood with their rifles at the edge of the passing herd, shooting any buffalo that strayed too close to the camp. The gunfire only disturbed a few of the shaggy creatures, and they loped off deeper into the herd. After the dead animals were butchered, the women gratefully added the meat to their larders.

On the third day the trail cleared, and Rod gave the order to break camp. The days slowly blended into dusty sunsets as they followed the river through western Kansas, until on the last day of September they crossed the border into Colorado Territory.

When given the news, Ida looked around at the same flat, endless plains and asked, "Is this all there is? It's so empty, and there ain't no hills, neither. I don't think I like Colorado." She crossed her arms and leaned back against the seat of the freight wagon.

"Let's see what comes up ahead. I heard there are mountains a large sight grander than those we left behind, Ida. You won't lack for hills." Carl glanced over at her, and saw that she wore a petulant look on her face. "You got no call to frown yet. We ain't stopping here."

"Carl, I am so tired of traveling that I could fairly scream. I want to find a pretty place to live, where you won't be always toting your rifle and your gun belt against those Indians your pa worries about. I'd favor a nice town, or even a little city."

"I promise you, you'll have a pretty place by and by, but it won't be in no town, nor city neither. We can't raise cattle in the city."

Ida sighed and gave Carl a long look. "You're sure about the cattle? You're bound to raise cattle?"

"Yup." His tone left no chance of argument.

She sighed. "Then I guess I'm bound to live where you raise your cows. But you will take me to see Denver City, won't you, once the cattle get sold?" Ida turned on the seat, using her most winsome smile.

Carl laughed. "Yes, we'll go see the sights. I reckon we'll go hunt up my Uncle Jonathan 'fore too long." He looked at her eager face. "If our house is up by then, likely we can go there on a wedding trip." The delight he saw in her eyes made him laugh again. "You surely do sparkle when you're happy."

"I declare! You do bring out the best in me, Carl Owen." Ida beamed. "I'll really sparkle some once we're wed, and away from all these prying eyes," she finished, looking around at the men, boys, and children on horseback.

Carl's blood pulsed harder in his veins, and he flicked the whip over the heads of the mules to cover the creeping red blush he felt moving up his face. He swallowed once, then matched her boldness with candor of his own.

"I don't reckon I'll be a shy feller, once we're in our own place and you're in my arms. There's going to be no campfire betwixt you and me, nor anything else."

Ida clasped her hands tightly together. "I reckon I'm having a mighty hard time waiting for that day."

"You'll wait." Carl nodded once, firmly. "I'll do you no wrong."

Ida dropped her hands into her lap and shrugged her shoulders. "Carl, what do you aim to use to build our house? I suppose brick ain't very plentiful hereabouts?"

"I'll have to see what's close to hand, Ida. Depends mostly on where we settle, I reckon. If Pa picks a spot this side of the mountains, there won't be logs nor lumber around. I heard tell of something called a soddy, though."

"That's a curious name. What's it mean?"

"It's sort of a cabin built of chunks of sod and earth."

"Sod? You mean dirt and grass? Carl," she cried out, appalled. "That ain't no better than a slave shanty!"

" 'Tain't forever, Ida. I aim to build us a nice home once the beef starts selling."

"That'll take years," she wailed.

Chapter 11

Fort Lyon began life as William Bent's second trading post, but by the time Rod Owen's group reached the fort, the Army had acquired it, changed the name three times, fortified it, and installed a small company of troops. Rod called on the commandant and found that the Indians were busy up north along the Platte.

"That's a mighty relief to us all, I reckon," Rod said. "We been expecting to have a fight on our hands any day."

"Well, it's safe enough right now. If you're going to take up land hereabouts, you'd best get on with it," the Major advised. "Winter's not far off, and you'll need shelter. When those freezing winds hit, you'll wish you were back in the States."

"Thank you kindly for the advice, but we're going on. I promised my wife she'd have trees." Rod tipped his hat and turned to leave, but the major spoke again.

"In another day or two you should catch sight of the mountains. Keep heading west, and you'll run into plenty of trees."

Two days later, before the travelers broke camp for the day's journey, Ellen walked over to Marie and pointed to the cloudy far-western horizon.

"Marie, I been looking at those clouds, and every so often there's something that looks like a blue cloud amongst the rest. Do you reckon it could be one of them mountains your pa keeps talking about?"

Marie's eyes followed Ellen's finger. The sun had risen enough to sparsely light the brown prairie around them, and a hint of chill pervaded the breeze that tugged at the girls' skirts. Marie shivered as she stared toward the west.

"I don't see anything." Then the clouds parted, revealing a far distant peak thrusting up into the sky. "Oh, Ellen, that's a real mountain. I ain't never seen anything so beautiful! Let's go tell my pa."

The girls found Rod hitching his team to the wagon. Marie tugged on his arm, trying to get him to go with her to see the mountain, but in her excitement, her words spilled out faster than she could arrange them into sentences.

"Whoa, daughter. What's your hurry?" he exclaimed.

Marie pulled him out from between the wagons to where he had a clear view to the west.

"It's them, Pa, it's really them. They're right back of those clouds."

"What do you mean, daughter?"

"The mountains, Pa. Ellen found the mountains!"

Again the clouds dispersed briefly, allowing Rod a glimpse of the peak.

"That must be Zebulon Pike's Peak. You remember, daughter, 'Pike's Peak or Bust'. Your Uncle Jonathan came out here then. Fifty-eight or Fifty-nine, it was. Hush, I never thought to see it." Rod gazed on the sight for a while, then called to his neighbor at the next wagon.

"Chester. Take a look at that. Your girl got the first sight of the mountains. They're just grand."

Chester stepped out from hitching up and looked toward the west. "There's nothing to be seen, Rod."

"Wait a spell. The clouds will clear, I reckon."

"Why, they're so *blue*," Chester cried, as the clouds parted again. "Muriel, look at this."

The word spread through the camp, and all the travelers stood and stared, relief etched on their faces. After a time, Rod called out, "Hitch 'em up. Let's get rolling, or they'll stay as far distant as you see them."

The girls stood together a moment longer, looking at the cloud-covered horizon, their hands tightly clasped in friendship.

"It's beautiful," Ellen whispered. "So wild and untamed. And the wind— I love the wind!"

Marie squeezed her hand. "You're like that, too, Ellen."

Ellen turned to her friend. "How do you mean?"

"You're beautiful and untamed yourself. Under that shy face you show the world, you're a wild, free woman, and I reckon I'm the only one as knows it. Don't I wish Carl did. He needs you, if he could only see it."

Ellen gasped and turned away to hide the red that she felt flaming her face. She had not told Marie about Carl's response to her fall from the wagon. That night she had felt his emotion flowing into her from his hands, almost like fire, and she knew that he had been badly shaken by his unsuspected passion. Still, he had gone back to Ida. Ellen had seen them walking out of the camp on the last night at Great Bend, and had seen Ida's face when they returned, and she knew that Ida was still Carl's intended.

"Don't you give up!" Marie's words pulled Ellen back from the verge of despair. "You can't give up till the preacher says the words over them. She ain't right for him, and I reckon he knows it. His soul is a-ragin', and he don't get much sleep, pacing around all the night long."

Ellen pressed two hands against her chest. "It can't be on account of me."

Marie pounced on the comment. "What do you mean? What's happened?"

"Nothing! That's why it can't be on my account. You know I say dumb things sometimes," Ellen mumbled.

"You never do. You always make perfect sense. You're the most sensible girl I know, and you never could tell a lie."

Ellen shut her eyes against the daylight for a moment, then

opened them wide. "There ain't nothing I can tell you," she blurted out, and ran blindly back to her wagon.

Near the junction of the Huerfano and Arkansas Rivers, Autobees' Plaza sat in the sun. Set back from the cabins along the bluffs, the stockade lay with the gate cautiously open, surrounded by corrals and baking ovens. The settlement was a welcome sight, and Rod took Chester Bates with him when he went to collect news.

Hailing the gatekeeper, an old Mexican man with shrewd eyes, Rod and Chester gained entrance to the stockade, and halted their horses by a post outside the main building. They dismounted and tied their animals, then entered the trading room.

A bar of planks laid on two barrels occupied one side of the interior; store goods filled the other walls. A rough wooden box on the counter was labeled "U. S. Mail" in black paint. There were three letters in the box.

Seated behind the bar planks, a slight, clean-shaven man drank milk from a whiskey glass while he munched on a sandwich and read a folded newspaper. He looked up at the approach of the men.

"You the owner?" Rod asked.

The man nodded his head, his cheeks full of bread and meat.

Rod hitched up his belt. "I'm Rod Owen. This here is Chester Bates. We aim to take up land on the Homestead Act. What can you tell us about this country?"

The man swallowed his food and smiled, putting out his large, square hand. "I'm Charlie Autobees, Justice of the Peace for Huerfano County, so I'm the man to ask. What kind of land are you seeking?"

"I aim to graze cattle, but my wife favors trees. Where can I find good pasture land and trees, both?"

Charlie Autobees spread both arms outward. "There's plenty of land in the County, so you got a powerful mite to choose from." He walked over to a map hung on one wall. "We take in pretty near all the corner of the Territory, from here to Kansas, but if I was to hanker after trees, I'd keep on southwest of here and hit for the Wet Mountains." He tapped the spot on the map. "They're plum full of pasture land, and they's a-plenty of water, and about now I 'spect the leaves are bound to be a-turning. Makes a right purty sight for the women folks to take joy in."

"You got any towns around here? We got a storekeep with goods and a blacksmith along with us."

"If it's towns you want, just follow the Arkansas. We ain't too far removed from Pueblo City. Down south there's a Mexican settlement to two. One called Leones ain't far down the Huerfano and the Cuchara. 'Course, down along the Santa Fe road, there's the settlements at Raton Pass, but they ain't a place for the ladies. They got a name for being tough towns." As he mentioned each place, Autobees traced the route on the map.

"How about farming?" Chester asked. "You got any place that'll grow wheat?"

"That'd be down along the Cuchara. You take the Huerfano down to the fork, then head up the left branch. There's folk settling in there growing beans, wheat, hay, and corn. You name it, and it grows down there. For your smith, now, I recollect they was needing one down to Leones. He'd get a warm welcome down that way."

"Rod, looks like I've found the place I'm looking for." Chester hitched up his own belt.

Rod looked closely at the map. "There's a choice of towns for Rand to set up shop in, and Tom's likely to find work down south." Rod turned to Autobees and put out his hand. The man took it and they shook. "We're obliged to you for your help. I reckon we file homestead claims here?"

"Yup."

They took their leave, and Rod looked back at the distance-shrunken stockade as they approached the wagons.

"Looks like our trails are separating, Chester. You're a steady man, and I've valued our friendship."

"This surely ain't good-bye forever, Rod. The women folk will want to see each other, not to mention the unfinished business with the young folks. We'll be a-visiting, I reckon."

"I'll be handy for house-raising and such, Chester. You can count on me and my boys for help when you need it."

"I know it, Rod."

The travelers gathered around Rod and Chester as they dismounted and walked into camp. Rod spoke first.

"Pueblo City is close by, on the Arkansas. Rand, you could set up your store there, or go further south where some farmers have a settlement."

"I'd just as lief settle near the mining activities," said Rand. "I'll take a look at Pueblo City."

"I'm ready to follow the river south," announced Chester. "There's good land for crops down there. Who'll go with me?"

"I will," said Ed Morgan. "Elizabeth is of a mind to settle near Muriel."

"Molly and me will join you," added Angus Campbell.

"There's a town down there needing a smith, Tom. Come along, settle near your kin," Chester urged.

Tom O'Connor flexed his heavy shoulders. "All this traveling has me hankering after the fire and the forge. Next to the fire is a pleasant spot to be, come wintertime."

"I'll go in with Rand to Pueblo City and pick up Carl, then head south for the Wet Mountains," Rod said. "If I picture it right, we'll be about forty miles northwest of you folks."

"Then this is our last camp together?" asked Carl.

"We go our own ways after the nooning," his father answered.

Carl glanced around the circle. A bond of strength gained from trials overcome joined him to these men: Chester Bates, strong and solid, quietly going about doing the right thing; Edward Morgan, thin and dark, his quick grin and friendly ways starting to return after the blow of his little girl's death; Angus Campbell, with piercing blue eyes and sandy hair; Tom O'Connor, brawny and restless, still mourning for his long-dead wife; and Rand Hilbrands, tall and fleshy, with a somber air. Now they were parting, and pain squeezed his stomach.

James had brought in an antelope the previous night, and Julia cut up what remained of it for dinner. Marie invited Ellen to eat, and the girls huddled together, dreading their separation.

Ellen looked at Marie, whose eyelashes were jeweled with tears.

"Don't cry or you'll start me off. You heard your pa. We won't be that far away from you. Only forty miles."

"Forty miles! Ellen Bates, that's as far away as Staunton or Winchester is from Mount Jackson. How often did you get to go that far away from home?"

"I think it's different out here, Marie. A body has to go far to get to any place from another. We'll visit back and forth. I just feel it in my bones."

Chester Bates arrived with Rand Hilbrands right behind him. "It's time to be off, Ellen. We'll see you, Mistress Owen, Miss Marie." Chester nodded to them.

"Before you go, Chester, listen a minute," Rand said. "I plan to have a little Christmas party for everyone come the holidays. You'll pass the word to your group?"

"I will."

"Then come look me up in Pueblo City on Christmas Eve, and we'll make merry in our new home."

Julia smiled. "Thank you for the invitation, Mr. Hilbrands. It'll be like long-ago times."

"Let's be off, miss," Chester said, taking Ellen's arm. She walked off with her father, looking back at Marie as long as she could. Then she got in the wagon, and it rumbled away with the others, heading southwest along the Huerfano River.

There was one more fort to pass before they arrived at the town, and Rod spotted it at noon on the following day.

"Fort Reynolds," he told Julia. "We'll stop to eat here, then get on the road again. We should reach Pueblo City before dark."

"It will be nice to see a town, and I know Amanda will be happy to settle here, but I'm not a city girl, Rod. One night will be enough for me."

Dusk turned the sky to lead when the party first glimpsed the lights of Pueblo City. Small adobe buildings and timbered shacks abounded on the outskirts. In the center of commerce stood a hotel, a squat affair of Spanish styling, short on grace, but long on hospitality. Even before they approached the front of the hotel, they could hear a fiddle squawking and a loud voice attempting to sing:

"I got a mule, her name is Sal, fifteen miles on the Erie Canal. She's a good ol' worker and a good ol' gal; fifteen miles on the Erie Canal."

Carl grinned at the sound. "He sings worse than me, Ida, but it's Friday night, and I reckon nobody minds much."

"I mind. I hope he don't think to go on all night. I was planning to sleep sound, in a real bed."

"That sounds mighty nice. If your pa pays me off tonight, I'll have the price of a bed, too." He blushed as his thoughts wandered back over his words.

"Oh, pooh," Ida said, flicking her fingertip across his nose. She sighed deeply. "How soon till we can wed, Carl?"

"Soon as the house is built, I'll come after you. Surely there's somebody in town that can marry us." Ida laid her hand on his arm and turned to look at him. Carl squirmed on the seat. "It won't be long now, girl. I'll come visit you if I can get away." He turned to look into her blue eyes.

"That'll be grand, Carl." She smoothed her dress across her knees, then brushed a speck of dust from her bodice. "I'll look forward to your visits."

Carl turned his eyes front in time to pull the team to a halt before the mules ran into the back of the Hilbrands' family wagon. He jumped off the high seat, went around the wagon, and scooped up Eliza, who was in danger of falling asleep, and as a consequence, of falling off the wagon.

He settled the little girl in his arms and carried her toward the front of the next wagon, where Rand met him with a canvas sack in his hand.

"Put Eliza up there on the seat. Thank you, boy. Here. I'll pay you now, in case your pa decides to take off in the night." He handed Carl the sack. "One hundred and fifty dollars."

Carl hefted the sack. "Seems a mite much just for driving a wagon."

"Take it, boy. I promised you a good wage. I'll make plenty off the goods."

Carl thanked him and went to the wagon to help Ida. He stood on a wheel spoke and took her hand. "Your pa paid me a hundred and fifty dollars, girl! I'm going to build us a fine house."

"With a fine feather bed?" She arched her brows and stood up.

"Don't tease me. A man's got only so much he can stand." He dropped to the ground from the wheel.

"I know," she answered. "Get me down from here."

"I don't know as I dare."

"Silly boy. I won't hurt you."

"I don't reckon you will. It's your pa I worry about."

"Papa?"

"If he sees me hugging you, I'll be in a fine jam."

"Will that get us wed sooner?"

"Ida! We need a house first. Now, are you going to behave yourself, or do I leave you up there all night?"

She looked from side to side, bent her head and closed her eyes, then opened her eyes and gazed at Carl. "I really can get down by myself, you know."

"I know. You done it before when you was mad at me."

She wiggled her shoulders at him. "But it's nicer when you lift me down."

He groaned. "Is this the good-bye you want?"

"Just a little peck, so I'll know you're coming back to visit."

"One little peck then." He stuffed the sack into his trousers pocket, reached up his arms for her, and she extended hers, laying her hands on his shoulders.

"You've got such a nice frame, Carl Owen," she murmured as he set her on the ground. "So strong. And you're so fine looking, too." She passed her fingers over his cheek. "Now, where's my peck?" She put back her head, lifting her lips to where he could reach them.

He gave her a chaste kiss, but it wasn't enough, not for Ida. "Please, show me you'll come for me," she breathed, and he took her into his arms.

He didn't mean to linger, but she was so warm in his arms, and so eager, so willing to receive his embrace. His lips covered hers again, and he pretended it was auburn hair slipping through his fingers.

"Doggone you, girl," he muttered when he finally broke free. "I'll visit when I can. Your pa will come looking for you in a minute. Good-bye." He loosed her and stepped back. *And you ain't Ellen Bates*, he thought, wondering if she would always be in his thoughts when he kissed Ida. Carl turned away and went to find his family, trying to shake the mood.

"Pa," he said when he saw Rod. "Rand Hilbrands paid me. I'll buy supper for us tonight."

"Sure. Let's see what Colorado folks eat."

Rod and Carl led the Owen family into the lobby and common room of the hotel. The appearance of the inn was rustic, for the chairs and stools were made of unpeeled pine logs and rawhide. A door led off to the right, where the aroma of meat drifted on the air. Another door, to the left, opened into the barroom, already crowded in the first hours of weekend freedom.

As Carl glanced around the lobby, Rand brought his family into the hotel. The Owens and the Hilbrands filled the lobby, and the dark-haired man at the desk looked angrily over at them.

"I can't put ye all up for the night," he growled. "I've got lots of folks in for the weekend, and I'm nearly full up."

Rand approached the desk. "I'll be wanting a room for my girls and a room for the wife and me."

"The best I can do ye is one room, but it's big and has plenty of room for spreading quilts and such. Ye can all fit in."

"This seems a poor excuse for a hotel, if you can't find rooms for your guests," Rand blustered.

The proprietor planted his feet on the floor and placed his fists on his hips. "This ain't your Grand Hotel, mister, and I don't believe ye made arrangements beforehand, neither. I gives ye what I has to give. If ye can do better than that, buy me out and I'll be off to the gold fields!"

Chapter 12

Rand looked at Amanda. She nodded her head. He scratched his ear, looked over at Rod, and shrugged his shoulders.

"I'll give you fifty dollars and a hundred pounds of flour. If you're anxious to be off, I'll be happy to help you pack your bags."

The dark-haired owner laughed and slapped his chest. "Ye can keep the flour. I'll take the cash and leave in the morning. My brother's holding a claim for me that shows signs of being the biggest strike in Colorado history. Ye won't see me keeping no flea-bitten hotel no more after tonight. I've got a fortune waiting for me over yonder."

Rand turned to his wife. "I reckon we've got a hotel to run, Mandy. We'll see if there's a place to set up the store." He glanced at Rod. "You won't have to look far to find us come Christmas time, Rod."

"You've a lucky streak in you, Rand. Ten minutes in town and already you're a leading citizen. We'll just eat and be on our way."

Rand gestured toward the dining room. "Go find a table and eat up."

Ten members of the Owen family followed Rod into the dining room, Roddy in his father's arms. The lighting—coming from six candles in wall holders—was dim, and Carl stopped to let his eyes adjust. He noticed that the tables, jammed with avidly eating men, were made of rough planks of wood, splintered along the edges, while the men sat on benches made of half-logs.

"Do you bring your own lamp to see by, Papa?" Julianna looked around curiously.

"It would make an improvement, I reckon, daughter." Rod laughed.

"Look, Rod." Julia pointed. "Those men are getting up. I figure there's room for us at that table."

Seven big men filed past the family, one holding his full belly and burping loudly. Another nodded to Julia and said, "Eat fast, ma'am. They clear the room at seven for the dance."

"A dance, Pa?" Marie's eyes sparkled.

"Not tonight, daughter. We have to be on our way early tomorrow. We'll be in at Christmas time, and there'll be plenty of dancing then." Rod sat down, and the rest of the group squeezed onto the benches.

A sturdy matron came over to the table and cocked her head to one side. "Buffalo steaks, beans and sourdough bread are what we serve. Butter and peach preserves is extra."

Rod pointed to Carl. "He gives the orders tonight."

"There's ten of us can do justice to that fare," Carl said, turning to Mary. "What's the young'un eat, Mistress Mary?"

"Bread and butter and peach preserves. And half a helping of beans."

"Bring what she said for the young'un," ordered Carl. "And bring all the rest of us butter and preserves."

First light saw the Owen wagons already on the prairie heading southwest for the mountains. A constant wind blew over the small hills and rocky outcroppings of the desolate countryside. Ahead lay the Wet Mountains, their wooded green flanks topped by moisture-laden clouds.

"That sight over yonder gives me a real peace, Rod. I don't mind traversing this arid land if I can live snuggled up against them sweet green hills." Julia gave a sigh of contentment. "I reckon if we get a nice piece of property up there, I'll say you kept your promise of trees, and right handsomely, too."

"With those rain clouds, there's bound to be water a-plenty

in this country. We need to look for a spring or a creek coming off those mountains, and there we'll build."

The next day, Rod stopped the team in a secluded meadow through which a creek flowed from the side of Greenhorn Mountain. Juniper and piñon trees surrounded the grassy field, and on the bench below them, bands of color showed where aspen and oak trees lived. Up the mountain, pine, fir, and spruce promised an evergreen world.

As he helped Julia to the ground, Rod asked, "How does this place suit you?"

Julia ran out on the thick carpet of grass. She whirled around, laughing. "This is home, Rod. This is our home!" She ran back and stopped, breathless, in front of him. "This is better than back in the Valley. We have all of this to ourselves." The motion of her arm took in the entire mountain and the valley of the creek below. "And no Yankees to drive us out. Oh, Rod, it's well-nigh perfect!"

"You've got a sparkle to you like a dozen gems, Julie. My heart leaps to know you're mine." He took her in his arms and looked around at his grinning sons. "Well, she is mine," he declared, and kissed their mother.

Julianna giggled and hid her face in her hands. "Why's Papa acting so silly, Marie?" she asked from between her fingers.

"He's so glad to be home, Jule," answered her sister, eyeing the rolling tops of the mountains before them. "You know, these mountains look like the ones we left in Virginia. I feel like I'm home, too."

"Well, if we're home, where is our house?"

"Julianna! Pa and the boys have to build it. You can't expect it to be here waiting for us." Marie turned and walked away.

Her sister followed, tugging on her skirt. "You mean we have to make everything, just like we done all across the country?"

"I bet you thought it'd all be here like back in Virginia, didn't you?"

"This is sure different than I expected. Marie, I'm scared of critters. I want a proper house."

"Who you been talking to, Ida Hilbrands? We'll have a house by and by, Jule, and Pa won't let anything get you; so don't go to crying on me. I want to go see that crick."

Rod sent Clay and Albert to water the stock and the teams, then turned to his older sons. "Well boys, it's time to sharpen the axes. I'll stake out my homestead on the south side of the creek, and Rulon, you can have the north side, if you like. We could put the cabins right opposite each other, and build a little bridge over the creek for sociability. We'll put a half-shelter behind the house for the horses and mules, and the cattle pens right out there, in the meadow. They'll have plenty of grass down there."

Carl scratched his shoulder. "I'm going to need me a homestead, too, Pa. I like that little bench land we passed just north of here."

Rod nodded. "That looked like a fine place for a cabin."

"I'm hoping there's a sweet water creek south of here," James said, eyeing the trees in that direction.

"As soon as we set up camp here, you can ride over and find a place you like," Rod said. "Pick your spot and drive your stakes." He looked around the sweep of the horizon. "We'll work on cabins for your wives as soon as your ma and Mary have theirs."

The men cut small saplings and made temporary shelters with the wagon covers until cabins could be raised. Julia arranged her kitchen goods on a pile of boxes, and set about fixing a fire ring for the Dutch ovens and iron skillets. Mary joined her while Marie and Julianna took Roddy for a walk to gather firewood.

"Here now, don't you go to lifting that heavy oven, girl," Julia cautioned, looking at Mary's flushed face with a critical eye. "You need to set and rest a mite. Just take a seat on that stool, yes, draw it up over here and put your feet up a while. There's no hurry to make the fire, for once. We don't need to start on supper for an hour yet."

Mary sat down heavily, and slowly swung her feet up to rest on a wooden box. "I'm fine, Mother Owen. Just worn out from traveling. It's so good to stop at last."

"Mary, you ought to be blooming right now, but most of the time you do look all tuckered out. What can I do to bring a mite of sparkle to those pretty eyes?"

Mary stared down at her hands. "I suppose I am an ungrateful ninny. I wanted Rulon back from the war for so long, and then he— It was hard."

"You did your duty and then some," Julia murmured.

"It wasn't only duty. Then, when he'd mostly healed, and I, well..." She laid her hand atop the swell of her abdomen and sighed. "Father Owen proposed that we make this journey. It's been so much longer than I thought. All along the way, I've been yearning for a home of my own. Now we've finally arrived. I must be grateful for that."

"We're all grateful to stop," Julia said, nodding. "Mr. Owen has a forceful attitude, but he wants the best for us all."

"I used to be frightened of him," Mary admitted.

"You haven't seen his tender heart."

"No."

"If you'd come to live with us after you wed Rulon, you'd have been bossing him around by now."

"Oh, I can't think so." She rubbed the bulge beneath her skirt. "That's not my place."

"Well, I suppose not. It's mine to keep him upright and flush the conceit out of his soul."

"Conceit? Surely not."

Julia laughed. "Mr. Owen needs a daily dose of reality and humility, else his opinion of himself will grow too large."

"Mother Owen!"

"You should have come to us, girl, then you'd know it. But during the war times, unsettled as they was, you probably got more food to eat from the store, living with your pa. I see now it was best."

Mary shook her head. "I wish I had been on the farm. You know how prickly Mama was."

"That's water under the bridge, Mary. You were a real help to her, even if she didn't reckon it at the time." Julia sat quietly for a few moments. "Thank goodness she's recovered her true self. I didn't like being at odds with her. Now you have the chance to live nearby and get to know us better. I hope you won't miss your folks too much."

"I want to make a family with Rulon at last, and not wish for my Mama."

"You've got a good start on that family. Rulon is a gentle man, but he's got plenty of strength for you to rely on. He won't let you down." Julia patted Mary's shoulder. "I now know what's wanted. I'll speak to Mr. Owen about building you the first cabin. You have more need than I do."

After several days of logging, enough trees had been cut, and the men raised Rulon's cabin. When the last shingle was finally bound into place, Rulon took his wife inside, shut the door, and remained there for a long time.

Julia hummed a song as she went about making supper, skinning a squirrel that Albert had brought her. She turned toward the snug little house, nodding approvingly at the smoke that puffed out of the chimney.

"I knew Rulon would make a good husband, given the proper chance," she said under her breath.

A long time later, Mary opened the door and stepped over the log doorsill, her eyes bright. She looked back into the cabin with her mouth curved into a smile, carefully shut the door, then hurried over to Julia and hugged her.

"Mother Owen, you're a dear sweet lady to let me have the first home." She laughed, the first time in months. "I'm mighty obliged." Mary shivered in the chill wind that suddenly came through the trees. "Rulon laid a fire. You'd best come inside."

"Does he know you're giving this invite?"

Mary clapped a hand over her mouth and giggled. "No. I'd best warn him you're coming."

Julia laid her hand on Mary's arm. "Never mind, then. I'll have my own hearth in a few days. You run along and get warm." She shooed her toward the little house, thinking, *Cleaving to your husband is the best way to make a family, Mary-girl.*

When the week was up, Julia had her cabin, larger than Mary's, with a lean-to kitchen alongside the large fireplace, and a loft divided into two portions.

Marie and Julianna tugged their big feather bed into the smaller of the rooms, spread it with sheets and a quilt, and then snuggled down into its warmth.

"Oh-h-h, that feels so good," said Julianna, shivering her chills away.

"It's getting right cold at night," agreed Marie, pulling the quilt over her head. Then she sat up. "I guess Carl's going to start on his cabin tomorrow," she added mournfully.

"Carl's getting married. Carl's getting married," Julianna sang out, then collapsed in giggles.

"Hush you," came her brother's voice through the wall.

"Save the noise for the shiveree," called out James.

"Quiet up there!" thundered Rod Owen from below.

~*~*~

The weather grew steadily colder as the men continued with the logging. James found his creek, and started cutting logs for a cabin for Ellen. Carl chose the wooded bench with a natural clearing in the center for his home site. An artesian spring rose just below the clearing, which became the headwaters of a little stream that ran to join the creek far below his father's home. Carl had staked out a homestead that took in both sides of the stream and down into the valley. Ida would favor the cabin being surrounded by trees, snugly tucked into the forest.

The walls of both cabins were half way to the top, and the Christmas party was ten days away when the good weather broke in late afternoon. White clouds laden with snow rolled down from the mountain summits. A freezing wind blew from the north, forcing Carl, working alone at the cabin, to pull his gray coat collar up around his chin. He saddled Sherando, headed him south, and told the gray gelding, "Take me to Pa's, boy."

The horse started off into the driven needles of snow. Carl hunched his back against the wind, crossed his arms, and stuck his hands beneath them. After a while, the trail lay through the sheltering trees between his cabin site and Rulon's, but at the end, there was still the meadow to cross.

Carl halted Sherando before he left the trees to let the horse rest. He dismounted and stamped his feet to restore circulation, beating his hands together to warm them.

"Sherando boy, this storm can't last long. I've got to get that cabin built before Christmas." Climbing into the saddle once more, Carl urged the gray into the biting wind. "It's only a quarter mile," he told the animal. "It's mighty cold, but you're tough, horse."

The moaning wind blew his words away as the icy blast hit them. On every side, Carl could see only swirling white ice crystals. He gave the horse its head, trusting its instinct to reach the cabin.

Sherando moved slowly, fighting the cross wind as it headed west up the meadow. The wind increased and tugged at Carl, almost dislodging him from the horse's back. Ice caked his hair and snow sifted down into his collar. Then they passed the bulk of Rulon's cabin on the right, and Sherando changed direction to cross the creek.

The horse paused at the log bridge spanning the water, and Carl saw that ice was forming at the sides of the stream. He shivered, and urged the tired horse to step onto the bridge.

"Come on, boy," he shouted over the keening of the wind. "Them logs are set solid."

The gray stepped tentatively onto the slippery surface of the logs, then skittered hurriedly across.

"That's a boy," Carl shouted triumphantly.

Snatched by the wind, his voice carried to his father's cabin, and a light shined out into the white yard as the door opened.

James blocked out the light as he came through the door and caught Carl, who was sliding off the gray's back.

James called out, "Clay, grab them reins and take care of the horse. I'll get Carl into the house."

"You're well-nigh froze, son." His father helped James assist Carl across the doorsill. "That blow came up mighty sudden. It's a wonder you made it back here."

Carl shivered, then said, "It's my fault I got caught. I want that cabin up and finished so bad, I let the storm take me by surprise."

Morning came without a change in the weather, and Clay had to lean heavily against the door to crack loose the ice binding it to the jamb.

"Pa, that storm's still a-blowing, and the snow's piled up next to the door. How am I going to get out to feed the stock?"

"There's always a way for a man to feed his animals." Rod went over to the door. He tugged it open and faced a wall of white. "Fetch me a stick," he told Clay. "Maybe it ain't packed down tight."

Reaching as high as he could through the doorway, he flailed the stick into the snow. "It's still loose. Get some pails, boys."

Rod buttoned on his coat while Clay and Carl brought the buckets. "Clay, keep that second pail until I need it. Carl, you empty the full ones into the washtub."

Rod scooped out a pail full of snow at the top of the doorway and handed it over his shoulder to Clay. Taking the other bucket, he scooped again. Repeating the process until he had a hole big enough to crawl into, Rod then wiggled his way out the door and entered the icy cavern. "Clay, give me that stick again." His voice boomed in the confined space. "We'll see how deep this drift is."

Thrusting the stick into the snow above him, Rod felt a light resistance. He coughed as a load of snow fell into his upturned face. "Get me a longer stick," he commanded, angry at the elements.

Carl handed him Julia's broom, and Rod took it with a jerk. He stabbed it upward and broke through into the howling morning. New snow burst into his cavern, blinding him for a moment. Then he broke loose more of the crusty roof, and packed the snow down on one side to make a ramp to exit the hole. Triumphantly, he pulled himself out into the storm, floundering in the cabin-high drift.

"By gum, Colorado does everything in a big way," he shouted down to his family. "I have never seen a blow like this before."

Rod slid down the side of the drift and felt his way around the cabin, stomping down a path as he went, and found the horses cold, but snow-free in their shelter. The animals stood nose to tail, huddling together for warmth. Carl soon joined Rod, stamping his own feet as he came.

"Pa, we better run a rope from here to the stock pens, or we'll never get there and back every day."

"Good idea, son." Rod took down a rope from the side of the shelter. It was stiff in the cold, so he held it under his coat for a moment. Carl did the same with a second coil of rope, then they tied the ends together. Rod fastened one end of his double coil to a pine log that jutted from the side of the shelter and stepped into the storm.

Clay joined Carl as their father disappeared into a white swirl. "I wish we'd built the pens right alongside the house, 'stead of out in the meadow." Clay blew on his hands, then pulled gloves from his pocket and worked his hands into them.

"You'll be glad we did, come summertime and the flies gather. Grab the rope. We'd best follow Pa close." Carl moved off into the blizzard.

The rope was tight and easy to follow, for Rod was leaning against the wind, fighting to reach the cattle pens. Carl and Clay caught up with him, and presently, Rod stumbled against a pine pole.

"I reckon we're here," he shouted into the storm, tying off the rope and climbing into the enclosure.

Carl and Clay followed behind him, spreading out a little to search the inside of the fence for the cattle.

"Shoot, they got to be here somewhere," Rod growled. "They can't get out of this pen." He let go of the fence rail and pushed out into the middle of the pen, and the wind bowled him over.

Carl stooped to help his father to his feet, then Rod continued to fight through the drifts, only to fall again. He got up, brushing the snow from a large black and white object in his path.

"Well, I found the cattle," he muttered. "Carl, that there Brindle cow won't be knocking you into the mud ever again."

Chapter 13

Rod Owen said nothing more once he and his sons checked the carcasses of the cattle for any chance survivors. He returned in silence to the cabin, where Julia read disaster in his face. She glanced questioningly at him, but received only a shake of the head in reply.

Julia turned to Carl, who enlightened her in somber whispers.

"Not one?" she asked.

"No," he said, shaking his head. "Not one."

Julia sat down and rubbed her forehead with one hand, feeling the weight of the news upon her brow. "Lord God, don't desert us now," she breathed in prayer.

Marie and Julianna wept openly about the loss of the cattle, while the storm raged on for three days. Finally, the sun came out bright and strong, and melted down a portion of the drift around the cabin.

Rod and Carl stamped down a path to Rulon's cabin and found his family snug and warm.

"The cattle froze, son," Rod told Rulon, speaking of it for the first time since leaving the stock pen. "I reckon we'd best make use of this sunshine, and drag them carcasses into the woods. I don't favor them bringing wolves and such down by the cabins."

"Can we get the hides off them?" Rulon asked.

"Maybe a few," Rod answered with a shrug. "It may be too cold to salvage them."

"Well, what are we standing around here for?" Rulon asked, pulling on his coat. "Let's get on with it. The day ain't getting any longer."

The men found the mules frisky and eager to work after their long and idle confinement. Hitching the animals to one of the dead cows, they hauled the animal into the forest. James and the younger boys joined them, and they worked throughout the morning, dragging the carcasses into the woods. Rulon and Carl skinned a few head of cattle before they found the task too difficult in the cold, but they were able to butcher the remains with axes and the two-man saw.

Returning to the house for dinner at noon, they stood in a bunch before the fireplace, warming their stiff fingers.

"Shore feels good, Ma," said a shivering James. "You can't imagine how cold it is out there. We dasn't stand around, for fear of turning into ice cakes, like Lot's wife."

Julia laughed. "That was a pillar of salt, boy. You need some study in the Good Book."

"I meant shaped like Lot's wife, Ma."

Carl looked gravely at James. "I reckon I ain't going to claim to be shaped like Lot's wife, little brother. Speak for yourself. Me, I'm a man grown." He hooted at James's affronted expression.

James threw up his hands. "Chiggers and fleas! It's mighty bad times when a body can't speak his piece around here without a lot of idle comment. You know I mean ice cakes in human form, not female form. I reckon I can tell what you got on your mind. You're just chafing to get that cabin of yours built, ain't you?"

Carl's face flushed red, and his brothers cackled and roared at his discomfort. "Hush," he drawled, "the only thing keeping me single right now is this dad blamed storm and a half-made house."

James's grin was crooked, then his face went somber. "The sooner you marry Miss Ida Hilbrands, the better I'll like it."

~*~*~

That night it froze. The snowmelt at the bottom of the drifts glazed into sheets of ice, and icicles hung from the eaves of the cabins.

Carl lay in his bed and listened to the sounds of the night. The roof boards above him crackled as they shrank in the dropping temperature, and somewhere in the forest, a tree split open with a pop, as ice formed in its heart.

Here in the loft he could see his breath, and when the hairs in his nose stiffened and froze, he knew the fire was out downstairs. He pulled the quilt over his face, and yearned for his own cabin, where he would keep the fire roaring all night, even if he had to chop wood all summer to fuel it.

He dreamed of a warm, sweet-smelling girl beside him in the bed, but could not see her face, for her back was to him. When he tried to turn her over, she became a lost cow, frozen in the storm. He cried out, "Ellen!" and awoke.

Sitting up in his bed, he anxiously looked over at James, and noted with relief that he still slept. He lay down again, chest heaving for a time, but sleep soon took him.

On the far side of the partition, Marie heard the cry, and bit her knuckle in frustration. *He'll still marry Ida*, she thought bitterly. *He's said he will.* She closed her eyes, praying for her friend, then fell into a restless sleep.

Two days were shrouded in cloud and freezing weather, but no more snow fell. Then two days of thaw lifted the hopes of the Owens in anticipation of the Christmas party in Pueblo City. The morning of the twenty-third, however, came without sun. A furious ice storm blew for four days, canceling any thought of leaving the cabin for travel.

Then Nature turned capricious, and brought along warm, fall-like days, and the men worked fast to finish Carl's cabin. On the third morning, a messenger rode through, bringing a note from Rand Hilbrands that the party was set for New Year's Eve, if the weather held. "Even if it snows again, come on in. I've got plenty of room, and some wonderful news," the note concluded.

"Mary and I ain't going anywhere," Rulon announced. "Her time is too near for traveling."

"Don't she lack a month yet, Rule?" asked Julia.

"That's right, but she ain't up to the trip. Go ahead, and I'll stay here with her."

Rod and the family left the next day, except for Carl, who wanted to put some finishing touches on the cabin before he left. "I'll be through by tomorrow morning," he said. "Sherando and me'll get there late tomorrow."

"Looks like we're going to a wedding as well as a dance, Rod," Julia said as they left in the wagon.

Yep, I reckon you'll have new kin before the week's up."

"I wish Ida had some cattle to bring with her," Julia murmured.

"Now don't fret, woman. I've been contemplating on what to do about getting us new stock. I'll take a few of the boys up to Denver City to look up Jonathan. If he can't put us to work, I'm sure he'll know of miners we can work for until we have some money. Then I reckon we'll ride to Texas and pick up some of them long-horned cows. I heard tell at Fort Lyon they're selling at three dollars a head."

"That's sure a fancy plan, Rod Owen. Don't forget to tote that strong box back to Jonathan."

Rod laughed at her easy acceptance of his scheme. "You're a surprising woman, Julia Owen."

"I reckon. And don't you forget it."

~*~*~

On the morning of December thirty-first, Carl awoke for the first time in his new cabin. He glanced around the dim room, satisfaction stealing over his face. He had built well, and he hoped Ida would appreciate the solidness and hard work that had gone into its creation. Looking up at the loft above him, he thought ahead to the children who would fill it, and smiled as he imagined himself roaring out, "Quiet up there!" echoing his father.

He sat up in the rope bed he had constructed against the end of the room. Fir boughs beneath him creaked with his shifting weight, and he recalled the comfort of the springy branches during the night.

Carl bent over and picked up his jean trousers from the stool near the bed. They were the pants he had bought in Kansas town, his newest clothes. They would have to do for the party, and for the wedding, and for many months of hard work to follow. He stooped and pulled them on, then finished dressing and went outside to the washstand.

The water in the bucket was clear of ice, and Carl felt good about the day. He washed, and shaved carefully with Rulon's razor, remembering that he must ride back to Rulon's cabin with it this morning before he left. He would buy a razor and such gear in Pueblo City when he arrived.

He stepped back into the doorway of the new house, and smelled the pungent odor of the newly cut wood in the box beside the fireplace. Ida would love this place, nestled into the clearing like it had grown there. Everything was ready for her to step into the room and take over the cabin to make it a home.

Some primitive caution, born of the howling storms he had undergone, made Carl roll a blanket and tie it to his saddle before he left the cabin. Then he tucked a double handful of jerky made from one of the frozen cows into a sack and tied that on the saddle, too. The same feeling urged him to belt on his pistol. He thought twice over that, telling himself a man didn't go armed to his wedding. He ignored the thought, and slung the gun around his hips. "I got a ways to go before Pueblo City," he muttered aloud.

Carl rode into Rulon's dooryard just as Chester Bates and his family broke into the clearing from the south.

"Company coming, Rulon," Carl pointed out as his brother stopped chopping wood to accept the razor. Carl cantered his horse over to meet the new arrivals in front of Rod's cabin, as Rulon followed on foot. "You all light and set," he called to the Bates family.

Chester dismounted from a tall brown horse and helped his wife dismount from her bay. Carl dropped off Sherando and ran to help Ellen swing off her dun mare as Rulon arrived to greet the Bates.

Carl grinned at the girl and teased, "You go astride now, Miss Ellen?"

She grinned back. "The wagon broke a wheel, and pa only had one sidesaddle, so Ma got it. I like to ride astride," she insisted. "I can tell what Dun Baby's going to do next. She likes to try to throw folks," she finished in a whisper.

Carl rubbed the frisky animal's cheek. "Where'd you get her?"

"Pa made up some furniture and traded to a Spanish gentleman for a string of horses. I think they're only half-broke, but I like that." Her eyes shone with excitement. "There's just lots of Spanish folks down where we live, and I'm learning some words already." She turned toward the stock pens. "Like, 'corral' means 'stock pen'." She paused. "Where's your cattle?"

"Up in the woods a piece. We had a little storm up here. Froze 'em solid as ice cakes, to quote James."

"Oh. I'm sorry," she said in a small voice. Her brow furrowed with pain. "That must be a big blow to your pa."

"He didn't say a word about it for three days, but you know Pa, nothing keeps him down for long. By now he's hatching a plan to get us out of this fix."

Chester came over to Carl and Ellen. "I'm sorry to hear about your cattle. And it looks like we missed your folks. Rulon tells me you're not going in to the party. I reckon we made this detour for nothing."

"No, sir. Rulon's the one not going. I am, and I'd be pleased to ride along with you. How are the rest of the folks? Are any of them coming?"

"The Campbells and the Morgans are back a ways in a wagon, but Tom O'Connor stayed to tend the stock. He says his kids are too young for a dance, anyhow."

Ellen laughed. "Tom O'Connor is courting a pretty little Spanish girl down in Leones. No dance in Pueblo City could drag him away."

"You don't say! I reckon there's something about this Colorado air."

Ellen looked puzzled at his remark. He offered no enlightenment, and she looked away, a little sigh moving her shoulders.

"Well, we'd better get, if we're going to make Pueblo by nightfall," Chester said. He helped his wife into her saddle and swung into his. "Carl, you young people have frisky horses, so why don't you take the lead for a while?"

"Suits me," Carl said He locked his fingers to give Ellen a boost. She held onto the high horn of the saddle and accepted his help by placing her boot into his hands. Then she was astride the horse, her long skirt flaring out over the cantle and down Dun Baby's haunches. The mare danced around, eager to be off again. Carl grinned at the sight, then mounted Sherando.

"That's a funny looking saddle," he said, grinning, as they started off. "What's that high thing in front for?"

Ellen patted the horn. "This here thing is for wrapping a rope around after you get it on a cow. I watched some Mexicans tending cattle down to home, and it's so exciting what they can do with a rope and a good cow pony. I've been practicing throwing a rope, but only when Pa's not around," she admitted, wrinkling her nose as she grinned. "He thinks a girl should stick to kitchen chores, but he could use some help when inside work is done."

"Sounds like you have your house all built."

"Pa put up the cutest little sod house. It ain't very big, but it's enough for the three of us for now." A lock of red-gold hair got loose from the rest and Ellen pushed it back into place. "Lawsy, I'm going to look a sight when we get to the dance."

Carl looked at her a long time. "I reckon you'll do," he said. "You look kind of carefree and happy, and full of fire."

Ellen blushed. "I never knew you had a silver tongue, Carl Owen," she exclaimed.

"I don't. You look so excited. You'll be the most fetching girl at the dance. I surely hope you'll save me a right smart lot of dances."

"Well," she said, looking down at the ground. "I'll think about it."

The trail they followed dipped into a stream bed, and Ellen slowed her horse to cross it. Dun Baby suddenly stopped and lowered her head to drink. Ellen kept her seat and laughed, then looked around her.

"She won't move till she's had her fill," she called to Carl, who turned Sherando and came back to the stream. "What a pretty valley," she said, smiling. "And that bench up there, with all those trees. I can almost imagine a cabin built in there. Why, I believe I do see a cabin up there!"

"You do," Carl said, grinning. "It's mine. Ain't it a purty place?"

"It's right lovely." Ellen eyed him closely. "Are you bringing Ida back, now that the cabin's built?"

Before he could answer, Chester Bates and his wife caught up with them.

"I reckon you're stuck there till she drinks the stream dry, daughter," Chester mused as he came alongside. "We'll go on ahead." He and Muriel trotted their horses out of sight toward the north.

Carl turned to watch them go, his heart pounding. He had almost forgotten Ida in his pleasure at Ellen's company. Slowly he faced the girl in the stream, setting his teeth and flexing the muscles of his jaw. "Yes," he said slowly. "She's expecting me."

Dun Baby quit drinking, continued across the stream and ascended the bank. Ellen pulled up alongside Carl. Her face was white, and she lifted her chin before she spoke. "I thought you had more sense than to ask one girl to dance while on the way to wed another, Carl Owen." Her green eyes seemed to be filled with brown sparks as she sat erect on her mare. Then she kneed the dun and started off across the rising valley slope after her parents.

"A man can dance until he's wed," he shouted, urging Sherando to follow her.

The rest of the journey was a misery for Carl. Ellen answered when spoken to, but the ease of their conversation had vanished. She rode beside him, but her excitement and joy were gone, and he shrank from the knowledge that he had robbed her of them. The bright, crisp day seemed gloomy and overcast to him. Finally, he rode silently through the tedious miles across the prairie.

Chester called a halt at noon, on the sandy bank of a waterhole. After the horses drank their fill, he allowed them to crop the brown buffalo grass on the plain surrounding the water. When the travelers had eaten and the horses were rested, they resumed their trip.

Five o'clock had come and gone before Chester Bates and his party rode into Pueblo. Rand Hilbrands' hotel was well lit for the festivities. Candles burned on every wall inside, and they found that the formerly dim dining room was ablaze with light. The tables and benches had been cleared away, and the space was reserved for dancing. Three musicians tuned their instruments for the next dance set.

Carl glanced around the room, excitement building in him in spite of his miserable trip. He did not see Ida, and turned to Ellen with fierce determination.

"I've seen you this far, and I'm claiming the first dance," he told her, and before she could deny him, he took her hands and pulled her onto the dance floor. Ellen allowed him to lead her into the gaiety, but her stiff movements betrayed her reluctance to dance with him.

"This ain't fair, Carl Owen," she whispered grimly, as he held her hands firmly in his.

"Nobody promised you life was fair," he grunted back.

When the music finished, Ellen removed her hands from Carl's and fled. He turned to watch her go, and saw Ida coming into the room from the kitchen. She wore a pale yellow dress, the same color as her hair, which was piled upon her head in a new style.

She seemed to see him, then her eyes slid past his in an embarrassed manner, as she continued her advance into the room. Carl felt his heart leap as he made his way through the press of people. She was as pretty as ever, and soon she would be his.

Ida stopped in front of a group of strangers, three young men and two ladies of expensive foreign dress. She greeted them warmly as Carl came up beside her. The strangers replied, and Carl heard the unfamiliar cadences of the King's English for the first time. He strained to understand the odd phrases and inflections they used as he nervously waited for Ida to break off her chatter and acknowledge his presence. Carl sensed a tensing in her, a strain in her voice as she continued her conversation with the people in the group.

Becoming impatient, and feeling a slow heat creeping up his neck at her continued snub, Carl placed his hand on her elbow to draw her attention. She stiffened, and glanced at him uneasily.

"Hello, Carl," she said coldly. "Can't you see that I am talking to my friends?"

A dark-haired young man detached himself from the group and came to Ida's other side, an air of protectiveness hovering over him. He glanced sharply at Carl and said in an aggrieved voice, "I say, what's the meaning of this? Take your hand off her arm, your boorish fellow."

Carl tightened his grip and turned to face this challenge. He looked closely at the Englishman, and saw that the young man was a few years older than himself, slight, and had a long, straight nose, a thin mouth, and a jutting chin. His swaggering manner suited his expensive clothes. Reading disdain in the man's pale eyes, Carl turned a questioning look on Ida, who avoided his eyes.

"I reckon I have a right to speak to the lady," he said, trying to get her to look at him. "I have to speak to you, Ida, and we'd best be alone."

"Say your piece here, Carl. Whatever it is, my friends can hear it, too." She finally looked at him, then away again, her eyes resting on the young Englishman and his party.

Amazed at her treatment of him, Carl dropped his hands and shifted his weight. "I reckon this has to be private, Ida." Then realizing the import of his message, he continued. "Hush, if you want your new friends to hear, that's proper. The whole town will know soon enough."

He grabbed Ida's hands, turned her to face him, and looked down at her lowered eyes. "I've come for you, Ida. The cabin's done."

Ida jerked up her chin and looked at him, then her eyes slipped sideways to look around the room, as though in a panic.

Carl spoke again. "We'll find a preacher and get wed, enjoy the party, and then we can go home."

Ida looked directly at him then, a strange light burning through her eyes. "No, Carl," she whispered, and pulled her hands from his grasp.

Pale Eyes stepped forward, muttering, "This is a muddle. Who is this chap, Ida?"

She waved a hand at the Englishman, stopping him in his tracks.

"Wait, Cecil. I have to tell him."

Carl focused his attention on Ida's eyes, trying to read her expression. "Who is this feller, Ida?" he echoed, his voice barely above a whisper. "Why's he acting so familiar with you?"

Ida flew to the offensive, stamping her foot and fisting her hands. "He has more right than you, Carl Owen. You said you'd visit, and I waited for you ever so long. You never came, Carl Owen, so you gave up any rights to me. Mr. Gilbert, here, came along and asked for my hand, and I figured it was mine to give. I'm getting wed, all right, but to him!"

Chapter 14

Carl staggered backward, as though Ida had buried her small fists in his belly. His jaw dropped, and he took a long shuddering breath.

"What's this man got that I ain't?" he shouted, his voice hoarse. Then he read his answer in her hard, glittering eyes, as she looked from him down to the gems sparkling on her finger. "He bought you from me," Carl grunted. "He bought you with pretty things, and you was fool enough to let him."

He bunched his fists to swing at the sneering stranger who had put his arm around Ida's waist, but two pairs of arms caught him from behind, and his father and James hustled him away from Ida and her beau.

"I'll be a pinch-toed son of a red-wattled turkey buzzard!" James exclaimed when he and Rod deposited a struggling Carl in the hotel lobby. "You've been double-damn-crossed, big brother." James scowled, looking as angry as Carl.

"Rand told us when we got into town, son. Ida convinced him she was free to marry," Rod said, scratching his head. He looked at Carl, then plunged ahead with the story. "This Englishman came into town and stayed. After a while, he asked Ida to marry him, and she went ahead and accepted him."

Carl paced the lobby, alternately gripping his hands tightly together and driving one fist into his other hand. He cursed Ida, her love of money, and her shabby treatment of him. Then his voice lowered as he cursed himself for falling prey to her charms. James retreated to the dining room, leaving Rod to deal with Carl.

"Why, Pa?" Carl turned to his father, his voice rasping. "I was good enough for her in Virginia. Why ain't I good enough for her now?"

"I don't have an answer to that, Carl. You cool off, and if you feel like you can keep your temper in check, you can stay and try to salvage this party. There are plenty of pretty girls here. But if you feel like making trouble, you go on home." He waited for a moment, then added, "I know you'll be angry at me for saying this, since I arranged your marriage in the first place, but now I think you got off luckier than Mr. Cecil Gilbert over yonder."

Carl glared at his father. His father stared back, waiting. Carl breathed hard, resumed his pacing, then after several minutes had passed, he stopped in front of his father and nodded his head. "I've come this far, so I'll take hold of Rand Hilbrands' party with both hands." He shook his fists in illustration. "That two-faced little fox won't get the best of me."

"If you can't hold your tongue, you'd best leave right now," Rod warned.

Carl slumped into a nearby chair. His body shook with released tension. After a few minutes he said, "I'll mind my manners, and I'll hold my tongue, but you can't expect me to smile."

"No man will ask that of you, son" Rod answered gently. "Come in and find a pretty-looking gal to dance with. The night is plenty young."

Carl nodded grimly and followed his father into the dining room. A dance was in progress, a waltz, and his eyes glanced over the swirling couples to find Ida. They found Ellen, encircled by James's arms, gracefully moving in three-quarter time around the room. She was smiling, then laughing at James's joke, then her eyes met Carl's and she looked away, face gone white.

He tore his gaze from her face, disgruntled that she was occupied when he wanted her company. But he could not keep from watching her, and when the waltz ended and James went to get refreshments, he was ready.

He came up behind her in the corner where she stood, apart from the rest of the party-goers, and placed his hands on her shoulders. She stiffened, and he bent over to whisper in her ear.

"I reckon I can ask you to dance now, and have no anger betwixt us."

Something in his shaky whisper made Ellen whirl around and stare up at him. Her eyes searched his face. "What do you mean?"

Carl closed his eyes for a moment, then opened them and looked straight into Ellen's. "I'm a free man, Ellen. Ida found somebody more moneyed than me, and she kicked me loose."

Carl saw the flame of joy that leaped into her eyes before she could lower her head. He said, "Pa said I should come in here and find a pretty girl to dance with. You're the prettiest one I know. Will you take a whirl with me?"

"James went—"

"Forget James. He'll be gone a while. Dance with me."

A shadow crossed her face, then she straightened and smiled a bit. "I'll do it."

"Thank you," he said.

Carl was able to dance with Ellen one more time before he came across Ida in a corner kissing Cecil. Anger rose up in his throat, threatening to choke him, and he knew the time had come for him to leave. He shook as he turned his back on all that he had worked for, and walked slowly toward the lobby door, his eyes glazed, fists clenched.

Someone reached out and touched his arm, and he started to shake off the hand, then realized that Ellen was standing there, trembling at the sight of his glowering face.

"Carl?"

"I've got to get out of this place. I can't mind my manners any longer." He turned his red-rimmed eyes on her, and she gave a little cry at the wildness in his face. "Come with me," he pleaded. "Come help me ride the meanness away." Then he turned and bolted through the door.

Ellen, shaken, jumped at the touch of a hand on her arm. She turned to see Marie standing next to her, smiling.

"I told you a time would come. Go with him. It's just his pride that's wounded. He calls your name in his sleep."

"Oh," Ellen gasped, and ran out the door.

The lobby was empty. Ellen grabbed a cloak from a coat rack beside the dining room door, and swirled it around her as she walked out into the darkness of the street.

Pausing to get her bearings, she looked down the street toward the livery stable. A lantern burned beside the big front doors, and she stepped off the hotel porch and hurried toward the light. The stable boy was asleep beside the open door, and she ran past him into the barn.

Carl stood beside Sherando, saddling the gray gelding by the light of another lantern. His face was gaunt in the lamplight. She walked toward him, and he looked up, surprising her with a wan smile.

"Good girl. I figured you'd come."

"What?"

"You're a stayer."

"Is that something good?"

"Means you stick to a task."

Ellen shivered. "It's cold tonight."

"We can leave right now," Carl said, ducking under Sherando's neck and going into the next stall. His voice floated back over the side of the wooden enclosure. "We'll get some exercise and warm you right up."

He returned, leading Dun Baby, already saddled. A grin spread over his face. "I took a chance on being ready, but I wasn't wrong about you."

The horses were rested and willing to run. Carl gave Sherando his head as soon as they were clear of the town, and the gray galloped off into the prairie. Dun Baby did her best to catch the bigger horse. After two miles, Carl pulled the horse up and let him breathe. He looked up into the night sky, and figured it was about ten o'clock.

Ellen reined in her horse when she caught up, and slid off onto the ground. She stood with her arms outstretched and turned slowly around, as if embracing the whole sky.

The moon slid out from behind a cloud and shed silver light on the radiant girl. Carl noticed the joy in her as she lifted her arms to the moon.

"I love you," she cried out. "Colorado, you're beautiful."

So are you, girl, he thought, and swallowed hard. *She looks like Ma did the day we came into the meadow. So different from Ida.* He scowled and said, "You'd best get in the saddle. It's a long ride to the Greenhorn."

"The Greenhorn? Ain't we going back to the dance?"

"No. I thought getting out into the air would help, but I can't abide seeing that double-dealing fox again." He stopped, and set his teeth for a moment. "Pa told me to go home if I couldn't mind my manners. I reckon I'm heading back home."

Ellen walked over to Sherando and looked up at Carl. "It's beautiful out here, but I don't favor being left alone in the prairie."

"I don't figure to leave you. Come along and keep me company."

He watched her face as she took a step backward, concern in her eyes. "That ain't fitting, Carl. I can't go that far alone with you."

"I don't aim to do you no harm," he said firmly. "It ain't in me to punish you for what she did to me."

She put a hand over her mouth and gasped. "What about my folks? What about James?"

He gritted his teeth. "James! You don't love James."

"I owe him my hand."

"You owe me your life!"

She sighed and backed away. He dismounted and caught her by the shoulders.

"Your folks will be along when the party is over. You can stay with Mary and Rulon. She'll be pleased at your company."

"Marie knows I came with you," Ellen said. "She'll know what to say to Ma and Pa." She pursed her lips and blew out a breath. "Folk'll talk, but I don't care. I would just be a mound of earth in the graveyard if you hadn't plucked me out of the way of those Yankees in Mount Jackson. I'll go with you."

Carl dropped his hands to his sides. "Thank you."

He went after Dun Baby, grazing on dry buffalo grass on a nearby hillock, and brought the mare to Ellen. He bent and made a stirrup with his hand for her and she swung into the saddle. Her frisky horse sidestepped, and Ellen pulled her up short.

"She'll run for me now, and you can't catch me!" she challenged. Then she was racing over the moonlit plain, and Carl scrambled for Sherando.

It seemed vastly important to catch her, to draw up even with her. Carl flung himself onto the gelding's back, and urged the horse forward with little grunts and mutters, as though all his energy was focused on the fleeing girl before him, leaving him with few words.

She had a good head start on him and held onto the lead for a half-mile, then the big gray started to catch up with the mare. Ellen turned to look back at Carl, her face alive with excitement as she drove her horse to keep up the pace.

Carl ducked lower over his horse's neck, willing Sherando to catch the mare. Then he was alongside, and stole a glance at Ellen.

She was grinning, and looked at him in triumph, hair streaming back from her face. She reined Dun Baby down to a trot, then cooled her off at a walk. Carl kept pace with her horse, patting the lathered Sherando.

"You act like you won," he chuckled, when he had caught his breath.

"Maybe I did," she answered, running her fingers through her tangled locks.

A snowflake drifted down from the sky and landed on Ellen's hair. It melted, leaving a drop of water sparkling in its place, then the moon disappeared behind a thick cloud as other flakes swirled toward the ground. Ellen pulled the hood of the cloak over her head and snuggled into the folds of the cape.

"I grabbed this cloak and ran. I don't know whose it is, but it's good and warm," she shouted in Carl's direction.

Carl looked around at the eddying flakes, and noticed that the wind was moaning and whining in his ears. It blew the thick flakes into his eyes, and he shut them for a moment. When he reopened them, Ellen was gone!

Chapter 15

"Ellen!" he yelled into the white blanket before his eyes. "Ellen, where are you?"

No voice answered him, no cry cut through the keen of the wind. "Where are you, girl?" he shouted against the wind's shriek. Still no human sound reached his ears, and he strained to see through the frozen curtain enveloping him.

Panic seized him. Ellen was lost; Ellen, who just moments before was glorious, wild, free. He turned Sherando this way and that, calling her name, trying to see through the storm. As he whipped his body from side to side in the saddle in his attempt to catch her voice in his ears, his arm brushed against his holstered pistol. He tugged on the binding loop and yanked the gun free, then fired it into the ground.

"Carl," he heard Ellen cry, her voice whipped in all directions by the wind.

He glanced wildly about. "Ellen," he bellowed, and this time heard her reply off to his left. He turned Sherando in the direction of her voice and called for her to stay in one place. Blindly, he followed her calls, hoping panic would not make her mute before he could reach her.

The wind puffed away a sheet of snowflakes, and he saw the dark cloak just ahead. He cried out "Ellen," as he reached her side.

She turned, clutching the cloak around her. "Oh, Carl," she breathed, and gave a great sigh of relief.

"We can't stay here in the open or we'll freeze," he told her, voice raised over the storm. "I wish I knew what direction I'm headed. With all this snow blowing around, I've lost my bearings." He reached over for her reins and looped them around his left hand. "If we're heading south, we'll reach the St. Charles before too long, and we can hole up on the bank."

"Dun Baby should be headed south. I never turned her. I pulled up soon as I lost sight of you."

"We'll go that way, then," he agreed, thankful for her good sense. "I reckon we can't miss the river."

Carl turned Sherando and started him off at a walk, wondering which was worse, to trot forward into the uncertain footing of the unfamiliar ground ahead, or to go at a walking pace and slowly freeze. He wished he'd paid better attention to the country as they had traveled through it, and he hoped the river wasn't as far as he thought it was.

He heard Ellen behind him, shifting in her saddle. The leather groaned in the frigid air, crackling louder for a moment than the wind could moan. Carl gritted his teeth and pulled his hat down lower over his ears, and hoped that Ellen was warmer than he.

The horses plodded along, stumbling from time to time on the uneven ground. Occasionally, Carl dismounted and led the way, stamping a path through belly-high drifts, but the cold crept up his legs, and even when he rubbed his ankles, the loss of feeling persisted while he walked, and he had to remount.

To his frozen senses, it seemed hours later that the horses nosed downward into a gully, and the sound of the wind died abruptly. Carl pulled Sherando to a stop and peered through his ice-encrusted lashes.

The horses had brought them to a narrow ravine, an ancient waterway, protected from the driving wind by an overhang of sandstone. Carl climbed swiftly out of the saddle, gripping both sets of reins in his left hand. He ducked under Sherando's neck, and stamping his feet as he walked, led the horses further under the overhang. Tying the reins to a creosote bush, he limped over to Ellen's side, his cold muscles cramping as he used them.

Ellen awkwardly dismounted and rubbed her hands together to move the blood into her fingers.

"I'm glad we're out of the wind," she said, her voice quivering as she shook with cold. "I reckon I'm near froze."

Carl helped her walk to a little cup-like depression in the wall of the stream bed and sat her down out of the storm. Returning to the horses, he unsaddled Dun Baby, patting her affectionately. "You're a good horse," he muttered. "A stayer like your rider."

He turned to Sherando and rubbed the gelding's muzzle and neck. "Let me get your saddle off, boy," he said.

His hand brushed against the blanket rolled behind the saddle, and he remembered the prompting to bring it along. Untying the blanket and the bag of jerky, Carl unsaddled the gray, and did his best to make the horses comfortable before he returned to Ellen's side.

"Sometimes I get smart," he told her. "Put this blanket around you while I see if these bushes will burn. And help yourself to the jerky."

Carl left the overhang and went out into the ravine to collect brush. Snow fell steadily into the little valley but the wind was cut off, and he could walk up the gully without fighting his way through high-piled drifts. The sky glowed with diffused moonlight, scattered by the clouds and the million snowflakes, and Carl could see where he was going, although he knew it was midnight or later.

Under one bank of the ravine he found an animal burrow lined with dry twigs and soft leaves. He cleaned it out and stuffed it all into his pockets for tinder. A few yards farther on, he came to an old scrub oak with several dead lower limbs that would be dry on the inside. He broke off as many of the dead branches as he could carry, then turned back to the overhang.

"Wish I had an ax," he told Ellen. "There's a big oak up the gully a ways. It would keep us in wood for a couple of days, if need be. Hush, the way these Colorado storms blow, we might need it."

He set to work building the fire, keeping it small, but big enough to warm them, then struck his knife against an old piece of flint he had brought home from the war. When the sparks landed in the tinder, he blew them gently to life, nursing the baby flames with bits of dry grass and leaves, then twigs and finger-sized branches.

When the blaze had a strength of its own, he got up and stepped back to join Ellen. As he let himself collapse beside her, Ellen offered him a piece of jerky. He took it and held it up.

"Seems a shame to eat this critter after it walked all the way across the U-nited States. A hungry man ain't got much choice, I reckon." He tossed the jerky into the air and caught it.

"Eat it, Carl. It'll give you strength." Ellen shrugged the blanket off her shoulders and threw it around him. "You look froze, so you'd best take the blanket. I'll get close to the fire."

"Ellen, I ain't going to get warm and leave you out in the cold. You take the blanket and get some sleep. I'm going to be fine." He held out the woven wool.

"You're *loco*, Carl Owen! I ain't about to let you freeze yourself on my account. Get over here and we'll share the blanket."

"You ain't afraid of what folks will say?" He took a bite of meat.

"In the middle of a blizzard? Not anymore. I reckon this storm in this country makes the rules a mite different." She eyed him sideways. "Besides, I have your word."

Carl smiled, then yawned as fatigue swept over him. "And I'm a man of my word." He scooted over next to the girl and enveloped both of them in the blanket. "My brother Peter used to tell me I snored louder 'n a mess of locusts. I never believed him, but I best warn you, just in case he wasn't lyin'."

She laughed. "That's silly, to worry about snoring. I always felt like my pa had a right pleasing kind of snore. I missed it all the time he was gone to the fighting. When he got back, even the tool shed was home, once he got to snoring away at night."

Carl lay back against the rock and earth wall. "Strange what little things will bring a body comfort, ain't it?" He chewed on the jerky. "A fire goes a long way to help a man forget his troubles." He took another bite. "You feel the same?"

There was no response from Ellen, and Carl turned to look. Her head nodded downward, her eyes closed. Carl put his arm around her and eased her head back onto his shoulder. "You're all tuckered out," he whispered. "It's good you sleep."

Ellen woke to the touch of pale sunrise on her cheek, which rose and fell with the motion of Carl's chest beneath her head. Something held her from moving out of the warmth of the blanket, and she discovered his arm around her shoulders.

She stiffened, then relaxed as she recalled her invitation to Carl to share the blanket. *I ain't never been this close to him before,* she thought, and remembered with a start the night she had tripped from the wagon and landed in his arms. But he had been another woman's man then, and now he was free, at least he would be once his injured pride healed over. She bit her lip and eased her head off Carl's chest. She wasn't free.

I ain't been free since the day Rod Owen said he'd give us food and a wagon if we'd go west with his family, Ellen thought, a sour taste rising in her mouth. She closed her eyes. Pa and Ma didn't tell me I was part of the bargain. But she knew, when they said, "We've picked out a husband for you," that Rod Owen had required her hand in marriage to his son as payment in full.

James ain't free, neither. The thought brought Ellen's eyes wide open. She'd heard he was courting Jessica Bingham, and wasn't happy that his pa had made a match for him. *He don't hate me, nor dislike me*, she reminded herself, swallowing her bitterness. *I simply ain't Jessica.*

She caught her breath, and held it so she wouldn't cry out. When she thought of James, no stir of passion tightened her body, no urgency bid her hold him in her arms. There was affection all right, like for a brother or a good friend, but no strong heartbeat or racing, heated blood that would melt her natural, modest barriers in their marriage bed.

Who could not love James? All the girls in Mount Jackson said he was handsome, with his crisp black hair and strong mouth. He was respectful, kind, and willing to work long, wretched hours to advance a good cause. Over time he had seemed resigned to the fact that they would wed sooner or later. Who would not love James? *I would not.*

Ellen turned her head, slowly, carefully, breathlessly, so as not to wake Carl. She gazed at his stubbled cheek and jaw line, which filled her vision. She took a shallow breath, and looked for signs of hurt or suffering. His sleep seemed peaceful, undisturbed. All she could see of his unlined face convinced her that there was no pain today. He slept deeply, looking younger than his twenty years.

She inched her face back until she could see his eyes, finely chiseled lids rimmed with light lashes closed over eyes as blue as a Colorado afternoon sky. There was no pain in the hair-shadowed forehead, in the molded ears, in the sculpted nose, or in the slightly parted lips, full and chapped from the cold. There was no pain in his countenance.

Carl ain't James, she thought, *and James ain't Carl. I would love this man.* Ellen suddenly felt overwhelming peace come over her, and she allowed her hand to sneak up to cuddle his cheek. The stubble of his beard, which blurred the strong line of his jaw, was soft under her fingertips. His eyelids flickered, then opened. He was instantly awake, and his hand trapped hers against his cheek.

"Good morning, Ellen. You've a mighty gentle way of waking a man. Was I snoring?"

"No." He had hard calluses on his hand. "The sun is up. We'd best travel while the weather holds." She pulled at her hand and he released it. Her face coloring, she sat up. "It's still cloudy, and we've got a long ride." She shook off Carl's arm and stood up, brushing the wrinkles out of her skirt.

He grinned, looking up at her. "I reckon I'm rumpled and crushed, but you look like a bouquet of fall flowers, rich and red and full of spunk." Carl got to his feet. "I'll see to the horses.

The clouds hovered low and dark, but the sun shone through enough for Carl to get his bearings as they started off. The plain shimmered white in the weak sunlight, the glare broken only by the dusky tips of sagebrush poking through the snow.

Sherando and Dun Baby struggled in the drifts, tiring easily from the exposure and lack of feed. Carl stopped often, rubbing the horses' legs to warm them.

They passed Carl's cabin in the late afternoon, and Carl saw Ellen's stealthy look at the house as they passed. *I'd give a nickel to know her mind*, he thought. *What does she think of me, after all I done that's hurt her feelings?*

The creek was slushy as they rode through, and Carl dismounted to wipe the horses' legs once more.

"It's a mile, mile-and-a-half to Rulon's" he said. He looked around at the darkening sky, mounted, and reached for Ellen's reins. "I reckon it's going to blow again. This time I ain't going to lose you."

Carl kicked Sherando up the side of the creek of the creek bed and onto the flat. He headed for the trees, pulling Dun Baby and Ellen along with him. The mare tossed her head and fought the lead, but settled down as she came into the shelter of the oaks.

Ellen tossed her own head. "It ain't even begun to snow. I could've ridden all by myself up to here."

Carl turned Sherando and eased him up to Ellen's side. "I ain't willing to take a chance on losing you to the storm again. I asked you to come out here with me, and I'm responsible for your safety. I don't take that lightly." He handed her back the reins. "There's a path through the trees. We can make it to Rulon's in a few minutes. I reckon Mary won't mind some company for supper."

"I'll be glad for a home-cooked meal. We didn't come prepared for camping-out."

Rulon's cabin looked solid and comforting when Carl and Ellen rode into the open a short time later. Smoke rose from the chimney, curling up into lazy snowflakes that now drifted down into the meadow from the leaden sky. Rod's cabin lay cold and frozen across the creek, snowdrifts halfway up the sides. Carl was glad of the welcome Rulon's home promised.

As they approached the cabin, a shriek sliced through the frozen air, and Carl drew his pistol.

"You wait here," he cautioned Ellen. "That sounds like a big cat, and it's inside the cabin." Carl dismounted, threw his reins to Ellen, and pushed through the snow toward the cabin.

A throat-rending scream came from the house, followed by Rulon's panicky voice.

"No, Mary! You can't! Not till Ma gets back."

Ellen flung herself from the horse. "Put up your gun, Carl. Mary's baby is coming." She floundered through the snow and pounded on the door. "Rulon, let me in. It's Ellen Bates."

Rulon opened the door and hustled Ellen into the room. "Thank God you're here. Tell her she can't have the baby yet, please, Ellen."

"Shush, Rulon. You're scaring her." She looked around and saw Roddy's big eyes peering from under the bedcovers where Mary lay, alternately moaning and shrieking. "Mr. Owen," Ellen exclaimed, "dress that boy and take him outside. He's big enough to help his Uncle Carl with the horses. You start a fire in your pa's cabin and stay over there. Send Carl back when he's done with the animals. I'll need his help."

Rulon followed her orders as Ellen approached the bed. "Hello, Mary. I've come to visit you. I reckon you need a mite of help."

Mary stared wild-eyed at Ellen, moaning as pain shot through her. "Ida? Where's Rulon?"

"Your man's gone on a little errand to the Owen's cabin," Ellen said, her voice soothing. "He'll be gone for a spell, but I'll be here, and I'll help you. I'm going to have a look around for some things I'll need. You rest easy, 'cause I'm right here." She took off the cloak.

You're Ellen Bates," Mary moaned. "That's Ida's cloak. I thought you was her." Mary took a ragged breath. "I can't last much longer. Two days I been a-laboring, and Rulon no help." She stopped to wheeze and pant, squeezing her eyes shut against the light of the fire. "He keeps bidding me to wait for his ma to come. Ellen, there ain't no waiting when the babe wants to come."

Ellen rummaged through Mary's trunk and found clean linens. She tore a sheet into pieces and brought the rags to the bed.

"I'll get water to wipe off your brow. I reckon you're thirsty, too."

"I ain't got time for being thirsty," Mary panted. "I can't hold back this baby no longer." Her voice rose in a wail of anguish.

"Mary, don't hold back. Let that child come." Ellen returned with the water, as Carl opened the door and stood in the opening.

"Rulon took over tending the horses. Said you wanted me here." He looked as though he'd rather be out in the storm.

"Carl Owen, you shut that door and come over here!" Ellen's voice was stern. She shoved the basin of water into Carl's hands as he tiptoed forward. "Wipe off her face, then sit behind her and hold her up."

Carl's chin jerked up, and he shot Ellen a look of pure horror. "I ain't climbing into that bed with my brother's wife," he whispered hoarsely.

"You hush and do what I tell you. I reckon she won't mind you more than a great lump of bedclothes. Get her onto the side of the bed. She should sit up to push that baby out." Ellen pulled back the bedcovers.

"You ever done this before?"

"I've helped my pa birth calves. I reckon it's the same, only smaller."

"Ellen Bates, I been through a war and across the country, but I never seen the likes of you before."

"I hope not," she muttered as Carl tended to Mary's dripping face. "Mary, before the next pain comes, try to get to the side of the bed."

Mary panted. "Ain't no time without pain." She inhaled, then stiffened and screamed into the ache and the agony. Carl flinched, set aside the basin, and turned to Ellen.

"Can you draw her forward?"

Carl nodded, his face blanched, lips pressed tightly together.

"Put her here onto the edge, get on the bed, and hold her up."

He gathered Mary up in his arms and lifted her to the side of the bed. Mary moaned. Carl let out his breath with a shudder and got behind her on the bed.

Ellen pulled Mary's bed gown up over her legs, and tugged it up around her waist. Carl squeezed his eyes shut. "Rulon's gonna kill me," he groaned.

"Hush up, Carl. Hold her tight." Ellen spread a towel on the floor below Mary's dangling legs. Carl held Mary by the shoulders, and she hunched forward, grunting. "You help, Mary," Ellen urged, holding Mary's legs apart. "Push that babe out. Don't give up yet!"

"I'm dying," Mary shrieked, pushing.

"No you're not," Ellen answered, kneeling on the floor. "You're giving life. Push again, Mary. I can see the head."

Mary obliged, her scream high-pitched and keening.

"Oh good. The head's out. Hold on, Mary, let me get the shoulders straight. Don't push!"

Mary panted, "I have to push."

"Wait, wait. Now, go ahead."

"Oh-h-h-h-h!" Mary gave a great push, bearing down with all her strength.

"Ah! Here's the babe." Ellen sighed. "You've done good, Mary." She wrapped the child in a piece of sheeting. "Carl, I need your knife."

Carl opened his eyes and dug into his pocket. He handed Ellen his clasp knife, which she opened and used to cut the baby's cord. She laid the child at the head of the bed. "Now one more push," she told Mary. "You've got to get the afterbirth out."

~*~*~

Ellen looked up from washing the struggling infant. "You can go get Rulon now," she said to Carl.

He wiped his sweating face with his shirtsleeve. "Good. I need some air."

Ellen laughed. "You look like you think you did all the work. Look at Mary. She's wore out from two days of struggle with this lively little one. It's sure full of ginger."

Ellen dried the child, wrapped it up in fresh cloths, and carried it to Mary, who cuddled the baby and held it close as Ellen walked Carl to the door.

He put on his coat and looked down at the girl beside him.

"You're full of ginger yourself." He held out his hand to see if it still shook. It did. "Look at that. I'm all undone, and you're going strong." His voice filled with awe as he continued. "I reckon Marie couldn't do what you just done, and I'm almighty sure *she* couldn't. You stand mighty tall in my eyes, Ellen Bates." Then he bolted through the door.

"It's a girl, Rulon," Mary whispered a few minutes later. "Look at all that hair. She's real lively, too."

"Ah, she's sure a pretty little thing. You give her a name?"

"I favor naming her 'Ellen'." Mary smiled.

"'Ellen Owen.' It sounds mighty fine, Mary. We'll do it."

Ellen got up from the fire where she was cooking supper. "No. Name the baby for your ma, or for Rulon's, but not for me. I ain't kin."

"You should be," Mary sighed. "Without your doing, I'd likely be cold and stiff by now."

"I just happened by. Name the baby for your ma or your sister."

"You can't deny me, Ellen. I can put your name to my child, and you can't do anything to prevent me. 'Juliellen Amanda

Owen'. That's her name. It's right and fitting." Mary sank back on the bed.

"As long as you don't put my name up front, I guess I can't complain." Ellen shrugged and returned to stirring the pot.

Carl eased in from the night, accompanied by young Roddy. He beat his hands together and stamped his feet, sending a shower of snow onto the floor. The youngster mimicked him, then shed his coat on the floor and ran to his mother's bedside.

"It's snowing steady, but the wind ain't come up yet," Carl announced, bending to pick up the abandoned wrap. "I made us a bed up to the other house, Rulon. Best we leave the ladies here after supper. Is that agreeable?"

"That's fine, just fine." Rulon pulled Carl over to the side of the bed. "Come see my daughter. Ain't she a sight? We named her after Ma and Ellen, and Mary's ma."

Carl rubbed one boot behind the heel of the other. "You give her three names? Ain't that a lot for such a tiny girl?"

"We think Juliellen Amanda suits her just fine. Ain't she a pretty thing?" Rulon lifted the baby and turned to his son. "Roddy, look at them tiny hands."

"Pa, was I that puny?" Roddy ventured to put out a finger to stroke the baby's hand.

Rulon laughed. "I wasn't around when you arrived, youngster. I was off fighting for Jeff Davis and the Confederacy, so I got limited knowledge in that line. Ask your ma."

"Was I puny like that, Ma?"

"You were strong and fat, Roddy. But all babies start small."

"Why, Ma?"

"They start out little so they can grow, Roddy, just like you." Carl scooped up the boy and planted him on his shoulders. "See how tall you'll be one day? 'Course you got to eat all your supper to grow this tall." He carried the boy over to the table.

"Let's help Miss Ellen lay the table, then you can start in on all that good food she's a-fixing."

Ellen turned and hid a smile behind her hand. "If you set that silver tongue to wagging, Carl Owen, you won't have no place in your mouth to put the food. Set the boy down and find the plates. I'll dish up from here."

"Yes, Miss Ellen."

She gave him a quizzical look, then turned back to the fire. Carl put Roddy off his shoulders and looked at Ellen's back.

The blaze of the fire backlighted her auburn hair, giving it the effect of a crown of flames. Silhouetted against the light, her slim form, moving with the rhythm of her arm, stirred up an excitement in his blood.

As if a burning coal had escaped from the fire and hit him in the pit of his stomach, fire spread up his chest and down his arms, leaving his fingers tingling, shaking. He tried to shrug off the feeling of burning that flowed through his blood, but he only remembered another time when he had felt this same excitement, at the bend of the river, where she had fallen into his arms.

The feeling built in him as he walked unsteadily to the shelf to get the plates, and lifted his feet as he walked the few steps to the fireplace. He put the plates on the hearth, not daring to risk touching Ellen's hand, and backed away to the table.

"Here, Roddy. Take the plates to the table when I fill them." Ellen looked at Carl. "I reckon your uncle's feeling faint. You'd best give him this first one. Rulon, come eat. Don't worry about Mary. I'll feed her while you men partake." She turned her attention back to Carl. "Are you feeling poorly? You look a mite strange."

"I feel . . . a mite strange," he stammered. Carl turned his head back toward his plate. "This food looks good. I didn't know I was so hungry."

"Well, you been through a mighty rough time for a man. I needed your help, or I wouldn't have put you through it." Ellen came to the table with Mary's plate. "I reckon I own you a right smart lot of thanks." She touched Carl's shoulder lightly as she walked to the bed.

He grabbed his shoulder where she had touched him, then let his hand fall to his side. "Let's eat, Rulon, before I lose all my strength."

"I'm going to say grace first. I got a lot to say thanks over."

"Ellen?" Mary whispered in the darkness as Ellen slipped into the bed beside mother and baby.

"It's me, Mary," she soothed. "Try to get some sleep. You're all wore out."

"I just remembered something. Rulon told me Carl was going in to my pa's party specially to marry Ida." Her voice was sleepy.

"I guess that was his plan."

"Well, you ain't Ida."

"I ain't Ida."

"Are you two wed?"

"No."

"How come you to be here, and where's my sister?"

"She's still in town, fixing to wed some English fellow. Right in the midst of the party she broke the news to Carl, and he took it powerful hard. He asked me to go for a ride, and we got caught in the storm. That's what happened."

"He didn't seem to be pining any."

"He didn't get a chance today. He helped me birth your baby."

"Did he act better than Rulon?"

Ellen chuckled. "Some better, but not much. He was scared. I ain't ever seen a man so white in the face. But he stayed in here, and he did what I bid him."

"I'm glad it was you came with him. Ida wouldn't have been any help. She ran into a corner and hid when Roddy came along. I'm glad James let you come back with Carl."

"You go to sleep now, Mary." Ellen patted Mary's arm, frowning. "Good night."

"Good night, Ellen. Thank you."

Chapter 16

Chester Bates rode into the clearing at noon the next day.

"Ellen!" he hollered out. "Ellen Bates, where are you?"

Ellen's heart quaked as she opened the door of Rulon's cabin. "Pa!" she called. "Pa. It's good to see you."

"Daughter!" he yelled as he hit the ground. "Where is that young hellion? I'll shoot him. I swear it! If he harmed a hair of your head—" He craned his neck, looking around for Carl.

"Pa, shush now. Calm down. Stop shouting. Carl didn't lay a hand on me." She took his arm. "Please, Pa. Don't go to shouting again. There's a new baby trying to sleep."

"A baby? What're you saying? Who's got a baby?"

"Mary Owen had her baby. I birthed it for her. No, don't you yell none. Rulon wasn't any kind of help. I had it to do, Pa."

Carl came out of the woods behind Rulon's cabin with an armload of deadwood. He dropped it on the woodpile and strolled over toward the visitor. Ellen looked wild-eyed in his direction and took hold of her father's other arm.

"There he is!" Chester cried, struggling with Ellen. "I'll wring his scrawny neck, taking you off like that, without a 'by your leave'. Carl Owen, I'm calling you out!"

"Pa, listen to me. Carl, get away! Don't you come over here. Pa, don't you dare touch him! I went with him willing. He gave his word I'd come to no harm, and he's kept it. Pa, listen to me!"

Chester struggled again as Carl strode up and came to a halt before them, crossing his arms.

"You piece of trash. You ruined my daughter," Chester bellowed, spitting on the ground. He tried to reach his gun, but Ellen held him fast, desperation strengthening her arms.

"Mr. Bates, I ain't touched Miss Ellen. I own I acted a mite foolish to ask her to ride with me on such a stormy night, but I was awful muddleheaded then. You got a right to take a poke at me for being a fool, but I don't reckon you should shoot me. I wouldn't harm Miss Ellen to spite Ida Hilbrands."

Chester swore, then went limp. Ellen realized that the heat had gone out of her father and released him. He went over to lean on his horse, taking several deep breaths, then turned back to Carl.

"I been so mad at you, I even took a poke at your pa. I 'spect I lost my best friend, and my wife ain't so pleased with me, neither. Ellen, you ma says you have good sense. I hope you ain't let her down."

"Pa, I told you, Carl gave me his word of honor. He's a gentleman. You know all Rod Owen's sons are gentlemen. You told me so yourself."

Chester swore again. "You're the only child I got, Ellen. I reckon I worry overmuch about you, but daughter, this ain't your ordinary turn of events. Things are new and different out here, I give you that, but some things never change. A girl don't go alone with a man, not overnight. He done damage to your name, and it ain't going to be easy to wash it clean. I'm taking you home, now."

"I ain't going, Pa. I promised to stay with Mary till she's up and about. It's a duty I have, and I won't leave her."

Chester looked helplessly at his big, hard hands. "You got me between a rock and a hard place, daughter. I can't fault you wanting to do your duty, for I taught you myself to carry through on a task, but you got a duty to your own self, too."

"Pa, when I rode off with Carl, that was a task I was carrying through. He was hurting real bad, and he needed a friend." She stood in front of Carl, facing her father.

"That's my point, daughter. There's some will say he needed

you to take advantage of. This is a compromising situation you got yourself into, right compromising, and no man'll want a wife with a smear on her name."

"That ain't rightly so, sir," Carl broke in. "I seen the pluck of your daughter, and what she can turn her hand to. I know she ain't done anything wrong, and I don't have to think twice."

He stopped short, face flaming. Looking down, he kicked a clump of grass that was poking through the melting snow. Then he shoved his thumbs into his trousers pockets, rocked back on his heels, and looked at the sky.

Chester and Ellen watched him, clearly fascinated, waiting for Carl's next words. Carl took his hands from his pockets and clasped them behind his back, then he spoke.

"I reckon if I've hurt Miss Ellen's name, I'm sorry for it. I don't know what James'll say in the matter, but I should have said this a long time ago. Mr. Bates, I'm seeking permission to court your daughter."

Rod Owen was back, bringing his wife, his daughters, and Muriel Bates. As he passed Rulon's cabin, Rod spotted his runaway son chopping wood with a red, scowling face. Then, driving up to the front of his own house, he saw Chester Bates sitting on the bench outside the cabin, back to the log wall, smoking his pipe.

Rod pulled the horses to a halt and helped the women and girls down from the wagon box. They went into the house, after glancing at Rod and Chester. Rod let the animals blow a bit, while he looked the situation over. Rubbing his cheek, which bore a new bruise, he looked at his friend. "Well, Chester?"

"Well, Rod," the other man answered. He paused to puff the smoke from his cheeks. "You had the right of it. He laid no hand on her."

"He seems powerful vexed about something."

"He is."

"Well?"

Chester exhaled. "He wants my permission to court her. I told him nay."

"James will be along in a bit."

Chester squinted at Rod. "I figured he has a say in this affair." He hoisted one leg over the other. "Has he spoke his mind yet?"

"No, but his glower is as black as his hair."

"Well then, we'll have to wait to see if he still wants to marry her. If not, I can't just give Carl free rein, what with Ellen staying here and all."

"Hold on. Who says Ellen's staying here?"

"She does. She won't go home with me. Claims she owes a duty to stay here with Mary and the baby, to help her get back on her feet."

"Mary? Baby? What are you telling me, man?"

"She brought forth a girl."

"Julia!" Rod hollered, poking his head into the doorway. "Julia, we got a granddaughter! Wife! Come out here. Chester, who helped her along?"

"Ellen says she did. It appears she and Carl came along just in time to ease the child into the world. Evening, Julia." He nodded as she stepped through the door.

"Rod, I could hear you bellowing your lungs out, but I missed your message. What's the trouble?"

"Mary went and had her child whilst we was gone. Ellen played midwife. It's a girl-baby."

"Well!" Julia sat down on the bench beside Chester. "I never heard the like! Chester Bates, don't you go too hard on that girl. I say the Good Lord sent her along with Carl, to help out Rulon's wife."

"Seems she's a blessing to everyone but herself," he grumbled.

Three riders came from the trees. James was in the front, his horse lathered, followed by Clay and Albert.

"Rod Owen, I'm fairly burning to go see that grandbaby of ours." Julia rose to her feet and saw the young men approaching. "I'll set Marie to stirring up supper. You get the boys to put up them horses, so you can come over with me, if you've a mind to do so."

"Of course I'll come. You'd think I was a lump of clay." He winked at Chester.

James gave his horse the minimum of care before he loped across the bridge toward Rulon's house. Carl saw him coming, and swung the ax into the chopping block. He dusted his hands together and waited.

"You double-dyed yellow-back sneak thief!" James yelled. "I ought to thrash you right here."

"You and who else?" Carl returned, his face hardening. He fisted his hands, and stood waiting in a crouch.

"Just me!" James didn't waste time, but swung at Carl, who dodged away and jabbed at James's face. Neither man connected, and they circled in the yard, trading loud insults.

Julia stepped out of the door. "Carl! James! What's got into the two of you? Hush, now. There's a baby here."

The young men straightened from their crouches.

"What's this about?" Julia demanded.

"He sullied Ellen's name!"

"I ain't! Nothing happened between us."

"Worse, he wants to steal her from me."

"I want to marry her, yes I do."

"She ain't yours to marry. Find yourself another girl."

Piercing wails from the vicinity of Rulon's cabin interrupted the argument.

"Boys!" Julia was between them now, her hands gripping their arms. "This ain't the time or place to have a ruckus. Shame on the both of you. The baby was asleep until you woke her up!"

"Sorry, Ma." James bowed his head and compressed his lips. Then he turned to Carl with narrowed eyes. "This ain't over yet." His chest heaved.

"No, it surely ain't," Carl agreed in a growl.

When Julia and Rod returned to their cabin, Marie was dishing up supper to the guests. James and Carl sat as far apart as possible at the table, apparently holding on to their tempers until they had eaten. Rod pulled Chester aside and asked, "Has James declared his mind to you yet?"

"No. He's eating first."

"The two of them was fighting up yonder." Rod nodded toward Rulon's place. "I been thinking, and I figure I've solved a problem or two. I'm going up Denver City way to find my brother-in-law and work in the mines. I'll take Carl and James along with me. Ellen can stay here as long as she needs to. Suit you?"

"That sounds fine. If they're away from Ellen, maybe they won't come to blows over her."

"Oh, I don't know about that," Rod said. He picked up a plate and approached the fireplace, and Chester followed. Marie ladled beef stew into their plates while Rod looked around the crowded room for a place to sit down. Seeing none, he leaned up against the wall. "But at least Ellen will have some peace whilst she tends to Mary."

"Yes." Chester leaned on the wall beside Rod. "Maybe while she's during her duty by Mary her mind will settle on doing her duty by James."

Rod shrugged. "Time will tell. By the way, I asked Carl to let the men sleep in his cabin tonight."

"We'll be a sight different company than he expected to have tonight. Ida sure played him false."

Rod dug into his food with his knife before answering. "I knew she was flighty, but I thought he could handle her." He poked a chunk of meat into his mouth and chewed it before continuing. "I reckon it was more than he could do, from down here. That stormy weather was back luck all around." He shook his knife at Chester. "Mayhap the best thing Ida ever did for Carl was to throw him over for that stuffy peacock she's set to wed."

"We'll see," Chester said, shaking his head. "When James speaks to me, we'll know which way the wind blows."

"I don't think he'll have the chance. We're leaving in the morning."

Denver City lay spread out between Cherry Creek and the South Platte, treeless and bustling. Log and mud buildings, some half completed, lined Blake Street where the business of the camp was concentrated. Some of the buildings were so hastily built that they seemed ready to fall down around the ears of the users.

Carl rode into town behind his father and two of his brothers. Rod dodged a freight wagon and edged his horse to the side of the road in front of a hotel. Rulon and James followed him, and Carl cut behind the stage once it had gone down the street. The men dismounted and tied their horses.

Pointing up the street, Rod wiped his face. "Rulon, you and James take that end of the street and Carl and me'll work this end. Ask after Jonathan Helm. Somebody's sure to have word of him. We'll meet back here for dinner." Then Rod entered the hotel and was gone.

Carl walked past the hotel front and ducked into the low

doorway of a freight office. The clerk looked up at Carl's question and shook his head. "Jonathan Helm? No, but I ain't been here long. You'll have to ask the boss. He's out, gone up to the camps for the week. Sorry."

"Much obliged." Carl returned to the street and let his eyes roam down it, then strode into the next business.

"If he's been here since Fifty-nine, likely he's at the diggings west of here. I ain't heard of no man named Helm here in town," said the merchant.

The banker squinted at Carl over his spectacles. "Helm? No, that's not a name I recall. Try up the street at the assayer's place. Maybe Upshaw knows of him."

"Jonathan Helm? Wait a minute. Let me look in the records," said the assayer. He rummaged through some cards in a box, humming a tune to himself. "Was he a big man, with heavy shoulders and a black beard?"

Carl felt excitement stirring in him. "That's him. Ma last heard from him about Sixty-two, I reckon."

"Well, here it is." The man pulled a card from the box." I did this assay for him in Sixty-four. A mighty good one, it turned out. Yes, Jonathan Helm struck it rich up to Gregory Gulch. That's Central City, you know, the richest square mile in the world. But I haven't heard from him nor done another assay since this one. Likely there's plenty of back door rock-crushers who call themselves assayers up there, telling him what he's got."

"I'm mighty grateful for the information, Mr. Upshaw. We been following after Uncle Jonathan now for nigh on to a year."

"Well, good luck, young man. Just go on up to the north fork of Clear Creek. Somebody up there can set you back on his trail, I figure."

Carl dashed back up the street, looking for his father. He ran from door to door, poking his head in each one, dodging passers-by on the street until he located Rod.

"Pa!" Carl called into the dimness of a saloon. He started through the door in a rush, then remembered his manners and settled down to a walk to approach the table where his father sat with a small bald-headed man.

"Son, your feet will arrive ahead of your brains, if you don't have a care. I reckon you found out something?" Rod grinned over his hat, which sat on the table in front of him. "Sam Whitney here gave me a good lead, too. Sit down and we'll swap our news."

Carl pulled back a chair and sat on the edge of it. "The assayer says Uncle Jonathan's got a claim up to Central City, Pa."

"I reckon that's where we'll head after we noon, boy. Sam, this is my son Carl. Carl, Sam Whitney from the mint. He says Jonathan has been a steady supplier for a brace of years now. At least, the stuff Sam's been working with has come out of Jonathan's claim."

Carl took off his hat and nodded to the man. He turned to his father and said in a rush, "Shoot, Pa, can't we leave now? We ain't seen him for a long spell."

Rod chuckled. "My brother-in-law was a favorite with the young'uns back home," he told Sam. "I reckon that's the way it'll be out here, too. Boy, we got to gather up your brothers and have us some dinner. Go poke your head out into the street and see if you can spot 'em. The sooner we eat, the sooner we'll be on the road." Rod adjusted his chair. "And Carl, no—"

"I know, Pa." Carl cut him off and rose from the table. When he pushed through the door of the saloon, the light and uproar of the street engulfed him, and he looked around for Rulon and James.

After a moment, Rulon came out of a door two buildings down on the other side of the street. He saw Carl and waved to him, beckoning him to join him.

Carl stepped off the walk and waited on the edge of the street for a chance to safely cross. A party of horsemen trotted their mounts through the business district, leading pack mules loaded with supplies, presumably for their mining camp. Carl crossed after the mules had passed, and soon was at Rulon's side.

"Carl, you know them cartridges you shoot in your Spencer? They got a pistol in here that uses them same things instead of cap and ball. You load them in the back of the pistol cylinder, fire 'em off, then push out the casings and whang in another set of cartridges. Fastest reloading I ever seen in my life."

Carl grinned. "I had one in my hands, once. It's a marvel, all right."

"The gun is for sale, little brother. You got any of that money Rand paid you? I mean just kinda burning away in your pocket?"

"I was saving it to get a load of goods for when Ida and I—" He stopped, scowling. "Let's take a look."

Rulon led the way into the dark store. The pistols were on display in a glass case under the hardware counter. Rulon pointed to the Smith and Wesson at the back, and addressed the clerk. "Show my brother the cartridge pistol," he requested.

The clerk, a brown-haired man with an eyeshade, brought out the blued steel revolver and placed it into Carl's palm. "This is a mighty fine gun," he began.

Carl sighted down the octagonal barrel.

"You have six chambers, .32 caliber cartridges is what you use, and you can be sure it's a mighty fine gun for a man to have out here," the clerk continued.

Carl considered. "You got the cartridges?"

"Plenty. I figure to have a steady supply, now that the Army's fixing to clear up the Indian problem. I'm an Army supplier, you know."

"I didn't, but I reckon I'll take the gun." Carl looked at Rulon. "Maybe if you treat me right, I'll let you try it out from time to time." A slow grin cracked his face. He paid, shoved the pistol down into his waistband, scooped up several boxes of cartridges, and whistled his way to the door. When he stepped through, he stopped with one foot in midair and froze.

He swore gently. "I bet I'm in trouble with Pa," he said, slowly putting down his foot. "I just now recollected why I came out to get you. Pa's waiting back at the Blue Belle Saloon." He gestured with his head. "Could you—nah, I'd best look for James right quick, and you'd best scurry over and get washed up for dinner. Pa's anxious to ride soon as we get our bellies full." Carl walked down the street beside Rulon.

"What's the hurry?"

"That's what I forgot to tell you. Him and me both got word on Uncle Jonathan." Carl stopped in front of the saloon. "You go on in. I'll look for James."

Carl walked down the street toward the hotel, where he pushed his way next to his horse and loaded the shell boxes into his saddlebags. He patted Sherando, then continued down the dusty road.

He caught up with James on the outskirts of the town, where he was asking after Jonathan at the livery stable.

"Come on," he told James, his voice rough and his face set. "Pa's raring to get on the road. We got word about Jonathan. He's up north a piece, has some workings at Central City."

"Where's Central City?" James asked gruffly, waving his thanks to the stableman. He followed Carl back up the street.

"Northwest of here, at a place called Gregory Gulch. It's on the north branch of Clear Creek."

The brothers stepped around opposite sides of a wagon and entered the saloon, maintaining a polite distance from each other. Rod and Rulon sat at the table with Sam Whitney. As Carl and James came up, the man stood.

"I'll be going along, Mr. Owen. It's been a pleasure to meet you." He shook hands with Rod. "I hope you find Jonathan doing well. So long, boys." Sam retrieved his hat from the table, put it on, and nodding to the barkeeper, left the saloon.

Carl and James pulled out chairs on opposite sides of Rulon and sat. Rod looked at Carl, and a grin creased his beard. "Rulon says you got you a gun that shoots cartridges, same as a rifle. He says it's the coming thing."

Carl chuckled. "Up to date, Pa. A sure-thing, modern invention."

"Well, I reckon it's fine to keep up with the times, if you can afford it. Just now, I figure we should put something besides a pistol under that belt of yours. How about it?"

"Let's go eat!" Carl said.

Central City was a raw, wide-open town set in the midst of scarred earth and muddy water. Devotion was offered to only one god here: gold was the ruler, and the offerings were single-minded efforts to acquire possession of it. Some of the worshippers spent their days wresting it from the soil; others made their prayers on the altars of whiskey-soaked bars in tents along the creek.

Here was a town built in haste. Tents and half-shelters answered the need for basic housing, with only an occasional log house thrown up by a miner with vision. Every man's energy was directed to his particular rectangle of ravaged earth. None was spared to build beyond a primitive level.

"Can you imagine Ma in a pesthole like this?" James wrinkled his nose in disgust. "I'm a dad-blamed fool if I ever take up mining as regular work. 'Taint fit labor for a horseman."

"Where do you reckon we should start looking for Uncle Jonathan?" Rulon craned his neck to take in all the sights of the miserable camp.

"Assay office ought to do it, I reckon," Rod said. He took off his hat and reseated it on his head. "Carl, see if yonder gent can direct us to the assayer."

Carl pulled Sherando off the trail and walked him up to a miner hurrying along in the same direction. "Begging your pardon, can you direct us to the assay office?"

The man stopped and pointed to a trail leading up the hill to the left. "Ye can't miss it. Last tent on the path, or so it was last week."

"Still lots of folks coming in?"

"Every day some new Cousin Jack comes over the hill." He spat into the dirt. "Ye haven't the look of miners."

"We're fixing to visit kin."

The miner laughed, expelling a hoarse, croaking sound. "That's a new story. Mighty original. Good luck." He hurried off, glancing over his shoulder at the four horsemen, as if he expected them to follow him with ill intent.

"Obliging fellow, but almighty suspicious," Carl reported. "The office is up the trail."

Rod kneed his horse up the path and the others followed. When the way became too steep for riding, they dismounted and led the horses, and Carl took the position of guide.

Another fifty yards up the path, they came upon the assay office, half dugout, half tent, burrowed into the hill at the trail's end. A mild breeze stirred the door flap as they walked up to it.

Rod called out, "Hello. Anybody inside?"

"Raise the flap and dump your sample. I can't get to it tonight," a raspy voice answered.

"No samples here. We want information. Do you have a minute to spare?"

A sandy-haired man with mutton-chop whiskers and a black vest over his shirtsleeves opened the tent flap. He looked around at the four men, then fixed his gaze on Rod. "Well?" he challenged.

"I'm Roderick Owen from down south of Pueblo City. These here are my sons. We've come inquiring for my wife's brother, and figured you'd be the likely man to know his whereabouts. His name is Jonathan Helm."

The man's face darkened. He put his hands on his waist. "You come a long way, but you're a week too late. His shaft fell in last Tuesday. They dug him out and replanted him in the graveyard yonder."

Chapter 17

Julia caught sight of the men just as they entered the meadow. They were leading a mule loaded with mining gear, and her heart began to flutter. Even at a distance, she could sense an air of dejection and pain in the slump of her husband's shoulders. Something was terribly wrong, and she counted the horsemen over and over to be sure there were four, all sitting their saddles. Her body steeled itself, back straightening, shoulders stiffening, as the men came nearer and she recognized Jonathan's leather strongbox strapped to the mule's back.

Then she ran toward the riders, clutching the over-sized wooden paddle she'd been using to stir boiling clothes. Her washing-day apron flapped in the wind of her hurry, making a whit-whit noise that momentarily distracted her from her goal. She stopped and glanced around for the source of the noise, then looked to where Rod was stepping wearily down from his horse.

She inhaled, sharp and short, dropped the paddle, and ran again toward the men, confused by how old her husband looked. Their sons drew the animals up beside Rod, shutting off the world with a semi-circle of horseflesh.

She was gathered into the strong arms she had missed this last month, and his beard scratched her neck as he engulfed her, burying his face in the hollow between chin and shoulder.

"Oh, Julie," he sighed.

"He's dead?" Soft, and low, and horror-struck.

"Oh, my girl." Rod turned, and with a look dismissed the boys, and they gigged their horses toward the house.

"It's not possible," she said.

Rod nodded.

"No!" she cried, and he held her, soothed her in the meadow as she sobbed.

She couldn't bear to look at the box, not for several days. Then Rod gently reminded her that it was hers, and that she should open it.

"I don't have the key. I left it on the mantle."

He carried it out into the yard and put in on the chopping block. Two shots from his .44 mangled the lock enough to pry it loose. Setting it before her at the table, he stepped back and waited.

Julia looked up at Rod. "He always took care of me, especially after Pa died." Her eyes brightened with tears, but she blinked them back and looked upon the box once more. "Ain't it strange? In all the years I didn't see him, I never missed him. I knew he was doing fine. Now he's gone, the hurt is powerful. Powerful." She sighed and gazed at the box, then lifted the lid.

A letter lay on a cloth, which covered the other contents of the box. Julia sighed again and picked up the letter. She glanced around at her family, took a deep breath, let it out, and broke the seal of wax that closed the flap of the envelope. The brittle wax shattered, falling onto the tabletop and into her lap. She paused for a moment, then removed the folded sheet.

"Dear Julia," she read aloud. "When Pa died, I worried myself sick about taking proper care of you, because you was such a dear little sister and I didn't want to go wrong. Then you went south for your cousin's wedding, which I thought was only for the summer, and somehow, overnight it seemed, you grew into a woman. Then you up and tied the knot with a fellow from down there in Virginia named Rod Owen. That was a shock to me." She paused to wipe her eyes with the corner of her apron.

"I had my reservations, but Mr. Owen's been good to you. However, I am still your big brother, so I'm leaving you a little something to remember me by. Lady Colorado yielded up her secrets to me, and I'm passing them on to you. The contents of this box are from my first strike, and it's all yours. Here's the deed and all, so whatever I leave in the hole is yours after I'm gone. Your loving big brother, Jonathan."

Julia removed the cloth from the box. Inside lay five leather pouches, tied up with rawhide laces. She lifted one of them, surprised at its weight, and put it before her on the table. With shaking hands she untied the laces and opened the mouth of the bag.

"Oh," she exclaimed. "I been complaining about toting this box around with us. It's gold, Rod, and a right smart lot of it." She sat back in the chair, pulling the strings tight on the bag. She looked at it for a moment, then replaced it in the box. Looking up, she caught Rod's eye, and she gazed at him for a long time.

"I tell you what, Roderick Owen," she finally said. "You take this here gold, and you ride down to Texas and fetch you a herd of them long-horned cows. You drive 'em up here and learn how to take proper care of 'em in this new land, and you build you a cattle outfit. I ain't likely to miss the treasure, seeing as how I never knew I had one." She saw he was set to protest, and raised her hand. "That's my wish, and if I die tomorrow, I want it carried out."

Rod took a week to get ready, making doubly sure that Julia was serious about parting with the gold. She only said, "The Lord moves in mysterious ways," and refused to discuss it further, so he plunged into preparations.

Rulon, Carl and James were sent out hunting, while Clay and Albert chopped firewood and helped their father butcher the game and dry the meat.

"I ain't going to leave you here needing food," he told Julia. "I feel bad enough leaving you all without a man for protection."

Julia smiled and patted her Sharps rifle. "I reckon I can still shoot well enough to discourage any prowler."

"That's so, but you keep a wary eye open. We ain't seen any of them Ute Indians I was told hunt up in these hills. Stay around close to the cabins whilst we're gone."

At the end of the week, early in the morning, Rod gathered his family for final instructions. He looked at the pile of firewood that Albert and Clay had split.

"I reckon we've provided for your needs, at least for a couple of months, but I'm nervous as a spring colt about leaving you all alone. I can't say for sure how long we'll be gone."

He turned to his wife. "Take care to keep sight of the girls, and don't let Roddy wander into the woods alone. That boy's taken to straying like a pumpkin vine." He shook his head. "Check up regular on Mary and Ellen. I wish I could leave Rulon, but I need all the hands I have to move a herd the size I plan to buy."

"We'll be just fine, Rod. Don't you worry none about us. Get them cows up here safe and sound." Julia moved into Rod's arms for an embrace. He nuzzled her neck, then kissed her.

"I aim to go and come safely, woman. I know I got a lot to learn, but I ain't too old to acquire knowledge." Rod released Julia and stepped into his saddle, and his sons mounted up. Lifting his hand in farewell, Rod turned his horse and rode at a jog toward the south.

Ellen watched the Owen men leave, then turned from the door of the cabin, hoping the dim light of the room was not sufficient to show her face. Mary had begged her to stay for company while Rulon was away, and Ellen had agreed, even though Mary was doing better, healthy enough to get up and share the work. Now Ellen knew that the days ahead would be lonely ones; she would not have all the work to keep her mind occupied.

She picked up the hairbrush her mother had brought with her things from Pueblo City, and began to arrange her hair for the day. The breakfast fire reflected off her locks as she brushed out the tangles, then twisted her hair into a coil atop her head. As she placed the last hairpin, she thought back to last evening, and the fierce light in Carl's eye as he insisted that Ellen walk with him to the creek.

"I've stayed away from you since I got back from Denver, not because I wanted to, but because I knew it was your pa's will," he said, face twisted and uncertain. "I'm going away again, and I got to say something to you. Please come."

"We'll need water for the morning anyway, so you just take the buckets and help me. Pa could not object to that."

She smiled to herself as a light leaped to Carl's eyes, and a grin spread over his face as he followed her in the near-twilight. She heard Carl whistling to himself as she approached the creek and sat down on a rocky ledge that formed part of the bank.

Carl hunkered down on the edge of the creek and dipped the buckets into the water. He set them out of harm's way, then settled down to watch the ripples in the creek as the water flowed over the pebbly bottom.

Ellen watched him from the corner of her eye. He looked determined, pursing his lips in thought as he gazed into the stream, apparently studying out what he had to say. He tossed a stone into the flow, glanced quickly at her, and directed his gaze again to the water.

When he began to talk, his voice was so low that Ellen had to strain to listen, leaning forward a little to catch every word.

"I ain't got much time, and I've got a lot to say. Reckon I'd best start." He looked around once more, then looked her in the eyes. "Ever since that night we had the dance on the river, and you fell into my arms off that wagon, I been mighty unrestful in my soul. I thought I had a girl to share my life. I was wrong."

He gulped once, then continued. "When I held you against me, and felt your heart a-pounding away, I knew I was a ring-tailed double fool for sticking with Ida. But I'd given my word, and I was stuck with Pa's choice."

He stopped a moment and shifted his weight. "After we went our ways to settle, I figured things would get better for me. I hoped I'd get some sleep, not have nightmares, what with all the hard work I was doing. I made my plans and built my house, and I got excited about getting wed. Then Ida took me by the tail and threw me out the door. I thought I was going to die, I was that prideful. But you were there, like a ray of light on a foggy morning."

He looked at her face, and she could see sweat beading his forehead, even in the chill of twilight.

"Shoot, I'm just going on and on. The important thing is, I got to see what a man rarely finds out before he's wed. You got a backbone of pure steel inside that soft form of yours."

Ellen felt her face burning in the evening darkness. She put a hand to her cheek. It was warm, and she knew she was blushing. Peeking back at Carl, she saw that he had stretched out on the ground on his side, with his elbow supporting his cheek, as though he were exhausted from the effort of talking.

"I ain't done," he whispered, and sat upright again, in one quick motion. "Now I got the freedom from Ida I need to court you, your pa says I can't call. He says only James has that right, and he ain't made it clear to your pa what his mind is. What I want to know before I go away for a couple of months is, do I have anything to look forward to on your account? If I can talk James into thinking he don't really want you after all, and then do whatever task your pa sets for me, are you willing for me to call?"

Ellen sat with her hands on her cheeks, wondering what to reply. Then she softly opened her heart to him as frankly as he had to her.

"Carl, I reckon I been willing for you to call from the day you plucked me out of the muddy street in Mount Jackson and cussed me from head to toe. I'll pray you can use that silver tongue for some good on James, and that my pa comes around to my way of thinking."

The last light faded, but Ellen knew Carl was still nearby from the deep breathing she could hear. Then she heard him stand up.

"I reckon that'll hold me for a couple of months," Carl said. "I'll carry your water to Rulon's."

She followed in the darkness, and he waited for her at the door, setting the pails on the bench. Then she was enfolded in his arms, and he embraced her tenderly as he whispered in her ear, "Ellen Bates, I love you!"

Then he was gone, his footsteps fading into the satin darkness.

Ellen shook herself free from the memory, then washed her face with the water Carl had dipped up the night before. Tying on her apron, she went to the fireplace and thrust another chunk of wood into the flames, for today he was truly gone, and the air in the cabin felt cold and damp.

The grizzled old man in the wide-brimmed hat shook his head. "I cain't figure how you aim to get them cows past the Comanches and Kiowas in the Panhandle. They'll grab up them cattle soon as they see you coming. You're a crazy man to try trailing cattle with the Indians all stirred up."

"I reckon that's my gamble. All I want is some hands willing to make the trip." Rod slapped his hand down on his thigh. "I always heard a Texas man was full of courage. I only need five or six fellers to prove me right."

The old man removed his hat and scratched his head,

reseated his hat, and took a swig from the glass on the table. He looked Rod over once more, then nodded. "Then I reckon you need to see Bill Henry. He's got him an outfit looking to hire out, but work's mighty scarce around here. Well," he shook his head again, "work ain't scarce, but money sure is."

"What's his experience with these longhorn critters?"

"He's trailed them a good mite, and he's a hard worker. I'd say his bad luck is your good fortune."

"Where do I find him?"

"Ask after him down at the livery stable. His cousin will know how to get a-hold of him." Sucking on his yellowed teeth, the man looked once more at Rod. "Well, I wish you luck. And keep your eyes open for the Carpetbaggers. They come down here with some new law called 'Reconstruction', and they're 'reconstructing' the whole countryside into their own pockets. They's made laws agin any man who fit for Davis and the Cause. You tread light here in town."

"I thank you for the warning."

Rod took his leave and sought out the information he needed from the stable hand.

The quiet young man in the patched shirt shifted his feet. "Bill Henry? You say you got work for him? He'll be mighty tickled to hear it. Things ain't gone so well for him of late. He's coming in to town tonight, and I'll bring him up to the hotel about suppertime. We'll meet you in the dining room."

That evening, Rod and Rulon took a table in the back of the dining room and ordered steak and beans. Carl and Albert occupied the table beside the outer door, while James and Clay sat in a corner against the window wall, where they could see everyone who entered from the hotel lobby.

"Why does Pa want us all spread out like this?" Albert asked

Carl before he wolfed down a bite of steak.

"He's a mite cautious, as usual. That old codger warned him about the laws down here. The sooner we hire on a crew of herders and light a shuck for home, the better I'll feel." Carl paused to spear a chunk of steak. "I hope this Henry feller can take the job. Being in a state where a man's got no rights makes me a mite cautious, too."

"Can them Unionists stop us from taking our cattle out of here?"

Carl spoke low. "I reckon them low-life carpetbaggers make up the rules as they go along, especially if they see a profit in doing it."

"I favor that Henry feller getting here with a powerful yearning to travel on with us. We come too far with Ma's gold to see any Yankees make off with the cows she bought." Albert sat up straight. "That there's the stable hand coming up the walk, and he's got another feller with him."

Bob and Bill Henry came through the door of the dining room, Bill brushing the dust of the road from his sleeves. He had light brown hair that curled over his shirt collar, and blue eyes that flicked around the room and settled on Rod, at the rear table.

From his seat two feet away, Carl looked over the powerfully built Texan. He wore a moustache that drooped over the sides of his mouth. His face, shaded by a hat with a wide brim, was brown and unseamed, and Carl guessed he was at least two years older than himself. Judging from the bulge of muscles in his thighs, he had spent most of those years on a horse.

The man spoke to his cousin in a low voice, "I reckon that's the fellow with the cows and no savvy on moving them. Let's go see what he has in mind."

~*~*~

Bill Henry swaggered across the room like he owned the whole of West Texas. His cousin Bob followed after, and came up to the table as Rod rose to his feet.

Bob nodded to Rod. "Mr. Owen, this here's my cousin, Bill Henry."

"Sit down, gentlemen. Can I offer you supper?" At the nod of the young man before him, Rod waved in the direction of the kitchen. "Two more places at this table," he called out.

Bill Henry sat down, and leaned back in his chair. "I heard you're looking for a trail boss and some hands to move cattle." His blue eyes never looked over at Rulon, but gazed straight into Rod's.

"I bought a herd, something over 1400 cows. I reckon I need help to get it to the Colorado Territory. I've raised dairy cattle all my life, but these longhorns are a different breed. I need a good man to show me and my five boys the proper handling of this herd. If that man was willing to stay up in Colorado and show us the rest of the beef cattle business, I reckon he'd be the right man for the job."

"You say there's six of you?" Bill tipped back his hat with one finger. "I know cattle trailing as good as any other man, and I know the rest of the business, but I ain't so sure about leaving Texas for good. I'm a Texas man born and bred."

"Well, I'm offering twenty-five dollars a month and room and board for the man who'll come with me and stay on to settle nearby. We got us a place of trees and meadows, grass a plenty, and water enough for all the cattle we can bring. You look like a canny man, and if what you tell me about yourself is true, you're the man for me."

Bill Henry frowned and sat up in his chair. "Seeing as how you're just come to Texas, I won't take that for insult. Out here we don't question what a man says he can do. A man's word is all he has, sometimes, and if he can't tell the truth about himself, he won't last long."

Rod grinned. "I thank you for not taking offense at my mistake. I reckon I'm still a little green around the edges, in spite of my gray hairs."

Bill cracked a thin smile. "You're a fair man to admit it. I figure you'll do. If your place is as green as you say, no offense meant, I could settle there while you learn the business."

"No offense taken. Do we have a deal?"

"Thirty dollars a month for me as trail boss, and twenty-five for the rest of the hands." Bill sat back in his chair and waited.

"Thirty for you?" Rod considered the matter for a moment, then shrugged one shoulder. "Deal."

"I reckon you bought horses? We'll take my cousin here as horse wrangler. I've got another prime hand in my outfit—Chico Henderson—and Sourdough Smith, who is a mighty fine cook, even if he is a little long in the tooth. Sourdough used to trap up in Colorado Territory, and he said he wouldn't mind seeing it again. We could use a couple more men, but if you're in a hurry, we can do it shorthanded."

"My boys are steady workers and fast learners, but if you think we need more men, hire them. We have to pick up the herd on Tuesday. Oh yes, I bought a hundred horses with the herd. I figure that should keep us mounted across West Texas and up the Pecos."

"You're not going through the Panhandle?"

"Too many Indians driving off stock up that way. We'll go the same way we came, through West Texas and up the Pecos in the New Mexico Territory."

"You remember coming through the Staked Plains? How do you figure to get cows across that desert?"

"As fast as I can. I figure we'll lose some there, but it's better than losing the whole herd to the Indians in the Panhandle."

"You're the boss, but I have my doubts about your choice of trails."

Rod's grin split his beard. A waitress brought two more platters to the table. "Like you said, I'm the boss. Get your crew and meet me at the Davis ranch early on Tuesday. Here's your food, boys. Eat hearty." Rod settled back in his chair and resumed eating.

"I tell you, Berto, it's them same tenderfeet we laid for out of Kansas City, them as drove us off from that little camp in the crick. I'd know that old man anywhere." Willy took a long slug of water from the canteen. "'Course he didn't see me in the back of the room, but now that I shaved my beard, he ain't likely to know me anyhow."

"And this man wants to hire cowhands, you say?" Berto Acosta looked around at his henchmen and tossed his cigar into the fire.

"Jellico told him to look up Bill Henry, but he's only got that old cook and Henderson with him, and maybe his cousin. The tenderfoot's going to need more hands than that."

"Are the sons with him?" Acosta asked, stroking his scarred right cheekbone with his forefinger.

"I counted five."

"And the hot-head, he is one of them?" The Mexican's grin chilled Willy's heart.

"He's there."

"I wonder where is that girl he fought for?"

"I asked around. They came down from Colorado."

Acosta stood up and looked around the group. "Amigos, we have to make a little trip to Colorado, a business trip. Tilden, Dawes, you will go into town tomorrow and hire on with this man. You will get word to Willy at the saloon of when you leave and what route you will take. We will follow behind, and when the work is done, we will take the herd and have our revenge.

And amigos," he threw back his head and laughed. "There is such a girl as you have never seen, a white goddess to enjoy, when the job is completed. It will be worth every mile!"

"That little dark-haired one is the filly I fancy," leered Rankin.

"I got first call on the one with the fight, that red-headed gal." Willy rubbed his chin. "I figure to tame her."

"If I got to eat trail dust and smell longhorns, I reckon I'll take a share," mumbled Frank Tilden, wolfing down his beans.

Pete Dawes ate a biscuit, his piercing blue eyes staring into the fire. When he had swallowed, he turned to Acosta. "Colorado's a far piece. You aim to get more than revenge out of this drive?"

"We will sell the herd after we take it from those tenderfeet. The cows will bring much money. There is more than pleasure to be had." Berto frowned. "You must gain their confidence. You must be trusted. Work hard, and do not complain. You will get a just reward, I promise you."

Chapter 18

Carl decided that riding drag on a herd of ornery, mean-minded, long-legged, slab-sided cows was the most punishing and dangerous job he'd ever attempted. Getting the long-horned critters used to the idea of grazing all in one direction took every bit of his concentration, and a good deal of muscle, besides. He saw why Bill Henry rotated the cowhands to different positions every day.

As they crossed the great dry desert west of Centralia Draw, the bitter alkali dust stirred up by thousands of hooves rose in clouds to choke the men and coat their bodies with briny white powder. Water barrels ran low, canteens were sucked dry, and thirst added to the cowhands' misery as they fought to keep the weaker cattle moving with the rest.

Bill Henry rode back from the head of the herd to speak with Rod.

"We won't bed the cattle down tonight. We've got to keep them moving toward the Pecos."

"The men are tired."

"It can't be helped. There's no water until we hit the river, and if you want to save your herd, you've got to keep them on their feet."

Rod let his breath out in a rush. "I'll tell the men back here."

"I'm headed up the other side to spread the word." Bill rode off, white dust following his trail.

~*~*~

Later on in the day, the cows bawled and moaned for water. Their tongues, coated with the roiling alkali dust, lolled from their mouths. Their ribs began to protrude from sunken sides like the bars of a wrought-iron window grill, and the suffering of the animals caused friction to surface among the men.

"Hey, you're letting one get by you!" warned Clay, as a wild-eyed cow attempted to slip past Carl into the freedom of the desert.

Carl's nerves rebounded, and he drew his gun halfway from its holster. "That's my lookout, you half-grown busybody. Get along, or I'll clip your tail feathers for you," he shouted.

Clay's face blanched beneath the coating of alkali already whitening his features, and he wheeled his horse away around the herd.

Horrified at his demented action, Carl dropped the pistol into its sheath and reined in to remove his hat and knead the back of his neck. "Hush, them cows give me such a pain, I came mighty near shooting my own brother. And now I'm talking to myself."

He slapped his hat against his thigh, raising a billow of white. "I surely do wish I was back in Colorado, paying court to Miss Ellen, instead of pushing a bunch of cow critters down the trail."

"Clay says he won't ride near you until we get over to the Pecos, son. What happened?" Rod's eyes skewered Carl's as they rode side by side at drag position that afternoon.

Carl took a small sip from his almost-empty canteen. "I don't reckon I blame him. If there's one man on the crew who's worse off than these cows, it's me."

Rod remained silent, and waited for more explanation.

"He was riding me about letting a cow through. I pulled my pistol and yelled at him. I reckon he worried I was gonna shoot him."

"We can't get our work done if we're fighting, Carl. You go—"

"I know, apologize to him." He bit his lip, then regretted the action as alkali hit his tongue. He spat, then took off his hat, smoothed back his hair with his forearm, and reseated his hat. "I suppose you want me to apologize to James, too."

"That would go a long way toward making peace in the family." Rod rode off a short distance and slapped the rear of a weary cow with a rope coil he held in his hand. "Hi-yup, there," he called, getting the animal started on the trail again before he returned to Carl's side. "I've found that a man's family needs to be peaceful to work well."

"Pa, I can't help that I fell in love with James's girl."

"Maybe not, but you can give her up with the same grace James showed about the Bingham girl."

"He carried on something fierce, as I recall." Carl attempted a grin, but noted that it didn't go over well with Rod.

"He got used to the situation and did his duty to court her."

"Pa, a girl don't want duty from her husband. She wants romance, devotion."

Rod's glare was chilling. "You mend your fences with your brothers, both of them."

Carl spat again. "Yes, Pa," he grunted, and hurried out after a steer, thinking, *I'll say I'm sorry, but I won't give up Ellen!*

After three grueling days and three sleepless nights, the herd neared the Pecos, and the cattle, smelling water, stampeded. Bill Henry and the hands riding at point and flank tried to turn the lead animals in on the herd to circle them. By this time, though, the exhausted cows were unmanageable, and they broke through the shouting, cursing cowhands and continued toward the river. As they ran, their horns banged together, creating a din of clack and clatter. Then the drumming of their hooves crowded out any other sound, even the futile gunshots the cowhands fired off in hopes of turning the herd.

Carl watched in disbelief as the lead cattle disappeared from sight, bawling in fright as they galloped off a cliff.

"Owen!" Bill yelled at him from ahead. "Get down that bank! Use your rope. Don't let them pile up and drown!"

Carl was halfway down the slope before he realized it, yelling, whooping, driving his horse down the steep incline. He hit the water with a great splash, and gasped for air as it cascaded on top of him. Grinning at the liberation from dust, he whirled his rope and snared a cow thrashing on top of a yearling in the water. "Hiy-hiy-hiy," he hollered, dragging the cow off the other animal.

"Keep 'em moving to the other side," Bill called. "There's quicksand yonder."

Carl rode back and forth in the water with the others, yanking struggling cattle to their feet and hazing them to the other bank of the river. By nightfall, most of the cows had crossed the river.

Bill Henry called to Rod from the water. "Mr. Owen, hold up and wait for me!" He rode out of the river, then climbed off his mount and strode over to Rod. "Six cows are bogged down in the quicksand and they're likely goners, and about twelve drowned at the start, but that's a small loss, considering."

"Considering what?" Rod growled.

"Considering they stampeded in."

"Am I to be happy I lost any?" Rod stared down at his trail boss.

"You're to be happy your crew is safe and you lost so few cows. You will lose cows, Mr. Owen." Bill widened his stance. "I can guarantee that. My job is to keep the numbers low and try to keep the hands alive and well."

"Then you're doing your job," Rod slowly agreed. He nodded at the Texan and rode away onto the flat, where the cattle were finally bedding down for the night.

Bill Henry held the herd in camp for a day, watering the cows until they'd had their fill before he gave the word to move them out again.

Two nights later, Carl rode slowly out to the herd, chewing on the last of his biscuit. He was to relieve James on night guard, and his nerves were taut. Earlier in the day, he had tried to speak to James, but his brother shrugged off the hand he'd placed on his shoulder, and walked away. Now he hoped James's weariness would work in his favor.

As he approached, he heard the twang of the jaw's harp as James played a song for the cattle. Carl made sure James saw him coming, and halted his horse in front of him. James continued to play until he came to the end of the song, then he lowered the instrument and blinked Carl's dust out of his eyes.

"Are they quiet?" Carl asked.

"All bedded down. They like the music." James sounded defensive.

Carl put out his hand. "Will you teach me to play that harp?"

James slowly raised his chin and stared long at his brother. He finally put the instrument into his shirt pocket. "I keep what's mine."

"I'm sorry things ain't smooth between us, brother." Carl dropped his hand, and brushed at his trousers.

"That's not my doing."

"I know, I know. I reckon I should have left Miss Ellen at the dance. I didn't, though, and James, I can't change that."

"You can leave her be." James's voice was husky.

Carl shook his head slightly. "It ain't as simple as that, brother."

"Sure it is. You just pull your heart out, cut it into strips, stomp it into the dust, and do your duty. I done it." James took off his hat and slapped it against his thigh.

"I don't want to do that."

James swore. "Then don't come to me with that thin excuse for an apology. You just tell Pa I didn't accept it."

"She wants me, James."

James swore again, kicked his horse away from Carl, and headed toward the campfire.

By the time Rod Owen's slightly diminished herd of cattle came through Raton Pass and entered Colorado Territory, Carl had a collection of sixty-three rattles from snakes he'd shot along the Pecos, a wild mustang, and a healthy respect for Bill Henry and his instructions.

"That Texan knows his business," he told Albert, as the two brothers rode along at the drag position. "Who would have thought he could teach us to twirl a rope and grab a cow with it?"

"I reckon," the youngest Owen son answered. "I'm just glad to be back in the Territory." He raked at his tousled hair. "I want a good, long, hot bath." Albert looked at the dirty blond locks spilling over the neck of Carl's shirt, and the red-gold beard masking the front of his visage, and a slow grin stole across his mouth. "From the looks of you, you'd better hunt up a razor when we get back. You smell scruffy as a mossy horn steer, too."

Carl rubbed his bushy beard and grinned back. "I reckon when a man's busy night and day, he has a right to grow himself a little face hair. As to smell, you don't take no first prize, little brother. When Ma catches a whiff of you, she'll plunge you into the wash kettle so fast you won't have a chance to get your clothes off first. 'Course, that'll save her some time and labor, having you wash your own filthy clothes at the same time you scrub your hide."

Albert's tanned face reddened. Grasping at a straw, he countered, "Well, you better have yourself a bath before you go a-visiting, or Miss Ellen will catch the first freight wagon back to civilization and take her chances with them rowdies we scared off back on the plains."

Now Carl colored, and rode off after a lagging cow, thankful for the action to divert his mind. He'd tried not to spend much time thinking about Ellen, because the memory of her face brought up the remembrance of Chester Bates refusing his proposal.

"James has the right to say yeah or nay whether he'll marry Ellen. You don't hold any cards there. You're not to speak to her, nor come near her in any fashion, until he plays his hand. If he won't marry her, you still have to wipe clean the blot you've set against her name," Chester had said, blue eyes drilling into Carl's. "You prove to me that you're a man of honor, then I'll consider giving my leave for you to court her."

As he swung around the heels of the cow he'd set after, Carl acknowledged to himself that he'd been a bit callous in observing that ban when he spoke to Ellen the night before he left, but now a great joy surged through him as he remembered her reply to his frenzied speech.

"Ha, ha, ha, ha-a-a!" he cried out, throwing his hat into the air. The cow he'd been following shied away and started toward the herd at a lope. Carl laughed again and trotted the horse back to retrieve his hat, bending far down to pick it out of a patch of Spanish bayonet. "Ellen wants me to call," he shouted to the hills. **"Ellen wants me to call!"** He gave another great whoop, then started after the moving herd.

"I heard quite a commotion back in your neck of the woods today," Bill Henry remarked around the fire that night. "Did you happen across some loco weed out there?"

Carl grinned and shook his head. "Uh-uh," was all he said.

Clay looked up from his plate, chewing his food. "I reckon he's fired up about us being back in Colorado. He thinks he's got a girl waiting for him." His voice was light and bantering. "I think she'll take one look at that set of fox tails he's got stuck on his cheeks, and she'll walk right into my arms." He ducked his head as the men around the fire laughed.

Carl wiped his knife blade on his jean trousers leg and stood up. "I reckon there ain't nothing wrong with a red beard, 'specially since it matches the color of her hair so nice."

Rulon looked up from scraping his plate. "It's a good thing James is out with the herd, Carl." He stood up and dumped the plate into the cook's washtub.

"James don't scare me," Carl retorted. "He'll come to see things my way, by and by."

"I don't think you should sell James short, brother." Rulon wiped his hands on his trousers. "He still claims Miss Ellen's hand."

"Well, I claim Miss Ellen's heart!"

Frank Tilden rose and put his dinnerware in the tub. Nodding to the others, he strolled over to his horse and mounted it, then moved off in the direction of the herd. After a few minutes' ride, he came alongside Pete Dawes, who—with James on the far side of the herd—was holding the cattle while the others ate.

"Go in and eat, Pete. No, wait a minute." Tilden took out a tobacco pouch and prepared to roll a cigarette. "They're all joshing Carl back there about his red beard. He says it's the same color as his girl's hair. She, I gather, is also under the claim of the black-haired brother. I thought the boss was going after some yellow-haired dame that's supposed to be Carl's girl." He licked the cigarette paper and carefully pinched it together. "I get a piece of that red-head when we've finished off the men, if I recollect rightly."

"I do recall your saying so." Pete's voice was quiet in the darkness. "There's a dark-haired one, too, ain't there?"

"That's Marie, the old man's daughter." The cigarette between his lips muffled Tilden's voice. A match flared in the night.

"I'm partial to dark hair," Pete said, sniffing. "I earned it, too. Trailing cattle ain't my favorite occupation."

"You'd rather plug Rebels full of holes, eh, Pete?" Frank laughed.

"Don't even have to be Rebels." Pete sat his horse in silence for a long time. "Just anybody I don't like." His saddle creaked as he shifted weight.

Frank felt a chill scurrying along his backbone, raising goose bumps. He hurried to change the subject. "You figure Berto's out there behind us?"

"He said he'd be there, didn't he? Berto don't tell no lies. I reckon he's going to close the noose pretty quick now. You look sharp, and don't get caught sleeping when he comes down on this bunch of high-thinking Rebels." Pete rode off toward the campfire.

~*~*~

When they had driven the herd past Edward Morgan's farm down on the Cuchara River, Ed and his sons had come out to meet them, and to keep the cattle out of the young corn crop. Tom Morgan told Rulon that Ellen was still up at the Owen's place, and Rulon passed on the information to Carl.

"I ain't seen her for such a long spell," he said, coughing on the dust the cattle raised from the prairie. "I'm almighty scared I'm going to take her right into my arms and hug her to pieces without asking her pa's leave."

"Not to mention, James's," Rulon said wryly.

Carl shrugged, and spurred his horse after a hungry cow trotting off toward Ed Morgan's field.

"I have a meadow picked out on the flank of the mountain," Rod said at dawn in the final camp near the homesteads. "It connects to another one higher up, and there's plenty of grass and water. We'll drive the cattle back in there and they'll pretty near take care of themselves all summer. That's good, because we've got plenty of work and lots of building to do down at headquarters."

Rulon nudged Carl. "Pa likes that word, 'headquarters'. He ain't called the cabins anything but that since we got back this side of the Colorado line. I reckon he's got a dream again."

Carl laughed. "He can dream all he wants as long as we got the muscle to bring it to life. I don't take no offense. I reckon I dream a mite myself."

Rod took the lead and showed where a game trail led through the trees toward the meadow he had in mind. All hands fell back into position around the herd, driving it along the narrow trail and preventing cows from breaking loose into the brush and trees.

Riding at flank position well back along the side of the herd, Carl found that keeping the cattle from wandering into the trees was hard work, and it left him little time for thinking how close by Ellen was. He turned the brown gelding he was using that day toward a cow bent on escaping through the underbrush. The horse cut off its route, and the cow loped back to the herd, bawling in protest.

"Brownie, you're one good cow pony." Carl patted his mount. "Let's get that steer up there."

Ducking under the overhanging limb of a juniper, Carl and the brown horse went after yet another errant steer.

Marie looked around, peering through the berry-laden bushes as she popped a blackberry into her mouth. "Where's Julianna? " she asked Ellen Bates. "Has that girl wandered off again?"

"I haven't seen her since we moved into this gully. I reckon we'd best go back and find her." Ellen craned her neck to examine the brambles through which they had come.

"Oh, let her find us. I'm tired of coaxing her to keep up."

"Marie, what if the Indians get her? Your ma will have our hides. Besides, we've got enough berries for the pies."

"Well, we have come pretty far today. You're right. We'd better go back." Marie turned to un-snag her apron from a bramble, and smoothed it down over her skirt. She straightened up and tugged her sunbonnet into place, then turned again and looked toward her friend.

Ellen stood in front of a big black horse, her hands pinioned behind her back. The scruffy, thickset man who held her covered her mouth with his massive hand. Ellen struggled, and her abductor laughed as the berries in her pail scattered on the ground.

Marie screamed, and the cry echoed back, bouncing on the walls of the canyon. A heavy hand clamped over her own mouth, and she tried to bite it, but the man only let go and slapped her across the mouth. She fell, scraping her arm on a rock as she went down. She screamed again, and the man reached down and yanked her to her feet. He turned her roughly around and tied her hands, laughing.

"Go ahead and scream till you're blue in the face, girlie. Ain't nobody out here to give a listen. 'Course, if your noise gets on my nerves, I'll slug you again." He tested the security of his knots, then whipped her around and leered at her, sunken blue eyes beneath shaggy eyebrows looking her up and down. His dirty brown hair hung to his shoulders, matted and tangled, and his beard was stained with tobacco juice and old bits of food.

Marie choked back her next scream, almost retching at the sight of her attacker.

"Rankin, you gag her up. No telling how far those cries will carry in this still air. We ain't far enough behind them riders to take a chance." Willy held his hand over Ellen's mouth, and he grinned at her as he let go. "You cry out and you'll get the same treatment as your friend. I ain't opposed to taming you good and proper, you little wildcat."

He tied Ellen's hands, then stuffed a dirty neckerchief into her mouth and shoved her toward his horse.

"We're going to take a little ride," he chortled. He mounted his horse and hauled Ellen up into the saddle in front of him. Rankin pushed Marie over to his horse and stepped into his saddle.

"You let loose a peep and I'll yank out your hair," he threatened the terrified girl. Then he bent down and jerked her up into his filthy arms.

Julianna scrambled behind a boulder as the men rode out of the ravine with their captives. She watched, breathless, as they passed three feet in front of her hiding place, saddle leather creaking with the added weight of the two girls. In silence she waited, long agonizing minutes until she was sure the men were gone, then she crept out from behind the rock and set off for home, running as best she could down the hills that lay in her path, heart thumping, pounding, choking up into her throat.

She heard riders coming behind her, and she darted into a clump of trees, hoping they hadn't seen her yet. Trying not to breathe aloud, she gulped air, waiting for them to capture her. Then, as they came alongside her place of concealment, she recognized the men, and cried out, "Papa, Papa! Help them! They been carried off!"

Chapter 19

"Julianna! Daughter, you're a welcome sight." Rod reined in his horse as his youngest child dashed from behind the tree. "You're not out here alone, are you?" He dismounted, and Julianna flung herself into his arms, sobbing.

"Oh Papa, they been took away." She burrowed her face into his chest. "We was picking blackberries, and two mangy old men came up and grabbed 'em. I heard 'em screaming and I hid when they went by. Oh Papa, you got to go after 'em!"

"Whoa there, Jule. Who got took?" Rod tried to calm the hysterical child.

"Marie and Ellen. They took 'em up toward the mountain." She waved her hand toward the looming Greenhorn.

Carl blanched and wheeled his horse back the way they had come, and James followed closely behind him.

Rod boosted Julianna up onto Albert's horse. "Clay, Albert, take your sister home. If there are only two of them acting so bold this close to the headquarters, there's likely more around somewhere. You stay there and see that your ma's safe."

Rod mounted his horse as his two younger sons rode down the mountain with their sister. He motioned up the trail with his head, and spoke to the others. "We'd best catch up to the boys, or they'll have the whole situation arranged without our help." Rod rode off in the direction Carl and James had taken.

Tilden looked at Dawes. Pete nodded his head in the same direction. "Let's go." They followed Rod and the other riders up the trail.

~*~*~

Carl drew rein in the blackberry canyon. Ellen's pail lay in the path, contents scattered and mashed into the dirt.

"They took them here, but they didn't linger," he told James through tight lips.

"We'd best wait for Rulon. He's the best tracker of us all."

"I'm good enough to follow these hair-bellied four-flushers. I ain't waiting for Rulon. They've got Ellen."

Carl alighted from his horse and fingered the hoof marks left by the kidnappers' horses. "Only one bug has scooted through here. They ain't been gone long." He stepped into the saddle. "Come on, James. Let's get them scoundrels."

James checked his pistol load, and made sure the rifle was secure in the saddle scabbard. "How are your firearms?" he asked Carl.

His brother drew his pistol and spun the cylinder. "It's full but for one chamber." Turning in the saddle, he loosened the flap of a saddlebag and removed the Smith and Wesson. "This one's ready to go. I keep all six chambers loaded, just for varmints." He tucked it down behind his waistband, then checked the rifle in his scabbard. "We'd best get a move on," he said, frowning. "Every minute their lead gets longer." He put spurs to the horse's flanks and followed the trail out of the canyon.

Heading south, he skirted the boulder Julianna had used for cover and picked up the tracks of the abductors. James came behind, and they took the trail leading upward, into the pine forest, then past a deep canyon that reached back up the mountain. The trail forked, and Carl took the branch that stretched into the forest, where the path soon lay under a thick layer of pine needles.

"I lost 'em," he sputtered, and circled his horse back to cast around for the tracks. He glanced up and saw his father and the other riders coming through the trees. "Well, here's Rulon's chance to go to work," he muttered.

When Rulon was in hailing distance, Carl called out to him.

"I lost the trail. You been tracking?"

Rulon grinned. "Does a red hound have fleas? You missed a turn back yonder. They headed straight into the canyon. I reckon they know you're following them now."

"Where they going? We ain't been on this section of the mountain."

Sourdough Smith, the cook Bill Henry had brought along, turned over the lump of plug tobacco in his cheek. "I reckon they're heading for an old cabin up there, below the crest of the ridge. I done some trapping through here, years ago." He spit a stream of tobacco juice into the brush. "I reckon I can still find it, if you want me to take you there."

"You find it," Carl said. "I'll be right behind you. Nobody but a lowdown snake abuses a woman where I come from."

Rod looked around at the riders. "I know I'm not paying soldier's wages, but who will stand with me and my boys to get those girls back?"

Bill Henry said, "Down in Texas, we go after scum like that for free." He turned to the others. "Any of you want to stay behind, you're declaring yourselves in favor of snakes and lowlifes."

Pete Dawes looked around at the sober-eyed Owen men. "Well, I shoot any snakes I come across," he said, spreading his lips open across his teeth.

"I ain't in favor of no lowlifes," grunted Frank Tilden.

Chico Henderson checked his revolver. "Let's go."

"You got my gun," added Bob Henry.

Sourdough led off, up the canyon on the left side, the rest of the riders following him on the dim trail, one by one, riding with their rifles loose in their scabbards and their eyes scanning the way ahead.

Carl felt a prickle in the hairs on the back of his neck. As he changed directions on a switchback in the trail, he muttered to

Rulon, "I don't like this. We're all exposed on the face of this wall. If they're laying for us, they can pick us off one at a time, and us with no cover."

Rulon nodded. "Keep your eyes peeled when we top that ridge."

The canyon wall was steep, and the horses were winded by the climb as they approached the lip of the cut. The ten riders edged cautiously into the open on top, and moved quickly into the shelter of the forest.

Sourdough pointed through the trees in the direction of the summit. "We've got a right smart way yet to go. Best we let the horses rest a while." He dismounted, and his horse shied against Frank Tilden's mount.

Tilden's horse reared, but the man kept his seat, cursing the cook. "I don't ride with rum-soaked, broken-down old codgers. Here's yours."

He drew and fired at Sourdough, but the horse turned as he pulled the trigger, and his bullet struck Bob Henry in the chest, knocking him off his horse.

"You stupid oaf," cried Pete Dawes. "Can't you do anything right?" His gun was out, and he shot Chico through the left shoulder. "Damn, you got me doing it now," he shouted, firing at Rod as he turned his horse to flee. His last shot also went high, and opened a furrow across Rod's skull. Then he was gone, and Tilden with him, and three men were down, their blood soaking into the pine needles.

Carl and Bill Henry started to ride after them, but Rulon called them back. "Let them go. I reckon I'd druther have them in front of me than behind, now that we know the set of their minds."

James and Sourdough bent over the injured men. Bob was the worst hit, struggling to breathe, fighting the pain of his shattered chest.

Bill went to his knees and looked at the gaping hole in his cousin's body. "Lie still," he growled, his face working. "You're going to pull through."

"Ah, Bill," Bob coughed, choking on his own blood. "Be sure they bury me in a patch of green. I never could abide the dust in Texas."

"Don't you go!" his cousin cried out, but Bob never heard him.

James stuffed moss into the hole in Chico's shoulder. "It missed the bone, tore up the muscle, then came out the back, so you won't die of lead poisoning," He untied Chico's neckerchief and used it to bind the wound. "We got to get you off this mountain and down to Ma. She can clean you up better." James looked around at Rulon and Carl, who were tending to Rod's wound. "How's Pa? Can he ride?"

"It's deeper than I first thought, but if he don't pass out, he's tough enough to make it." Rulon helped his father to his feet. "Dizzy, Pa? This fight's over for you. You need to get Chico down where Ma can put him and you to rights."

Rod shook his head to clear it. "I got to what?" he asked, obviously confused by the bullet crease on his head.

"Go home, Pa. We lost Bob. Take his body down home. Ma will patch you up."

"I should have had more sense," Rod muttered, seemingly getting his thoughts straight at last. "Them eyes always had something in them I didn't like." Drying blood covered one side of his face.

Rulon brought Rod's horse over to him and helped him to mount. James had Chico in the saddle and handed the reins to Rod, then patted the neck of Chico's horse. Carl tied the reins of Bob's horse onto Chico's saddle while Sourdough and Bill secured the blanket-wrapped burden of Bob's body across his horse.

"Don't stop until you get home, Pa," said Rulon, slapping Rod's horse on the rump. The animal started down the trail.

"I hope Chico can stay on that horse," James said. "He's lost a passel of blood."

"He'll do," said Bill. "He's got sand in his craw."

Sourdough was up on his horse. "That cabin's still a good piece distant," he reminded them. "We need to ride to catch them fellers before nightfall."

Carl's blood boiled him up into his saddle as he remembered that Ellen was in the hands of men like Dawes and Tilden. "I reckon the odds are getting well-nigh even now," he shouted. "They got four, and we got five."

"We know about four," Rulon corrected. "The way Dawes and Tilden chewed up the trail, I can't tell if anybody else has been along this way."

Sourdough led off again, Rulon beside him to check the trail, and the other three came in a bunch behind. The horses were rested, and they made good time, climbing the gentle slope of the mountain through the pines and firs that girdled its higher reaches.

Three hours before nightfall, Sourdough called a halt.

"That cabin ain't but a half mile or less through them trees," he said. "It's partly a dugout into the side of the mountain. We'll surround it easy, for there ain't but one way in, but they've got them girls, so they have a fair hand of cards, too. What you might call a Mexican standoff. When dark falls, we can get in real close, but if we go to shooting, we might hit them girls."

"Best we sneak on up there and have a good look," Bill said. "Can't harm nothing to know how the ground lies."

Dismounting, they picketed their horses in a protected hollow where they could graze, took their rifles, and set out on foot.

Rulon saw the cabin first, its log front protruding from the side of the mountain, and reached out to tap Carl on the shoulder.

"Yep," whispered Carl, crouching behind a pine trunk.

James came silently behind them, and whispered, "Where do you think they put their horses? I went a piece to the right, and there's no cover close in big enough to hide four horses. They ain't in the woods, or we would have heard them."

"I reckon if I was them, I'd want my horse close by," Rulon reasoned. "We'll circle to the left and check. The mountain ain't swallowed them up."

Sourdough appeared behind a neighboring pine. He glided over to join the three brothers.

"That cabin's weathered some since I was last here. The roof's in bad shape. Another storm will knock it down, and then the front wall will fall in." He looked back toward the cabin and spotted a rifle barrel poking through the front window. "I reckon they know we arrived."

A bullet whanged into a tree behind them, and the four men ducked into the brush, spreading out to cover the entire front of the cabin.

"Ah ha!" rang out a cry. "We have meet again. And this time you will not have the good luck."

Carl's stomach churned. "It's Acosta," he exclaimed. "I should have finished him off back in Kansas City."

"We should have ground his bones on the prairie," James responded, gritting his teeth.

"I must thank you for the gift of these lovely young *muchachas*, but where is the other one, the *diosa blanca*? I have been yearning to pay my respects to her."

"Yearn away. She couldn't make the trip," Carl yelled, and moved back from his position.

Another slug whipped through the air, barking the tree where Carl had stood. "He can shoot," Carl whispered from his new bush.

A twig snapped off to the left, and Carl swung his rifle to cover whoever was approaching. After a moment, Bill's head moved into view, and he hissed, "Stand easy. It's me."

He motioned for the men to join him, and they all moved out of rifle range to confer. "I been scouting on the left, and there's no sign of their horses." He paused a moment, puzzlement twisting his face. "I heard a whinny once, but I'll be switched if I could locate them." He glanced around at the other men. "Any luck on the right?"

"Nothing," James answered. "But we know who's in there now. Feller by the name of Berto Acosta. We tussled with him back in Kansas City on our way out here."

"Berto Acosta? He's got a black name in Texas," said Bill. "Cattle thief, stage robber, murderer: he's done it all. I wondered where Dawes and Tilden blew in from. It pains me to find I hired a pair of spies and murderers." Bill scowled and looked fiercely at the old trapper and the brothers. "I got a bullet with Tilden's name on it. Don't you forget that. When the time comes, he's all mine."

Rulon rubbed his cheek with his left hand. "Sourdough, you stay in that cabin long? When you was trapping?"

"Two winters I holed up there. But I didn't just trap. When I had nothing to do, I'd take a pick and do some hacking against the back wall. I'd heard tell there was a vein somewheres, but I never found it. I must have moved three ton of rock out of there for my trouble, but nary an ounce of gold did I find."

"And folks stayed in there since then?"

"Before and since. Folks have been moving up and down through these hills for centuries: Indians, Spanish, trappers, and prospectors. I don't know how old the cabin is, but over the years, many a body's bound to have stumbled onto it and put it to use."

Rulon could barely contain his excitement. "You reckon one of those bodies could have dug clear through the hill? Made a back door?"

"There was a bear's den over yonder. I left the old she and

her cubs alone." He ran his fingers through his white thatch of hair. "If some feller with more brawn than brain camped in here long enough, he could have tunneled through to the den. They could keep horses in such a tunnel."

"It's coming on dark in an hour or so. Now's the time to find that den, or cave, or tunnel." Rulon turned to Bill. "Take me over to where you heard the whinny. If there's an opening, we'll find it and see if it connects with the house. Carl, you and James go to shooting from different positions, to make them think we're all out here. Sourdough, you go to the right and give them a cross fire. If Bill and me find a back way in, you'll know it by the commotion. Give them a rush when you hear us blast our way in."

"I thought this was my fight," Carl growled.

Rulon thumbed his nose with his knuckle, and put his other hand on James's arm to keep him still. "I figure we three got equal shares in it, seeing as how it's our sister over yonder. And Bill has a stake because of Bob. Sourdough knows this place." Rulon looked around at all the men, then addressed Carl again. "Your job is to get in there with these two and fetch the girls out when Bill and me stir up a ruckus."

Waiting was pure agony. Carl bellied down in the pine needles and crawled to a fresh position from time to time before he sent a bullet singing into the hill above the cabin roof, but the time he spent waiting for return fire and for Rulon's diversion was time spent chewing his cheeks in frustration.

James scooted around in the woods to his left, shooting above the roof each time he moved. Carl wasn't sure where Sourdough was, but he knew the old man was somewhere on the right, shooting occasionally, and waiting for the ruckus Rulon had promised.

After his third shot at a dead branch overhanging the roof, Carl noticed that the debris knocked off by his bullets wasn't collecting on the shingles. It disappeared each time, dropping into the cabin.

"James," he hissed, when next James came close. "Look at this." Carl threw lead into the dead branch, and a chunk dropped into the hole. "I'll wager I can get up above there and drop through that hole into the cabin."

"Yup, and wind up looking like a piece of Irish lace. That's a sure way to an early grave. You keep down here and do what Rulon told you."

"But if I'm up there, I can see down into the house, and find the girls. Then we won't go in blind. It's a good plan, James, and I aim to try it."

"Where am I supposed to shoot if you're in my sights?"

Carl pursed his lips for a moment. "Sometimes I get the idea you would favor putting lead into me," he said, and compressed his jaw. "We don't see eye to eye anymore."

"I don't stoop to murder," his brother growled.

Carl nodded. "I'm mighty thankful for that," he said, then slipped into the forest to circle around.

Moving warily, in case there was a guard in the forest, Carl crept through the pines, avoiding the sticks that littered the brown pine-needle carpet beneath his feet. Turning south, he walked toward James's left, edging toward an arc of brush that might afford cover to his scramble up the slope.

He stopped at the edge of the clearing and glanced back at the cabin. The window on this side would show a fine view of him when he dashed into the open. He hesitated, and then James fired a volley of shots above the roofline.

"Thanks, little brother," Carl muttered, and ran, doubled over, into the clearing as answering shots thudded around James's position.

Carl hit the rise of the mountain going full blast, and his momentum carried him up the first ten feet. Then he flattened out on his belly, scooting the Spencer ahead of him, aware that his movements could be sensed through the thin brush between him and the cabin window. Being careful not to scrape the barrel and action along the rocks, Carl moved first the rifle, then himself, up the steep, rocky hill.

To get above the cabin, Carl saw that he would have to swing out onto a crumbling ledge above a sharp drop. The ledge gradually rose about fifteen feet before it angled down toward the roofline. There was one spot where he could probably be seen from the window, before he got high enough to be out of view, but there he would be on his own. James could not risk shooting then, for fear of hitting him.

Holding his breath, Carl eased out onto the ledge, praying that it would hold his weight. He clung to the rock face, slowly letting the air out of his lungs. One shard of rock tumbled off the ledge, but the rest held, and he moved, inch by inch, along the rising shelf of rotten rock.

Then he was at the spot where anybody looking through the window and glancing upward could see him plain as the wattles on a tom turkey. He stopped, feeling the skin of his exposed back crawling with raw nerves. One pebble, bounding down the face of the hill, might alert the inhabitants of the cabin and send a bullet into his back. One misstep, and he'd plunge down the sheer cliff face to his death.

There was no sound from the cabin, no gunfire and no voices, and the stillness made Carl's palms clammy. He could feel drops of sweat trickling along the valley of his spine. Rulon had had plenty of time to find the mouth of the bear's den and make his way with Bill through the tunnel.

The silence below was worrisome. Maybe there is no tunnel after all, he thought. I'm up here, set for disaster, with no remedy close at hand.

Carl scrunched up his face, tight as he could, then let it go slack, hoping to slow his breathing. His left arm ached from the effort of keeping the rifle free of the rocks, safe from striking with the telltale clang of metal against stone. He elected to move now in short, deliberate progressions, and it seemed to him that eternity could not be as long as this trip across the field of fire from the cabin.

Slowly, Carl inched his way up the ledge. He thought his heart must be beating loud enough to alarm the ruffians below him. Then, slowly he turned his head and looked over his shoulder toward the cabin. He could no longer see the window, and knew that he was safe from view.

Now was the time for speed, and his bunched muscles cried out in agony as he took hurried steps down the ledge to the place where he had aimed his rifle so many times. He fingered the dead branch where the bullets had stripped off the back, then looked down, into the dark interior of the cabin.

There was not just a single breach spreading between two roof beams, but a large hole that gaped open to the sky where several of the beams had rotted away. Carl looked up and signaled to James the size of the hole, framing a circle in the air, then he peered down again, hoping to locate the girls.

The ruckus began with a mighty concussion beneath him, and Carl felt himself slipping into space, caught off guard as he tumbled into the void. He fell heavily on his left leg and collapsed. Debris from the rotted roof struck his head and shoulders, and when he tried to get up and back himself into the corner of the room, he knew by the way his leg folded up under him that it was broken.

Using his Spencer as a crutch, he crouched in the dim room and pulled the Smith and Wesson from his waistband, aware of the terrific din coming from the rear of the cabin. Rulon and Bill must have got through, for bullets were whanging and spattering behind a hanging blanket. A man yelled in pain, and the sound filled the hollow with echoes.

Then he saw the girls, tied together behind the overturned table by the front door, and heard them shrieking a warning to him. He half-turned, his pistol feeling like a living part of his hand, and heard Pete Dawes exclaim, "How'd that tenderfoot get in here?"

Carl shot across his body, and heard the thunk of his bullet entering Dawes' chest. He recognized his own voice saying, "That's for Chico, and this here's for my pa," as he fired again, his slug going into the bridge of Dawes' nose.

Carl felt the jolt of the lead from Dawes' last shot as it hit his left hipbone, and thought, *That leg's gone*, as he spun around with the blow.

He landed up against the window that had worried him, while he was out there on the mountain. His rifle was gone from his hand, laying several feet from him on the floor. Knowing he couldn't reach it, he shifted the Smith and Wesson to his left hand and drew the Colt from his holster.

Willy thrust away the blanket and threw himself across the room, trying to get behind the girls, but Carl's shots stopped him, and Willy fell, sprawling on the dirt floor.

Now he had to find Acosta, but Carl couldn't see him in the gloom of the fading light. Powder smoke hung heavy in the room, choking off the oxygen and blurring his vision. Shots still rang out from time to time in the tunnel, and the pounding of boots on the hardpan outside let him know James and Sourdough were on the way in.

Where was Berto Acosta? All the revulsion he had ever felt

for the man rose in his chest, squeezing the breath out of him. He inhaled the putrid air of the cabin, shuddering as the numbness from his leg wounds wore off. His head felt like it was floating, and each time he moved, the bullet hole opened, gushing blood. He knew he had to find Acosta now, before he passed out.

The door splintered under the butt of James's rifle, and fresh air moved into the room as he enlarged the hole. James wiggled through, lifted the bar, and swung open the shattered door. "Where are they?" he hissed, then grunted as he located the girls.

"Get them out!" Carl yelled, and heard his brother hustle the girls through the doorway. Now he had to find Acosta and make an end to the man's corruption.

Carl holstered his Colt and, dragging his leg, using the rough furniture as props, he crossed the room and stumbled over Willy's body. He avoided Dawes, whose surprised eyes would never take the measure of another man, and hesitated before the blanket that marked the entrance to the tunnel. The hair rose on the back of his neck. He drew his Colt again, then swept the blanket aside with the pistol in his left hand, and froze.

Berto Acosta stood beyond the blanket, the fingers of his left hand caressing the scar where Carl had split his cheekbone. His gun was leveled at Carl's heart.

"You!" the man hissed. "You are just a *muchacho*, but you have spoiled the face of Berto Acosta, and kept from him the delights of the yellow-haired girl. No one, no one keeps me from having my way. Now you die."

Carl saw the furious black eyes narrow and he brought down his left arm just before Berto fired, turning it to knock aside the barrel of the gun, and the bullet whizzed by under Carl's arm.

Grunting, "I don't die so easy as that," Carl half tackled, half fell on the big Mexican, and felt the concussion of Berto's second shot going off next to his head. Carl landed with the barrel of his right-hand gun tucked into the soft flesh of Berto's throat, just where it jutted out to form the floor of his mouth, but he didn't hear the shot. He knew he fired by the jump of the Colt in his hand, and by the sudden slackness of the Mexican's body.

Rulon's legs came into sight as Carl brushed the back of his left hand alongside his head. His hand came away from his head warm and sticky with his own blood. Then the gloom of the tunnel gathered around him, and he slumped into the darkness over the body.

Chapter 20

Carl opened his eyes to a blinding light and a fuzzy, isolated feeling. The side of his head throbbed with pain, and when he shifted his weight to get out of bed, his left hip and thigh answered the motion with a jolt and ache of agony that threatened to send him back into blackness. Catching his breath, resting a moment, he recognized his father's house, and knew he was in his father's bed. No one seemed to be in the room, and Carl lay back and drifted into the welcoming darkness.

When next he woke, it was night, and he was in his own bed, in his own cabin, with the same pain and fuzzy, cottony feeling inside his head. He became aware of a restraint on his left leg, and looked down over his beard to investigate. Someone had bound a set of narrow, thinly split cedar shakes to his thigh, from hip to knee, and his pants and shirt were gone.

The ache in his thigh told him that he had not been mistaken about breaking his leg. He tried not to shift his weight as he reached down to probe the sorest part. The leg was swollen and tender, and hot to the touch.

As he reached over to retrieve the comforter that had slipped off to one side, his elbow brushed against a bandage on his hip, and he gasped with the pain that came awake, brutalizing his nerves. Taking long, shuddering breaths to fight back the agony, he remembered the last bullet from Pete Dawes' gun.

Gritting his teeth against the torment, squeezing his eyes shut to blot out the pain, Carl waited until the nerves he had awakened slipped off into a place filled with dull, scraping razors, and he could bear to open his eyes again.

James stood over him, candle in hand, face clean-shaven. His mouth moved, but no sound reached Carl's ears.

"You don't got to whisper just because it's night," Carl said, then frowned. "Am I talking out loud?" he asked.

James nodded and moved his mouth once more.

Carl put a finger into his ear and wiggled it, unsuccessfully, for there was nothing save the fuzzy, stuffed sensation. His head ached, and he raised his hand to find another bandage, bound on by a cloth wrapped around his head.

"Hush, I can't hear my own voice. What happened to me?"

James frowned and put the candle on the floor. In the eerily flickering light, he pantomimed drawing a gun, aiming it and pulling the trigger. Then he put the pretended weapon alongside his own head, just above the left ear, and made his hand move as though it held a bucking pistol. Then he fell to the floor.

Carl recalled the struggle with Berto Acosta. "Did I kill him?"

James's face appeared over the side of the bed, and he nodded emphatically, looking grim. He started to speak, then shrugged his shoulders and pointed to his throat with the imaginary Colt

Carl heaved a sigh, and closing his eyes, went to sleep.

Daylight brightened the room, and Carl sat up. Then he wished he hadn't and he lay down again to wait for the pain to subside. A buzzing filled his head, and he shook it to clear away the annoyance, but it stayed with him.

"Shoot!" he said aloud, and thought he heard the word echoing faintly back to his right ear. He sat up again, ignoring the pain that jolted through him, and shouted, "Hey!" Again he heard a faint version of his voice. "Hallelujah, I ain't completely deaf," he chortled. Then he became very still, holding his breath and straining to hear any sounds through the cotton in his head.

A thudding sound came through the window, and after a bit, he identified it as someone chopping wood.

"Glory be, glory be!" he whispered, sinking back into the feather tick.

A bird sat outside the cabin on a roof pole, twittering its morning adoration of the sun, and Carl thought there wasn't a sweeter sound on earth than that muffled bird song.

James came clumping into the room and dumped a load of fireplace logs into the fuel box. "That sounds wonderful," Carl called from the bed.

James whirled around. "What?"

"I heard the logs drop. I reckon I got a mite of hearing back."

His brother came over to the bed and pulled up a stool. He sat on it and peered at Carl. "It's about time you came back to join us. It ain't fun playing nursemaid to a feller who won't even say 'Thank you kindly, sir'."

Carl fingered his quilt. "How long have I been out?" He turned his good ear to catch James's reply.

"Eight days. You got a right smart furrow alongside your noggin. You and Pa, you're a pair." James laughed, and Carl smiled to hear it. "How in six little beans did you stay on your feet to finish off Berto Acosta? You got you a hole in your hip big enough to stick a fist inside, not to mention your leg's broke."

Carl sorted through the muffled sounds for a moment, piecing them together into words. When he figured he had the sense of them, he grinned. "Just ornery." He peered around the orderly room, and spotted the bedroll James had used during the night. "You been keeping this place clean?"

"No." James's voice held a hint of rancor. "You got a day girl comes in and cleans up and changes your bandages."

"What?" Carl clutched the comforter up over his chest.

James smile didn't reach his eyes. "She only tends to your head. You ain't got cause for alarm. Besides, her pa heard about our little fracas, and he's coming to take her home to the Cuchara."

"How soon?"

"Tomorrow. Not soon enough for me." James scowled and turned his back, then muttered, "You want anything to eat?"

"What's that?"

James turned around, his face once again smooth. "I said, do you want something to eat?"

Carl weighed the matter, wondering if the hollowness in his belly came from hunger or sorrow at the news that Ellen was leaving. He looked up at James. "I'll try something. James, I got to see her before she goes."

"You want me to carry that message?"

"I'd take it as a favor."

"I won't do that, but it don't make no difference. She'll bring breakfast by before too long." He went to the row of pegs against the wall. "Seeing as how you're going to have company and you awake to know it, I'll rustle up a shirt to cover your nakedness." He fingered a few pieces of clothing hung on the makeshift dowels. "You ain't got a big selection here, but I reckon this one'll do." James brought back an old shirt of Peter's that their mother had passed on to Carl.

Carl shrugged in on, finding it a tight fit, and trying to ignore the pain from his hip. "How long you figure I'm going to be laid up?"

"Oh, Ma calculates about a month of loafing will cure you or kill you. She says you snapped that bone clean in two, and your leg swelled up twice its size before we got you off the mountain. It took the whole bunch of us to set it, and you cussing and hollering the whole time. My, you about made me blush to hear it."

"What's that? Blush, you say? You ain't never blushed in your life, you're that brazen. Besides, I don't recall any such a thing."

"That don't mean it ain't so. I reckon I didn't even know some of them colorful words you was spouting. Pa was fit to be tied at the words you used."

Carl tried to sit up. "I never. James, you're pulling my leg."

"I don't think you'd allow that now that you're conscious. That leg pains you a mite, I can tell. Here, let me help you sit up."

Carl stiffened as James raised him to a sitting position. He felt dizzy with the shock of the movement.

"Shoot! That hurt you. I'm sorry, Carl."

Carl shook his head. "Nothing you could help, but I don't want to get in the way of no flying lead again for a long spell." His head still whirling, he eased himself back on the pillow James had propped against the wall behind him. "Did you get the bullet out?"

"Not me. Ellen fished it out." At the look on Carl's face, James added, "It wasn't a time for modesty, big brother. You was pumping blood all over the floor, white as a ghost, and she dived in and ripped a hunk off her skirt to keep you from dying right then and there." He shook his head. "She's one level-headed gal."

Carl groaned. "That's throwing powder on the fire. When her pa finds out I was uncovered in her sight, I ain't never going to win that girl's hand."

"Suits me just fine, since she's my girl,' James growled. "Don't you worry none, though. You was covered decent the whole time. We didn't pause to pull your britches off, or it would have been all over for you."

"You can drive a body crazy, you know that, James? Half the time I ain't sure I'm hearing you clear, and the other half I reckon you're standing there making up the whole thing out of your head."

"I ain't. Miss Ellen is a remarkable girl. Pa claims our betrothal is broken off, but I still count her my own." His face was set in determined lines. "You ain't won her hand, big brother. Nor have you won over Chester Bates."

"You get out of here before I rise off this bed and whup you," Carl threatened, his face gray and drawn. "I snuffed out the breath of three men who aimed to keep Ellen from me. I ain't proud of it, but I had it to do. I'm going to win her hand, even from you, little brother."

"We'll see about that." James turned on his heel and went out the door.

Carl dozed for a while, and then awakened as a hand touched him on the shoulder. He opened his eyes, hearing the buzz in his ears again. Ellen sat on the stool, smiling at him, a bowl of porridge in her hand.

"James says you've been awake. I allow I'm right thankful to see it."

"You'll have to come around to this side of the bed," he said. "I don't hear so good on that side." His heart pounded at the sight of her, sitting there in a faded green dress that couldn't detract from her fresh, alive face.

"I reckon you're hungry," she said once she stood at his right side. She looked around for a chair.

"Take a seat on the bed," Carl said, patting the place. "I'm a mite shy of strength to lift a spoon."

"You poor thing," she murmured, sitting gingerly on the edge. "I reckon I should have brought broth."

Carl smiled. "No, I need something to give me meat on my bones. Look how thin I got."

Ellen looked at him, noting the tightness of the shirt over his chest. "You appear to have filled out some."

Carl looked down. "Shoot, this shirt belonged to Peter when he was a young'un. I don't know what become of my shirt."

"I've got it over to Mary's. You bled a fierce lot all over it. I didn't know you were ready to get up and dress, or I would have fetched it along." She smiled.

"I ain't ready to dance a reel, but I reckon I need something to cover my body."

Ellen looked down at the bowl. "I don't mind," she whispered. "You got a right nice looking chest." She glanced up at Carl then, challenge in her eyes. "You have been so close to dying on me. I don't want to take the chance of losing you now." She bit her lip. "I aim to tell Pa it's time he let me wed the man of my choosing. I'm going down to the Cuchara and bring back the Spanish mission priest. It don't matter to me what words he uses, so long as they mean I'm your wife." She picked up the bowl. "Eat, now. I don't figure to give you more than three, four weeks to get well before I come back, so you be ready, you hear?" She blushed, rosy red in the light from the window, thrust the bowl into Carl's hands, and ran out the cabin door.

Carl grinned, and lifted a spoonful of mush to his lips. "Well, I'll be switched," he said, and shoveled the food into his mouth.

Soon after he arrived from his farm the next day, Chester Bates knocked on the door of Carl's cabin. Carl bade him enter, and Chester came around the doorjamb, his face flushed red.

Carl lay back on the bed, trying to quiet his quick breathing, steeling himself for Chester's harsh words.

The man came to the bedside, took off his hat and gripped it hard, his knuckles blanching white from the effort.

"I reckon I owe you my daughter's life, boy. I'm mighty sorry you got shot up that way. Your pa tells me Rulon despaired for your life before he got you home."

Carl let out a long breath. "I didn't know that, but I ain't sorry. I'd do it again to prove what that girl means to me." He felt drops of sweat forming on his forehead, threatening to trickle down to sting his eyes and betray his nervousness.

"I ain't an unreasonable man. Ellen's my only child, and I set great store by her." Chester's voice shook a bit. "I always wanted the best for her. I reckon she and her ma got the worst during the fighting, being left with a tool shed for shelter." Chester's voice took on a hard edge. "A tool shed! I swore they'd have a chance to forget all that. Your pa helped considerable that day when he rode up with his plan to come out here." He looked at his white knuckles.

"Pa needed you all to make a big enough party for traveling safe."

"He cared about us, too. A lot of water has gone by since that day. James—" He paused uncertainly. "And now it appears Ellen wants someone else to give her the best of this world. She spoke me quite a speech this morning." Chester paused again and sank down on the stool.

"She did?"

"She did. I reckon this is the day a father hopes will never come, but it always does. This is the day I take that little hand that's been in mine for these few years and place it into yours."

Carl's head came off the pillow an inch or two, but he didn't say anything.

"You proved you're a man who will lay your life down to save hers, and a father can't ask more than that." Chester rose to his feet.

"Are you giving your consent for me to call on her?" Carl whispered.

"Boy, I don't think you get my meaning. With feelings like you got, I'm playing it safe. I brought Mrs. Bates along, and a friend of ours. His name is Padre Gallegos, he's a priest, and he's here to marry you."

Carl sat bolt upright, disregarding the stabbing pain from his leg. A burning filled his chest, rushed into his throat. His arms shook as he supported himself in the bed. "My ears have been playing tricks on me the last couple of days, but I swear I heard you say you brought a priest along to marry me." He cracked a grin through his beard. "Hush, I don't want to marry no priest. I want to marry Ellen."

Chester stared at him, then clapped his hat on his head and roared into laughter. "Ellen's going to have a bit of humor in her life, I see. That's good. That's mighty good," he chortled, and strode through the open door.

Carl turned and looked out the window. Ellen stood in the dooryard, holding her hands clasped together. Joy flashed over her face when her father spoke to her. She threw her arms around him and hugged him tightly.

Lying back on his pillow, his heart pounding, Carl looked around at the room he had built with his own labor. This was a home worth the sweat and effort, and here he would build his life and work toward his dreams.

And Ellen would stand tall beside him.

The End

Take a Sneak Peek at

Spinster's Folly

Book 3: The Owen Family Saga

Excerpt from *Spinster's Folly*

Marie Owen pressed forward through the crowd that surrounded her brother Carl and his new bride. She pushed her way across the patch of trampled grass in the Colorado meadow, trying to get closer to the bridal pair. She could barely see Ma hugging on Ellen. Mrs. Bates dabbed at her eyes. Mr. Bates stood alongside them, looking stern. Pa stood back a bit, looking pleased with himself.

Someone in a great hurry to leave the site of the makeshift altar bumped Marie's shoulder hard, and a flailing hand knocked her bonnet askew. She cried out, "Have a care!" as she turned to see who had been so heedless, then shook her head as she realized it was only her next older brother, James, fleeing from Carl's triumphant grin.

"You behave, James," she muttered, loosening the strings beneath her chin so she could straighten her headgear. When she was satisfied that it was once again firmly in place, she returned to her purpose of reaching her best friend.

Her youngest brother, Albert, was her last obstacle. He had wormed his way to the front of the crowd, and was enthusiastically engaged in kissing Ellen's cheek. Marie elbowed the youth aside, reached her friend, and threw her arms around her.

"Lawsy," Marie whispered in Ellen's ear as she hugged her tight. "I'd begun to fear this day was never comin'. Now you're truly my sister!"

Ellen pushed back from the embrace slightly, her green eyes shining like dewdrops above her freckled cheeks. "It was so sudden. I didn't figure Pa would bring the priest with him." Her voice quivered. "Who would have thought . . ." She scanned the meadow, craning her neck as she looked back and forth. "Where is James?"

Marie squeezed Ellen's arm. "Now don't you fret about him on your weddin' day. He'll get over his disappointment."

"I want to tell him I am sorry."

"Don't you bother. He's been acting like such a ninny. It was plain as the nose on your face that you loved Carl and not him."

Ellen ducked her head, but when she raised it a moment later, her radiant smile bespoke her happiness.

Marie couldn't help kissing her cheek. "I'm thrilled for you," she murmured, and gave Ellen another hug.

"I cannot believe this happened so fast," Ellen whispered. She took a deep breath, then turned to look at Carl, who was sitting himself down on a chair, his face white.

Ellen's smile disappeared, and she turned back to Marie as people shoved against them. "Carl's bleedin'. I must get him to the cabin." She gripped Marie's shoulder. "You'll be next to marry," she said in a rush. "I see the way Bill Henry looks at you."

"What?" Marie protested, but Ellen had slipped away, entreating Rulon and Clay Owen to haul up the chair and carry Carl to the house.

Marie stood rooted in place by her friend's astonishing words. She watched a crimson stain spread across the hip of Carl's trousers, and a shiver of fear coursed down her spine. Carl had been wounded in a shootout with kidnappers. Surely he wouldn't bleed to death because he got out of bed to marry. Ellen was as good a nurse as anyone hereabouts. She would take ample care of Carl and pull him through this bad spell.

"James!" Ma's sharp call cut through the babble of voices.

Marie turned to see what had alarmed her mother, and saw James loping into the forest. She breathed out in exasperation.

He had been so temperamental lately, stumping around like a bear with a hangnail.

"Rod, go see—"

Marie went to her mother's side. "He's fine, Ma. Give him a fortnight to clear his mind, and he'll be the light of your eyes again."

Ma grasped Marie's wrist without looking at her. She spoke low. "Daughter, he's not fine. Make your pa go after him." She glanced down at her clenched hand, opened it, and let Marie go free. "Tell your pa—"

"James is man-grown, Ma."

Her mother seemed not to hear her. "Good, Rod is going." She called out, "Bring him back," sighed, gave herself a shake, then turned her attention to the departing newlyweds.

Marie shrugged her shoulders and followed her mother's gaze. Ellen walked beside Carl, fussing a little, patting his hand. His brothers carried his chair toward the little log house Carl had built with his own hands to receive his bride. No matter that his wife wasn't the one Pa had intended for him. It seemed such an age since Pa had connived to arrange marriages for two of his sons before they'd all fled the ruins of the Shenandoah Valley and headed out here to Colorado Territory. Carl's betrothed, Ida Hilbrands, was long gone.

"Good riddance," Marie said aloud.

"Good riddance to what?" a young female voice asked behind her.

Marie jumped and whirled to face her younger sister. "Julianna! Don't creep up on me like that. It's not ladylike."

"What do you know about being a lady? More like a spinster, if you ask me."

"Spinster? Don't you call me names!"

"I will if I want to. You're gettin' awful long in the tooth, Marie. You've got no beaus in sight, but I do. I'll be married soon."

"You're lyin' to make me feel bad. You're only thirteen!"

"I'll be fourteen soon," she simpered. "Mama wasn't much older'n that when she and Papa wed."

"You're ridiculous, Jule. Nobody marries so young anymore."

"And you're an old maid, 'cause you're overripe. Papa surely wasn't thinking when he left you off his marryin' list." She swished her skirt with both hands and stuck out her tongue.

Marie felt warm blood rising into her neck and face at her sister's insolence. "Leave Pa out of this," she barked. "You see how well his plans turned out." She gestured toward the departing couple. "True affection conquered his meddlesome—" She fumbled for a word, then spat out, "meddling. Ellen is happy, and so am I."

Julianna smirked, pointing toward the forest. "James ain't happy. He stomped off. Papa went after him, glowerin' almost as much as James."

Marie balled her fists, glaring at her sister. "Thank you for telling me something I already know, Miss Snippety Nose. James'll mend, given enough time."

"But in no time at all, Papa will have to put you on the shelf. Nobody will even look at you by Christmas, old maid!"

Marie turned and stalked off toward the plank tables set out under the oak trees nearby. When Ma had found out Carl was rising from his bed to get married, she had bustled about—with the aid of Rulon's Mary—and put together a special wedding dinner. Well, special, if you count honey drizzled on corn cakes as special. Add the meat pulled from the bones of a few roasted chickens, gallons of milk, cold from sitting in stone crocks in the spring, and the meal could pass as special.

No matter what irritating things Julianna may say, Marie couldn't take the time to tussle with her. There was aplenty of work to do today. Even so, she felt burgeoning anger consuming her good sense as she eyed a washtub full of tableware sitting on the grass beside the table. Which of her brothers had left the dishes on the ground instead of putting them on the table? *Inconsiderate clod!* She bent over, pulled a stack of tin plates from the tub, and slammed them onto the table. Her ears rang with the cacophonous sound. She retrieved a second bunch of plates, dropped them onto the first pile, then grabbed a double handful of tin cups, which she banged down on the planks, not caring if she dented them.

After a few moments of rebellion, reveling in the clinks and clanks of the tinware, she straightened up, put her hands at her waist and stretched her back. Then she blew an escaping lock of hair out of her eyes and twisted the kinks out of her neck. Remembering that—despite Carl and Ellen's hasty withdrawal— there were still plenty of folks to feed, served to pull her out of her misery and helped her transform back into sensible, responsible Marie.

The Spanish priest robed in brown was the first to enter the shade under the oak trees, wiping sweat from his forehead with his sleeve. The Texas cowboys followed, discussing the possibility of a shiveree that night. Mr. and Mrs. Bates came along with Ma. Pa was nowhere to be seen, but the rest of the family pressed forward, intent upon taking nourishment after the arduous work of getting Carl wed.

Marie hurried to get behind the food-laden table to serve as her younger brothers pushed and shoved to position themselves at the head of the line in order to grab generous portions. Marie smacked the backs of their hands with the bowl of the honey spoon.

"Ow!" howled Albert. "There's no call to beat me."

"Guests first," she replied, pointing with the spoon. "Get yourselves to the back of the line."

Clay licked honey off the back of his hand and glared at Marie, but obeyed without a word.

Mr. Bates escorted the priest to the head of the now-orderly line, accompanied by many polite gestures on the part of both men. Marie smiled at the priest, racking her brain for something to say, then, as she heaped his plate, remembered a Spanish word she'd heard recently. "Señor," she said, and made a bobbing sort of curtsey.

"*Muchas gracias, muy amable,*" he said, smiling back at her and making little crosses in the air over the food table.

"Muchas grachius," she parroted back, wondering what she'd just said as the priest moved on.

By and by, everyone who had crowded around the table had their plates full, and all were engaged in seeking places to sit to devour the comestibles. After consolidating the leftovers, Marie picked up a plate and fork.

Just then, an excited voice called from the woods, "Hey, James is riding the mustang!" The Owen brothers and the cowboys abandoned their plates and cups on the grass and hurried off to see the spectacle.

Marie watched them go, then forked up a bit of chicken, put a corn cake on her plate, and drenched it with honey. She found a place to sit by herself on the grass, and bit into the sweetened breadstuff. The bland corn cake reminded her of all such dry mouthfuls she'd endured in the years since Lincoln's Northern soldiers had come marching into Virginia. As she chewed, she wished she'd thought to get a cupful of milk. Eventually, the honey helped ease the ground corn down her throat. She dearly hoped Pa would trade a beef cow or two for part of Mr. Bates's wheat crop after harvest time. Wheat bread would be such a welcome change.

Young Roddy, Rulon's boy, came galloping under the oaks astride a stick Pa had fitted with a stuffed horse head made of burlap. "The horsie bucked," he announced in a high, shrill voice. "Unca James fell off." He pranced around his mother. "Mama, he said bad words."

Marie didn't fight the chortle the boy's comment brought upon her. *I reckon he did*, she thought, covering her mouth. *James don't like blemishes on his reputation as a horseman.* She watched Mary bend over and exhort her son about sticking close to her. *That baby's growin' up. Good thing Mary's got a new wee one to dote on.*

Her good humor faded as her heart constricted. She had empty arms and no prospects for a man to help her fill them with a babe of her own. She wondered if Julianna's words about her being an old maid had any truth. She was eighteen years old, after all. She closed her eyes and felt a chill move up her spine.

Rulon had taken Mary to wife years ago, just before he went to the war. Roddy had come along in the due course of time. Now Carl had wed Ellen. When was her time to marry and have a family? Had it passed her by when Virginia got tangled up in that cursed fight? Marie shivered as the chill enveloped the rest of her body. So many young men had gone for soldiers. So many hadn't returned home once the fighting was done. Now she was way out here in Colorado Territory. Her chances for finding a suitor weren't showing any more promise than they had during the "Unpleasantness." ∞

ABOUT THE AUTHOR

Marsha Ward writes authentic historical fiction set in 19th Century America, and contemporary romance. She was born in the sleepy little town of Phoenix, Arizona, in a simpler time. With plenty of room to roam among the chickens and citrus trees, Marsha enjoyed playing with neighborhood chums, but always had her imaginary friend, cowboy Johnny Rigger Prescott, at her side. Now she makes her home in a forest in the mountains of Arizona. She loves to hear from her readers.

Connect with her at:
Website: http://marshaward.com
Blog: http://marshaward.blogspot.com
Email: marshaw@marshaward.com
Facebook: https://www.facebook.com/authormarshaward
Twitter: https://twitter.com/MarshaWard

Do subscribe to Marsha's VMA Readers email list to receive advance notice of coming book releases. https://is.gd/rBXkA4

www.ingramcontent.com/pod-product-compliance
Lightning Source LLC
Chambersburg PA
CBHW050020180626
46810CB00002B/504